Sara

UNSTABLE

L.A. Bank

UNSTABLE

L. A. BRINK

THE PAPER HOUSE
PUBLISHING

Copyright © 2023 by L. A. Brink

All rights reserved.

No part of this book may be reproduced in any form or by any electronic or mechanical means, including information storage and retrieval systems, without written permission from the author, except for the use of brief quotations in a book review.

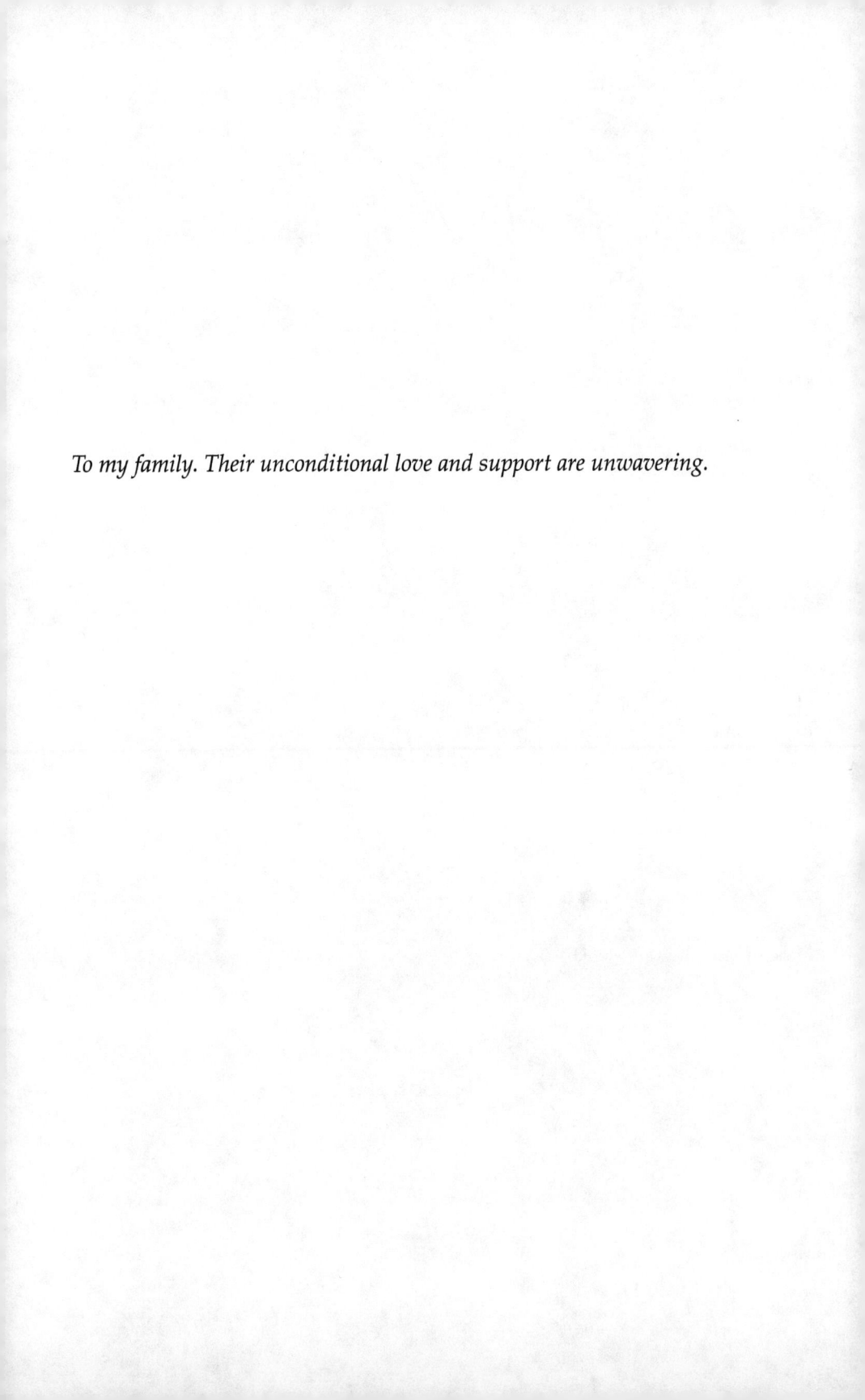

To my family. Their unconditional love and support are unwavering.

1

I CAN'T BREATHE. My eyes snap open, hoping to see who or what has hold of me. From the darkness I manage to make out a human figure, with their outstretched hand, a vice grip around my throat. My survival instincts kick in. I try kicking my legs against the bed, nothing. I focus on moving my arms to fight my attacker off of me, still nothing. It's like my whole body is encased in concrete! All I can do is lie there, motionless, gasping for air. Unable to stop what is happening to me, I stare wide eyed at the terrifying hooded figure above me with the knowledge, I am going to die. Hot, salty tears pour from my eyes down the sides of my face, my lungs burning as I make my final attempts to fill them with air to no avail. Accepting my fate, I close my eyes. I feel myself about to lose consciousness as my final thoughts race through my mind. *Why isn't Marc helping me? Did my attacker already subdue him? Is he still alive? Will I see my girls again? Is this the end?*

Suddenly, the vice grip leaves my throat. My lungs immediately fill with air, realizing at the same time that my arms and legs are no longer encased in the feeling of concrete and are moving freely at my will again. My hands fly to my throat, still gasping for air. Jumping from the bed, I stand ready to face off with my attacker, but the room is empty. I look frantically around the room for the intruder, wondering why, when they were so close to killing me, they decided to let me go. I'm so worried about the intruder I didn't even notice that Marc is still in the bed next to me, sitting straight up, reaching toward me, pulling me to sit beside him.

"Babe? Are you okay? What's wrong?" His voice is a mix of concern and sleep while he rubs slow circles on my back trying to console me. I close my eyes, focusing on my breathing and the feeling of his hand on me. "Did you have a bad dream?"

"Someone...someone was here, they were, they were choking me!" I tell him through my gasping breath, feeling fresh hot tears roll down my face. Before my eyes, I watch the sleep dissipate from him as he jumps from the bed on high alert, grabbing the bat from under the bed.

"What? Where? They were here? In the room?" he asks, focused on moving toward the hall. "I didn't hear anything; did you see where they went? Stay here while I check on the girls." He swiftly makes his way out of the bedroom, avoiding all the creaking floorboards. The bat is gripped tightly in his hands, poised in the air ready to swing at a moment's notice.

While he's gone, I focus on my breathing trying to think of what made this whole encounter feel...off. I try to remember everything. The "not being able to move" feels so familiar, but how? No one has ever tried to kill me in my sleep before. That's when it dawns on me, the feeling of not moving, not being able to speak, and seeing things that look so real, but aren't. I instantly feel foolish not only for causing Marc to panic, but also for not recognizing what was happening sooner so I could implement the calming techniques I learned years ago. I used to get sleep paralysis almost every night as a child.

"I'm fine." I say to myself as I let out a strangled breath. I get out of bed and tiptoe downstairs to find Marc. He's making his way through the kitchen when I get his attention. "I'm okay, there's no one here," I say embarrassed. "I think I actually had a sleep paralysis episode... I'm so sorry to worry you; are the girls, okay? Did you wake them?"

"Oh my god, babe, you scared me half to death!" he says, blowing out a frustrated breath running his hand through his hair. "No, they're still sleeping. Are you sure that's what it was? You seemed really sure someone was in here."

"Yes, I'm sure. Come on, let's go back to bed," I say, taking his hand to lead him back upstairs. My eyes are starting to adjust to the darkness; I can see Marc looking at me with hints of worry on his face. My voice is still hoarse, but I am finally able to breathe normally, and my heart rate is slowing down. He places the bat back under the bed so we can settle back into the covers. I lay my head back down to my pillow and look over to Marc who is now looking down at me.

"You haven't had one of those in a while. Are you sure you're, okay?" he asked, circling me into his comforting arms. "Come here, I'll hold you while you try to go back to sleep."

As good as it sounds though, I have to get up and check something out first.

"One second, I'm going to splash some water on my face and get a drink." I reluctantly leave his comforting embrace and start to get up out of bed, putting on my soft robe and slippers before heading out of the room. I look back to see he is already drifting off to sleep again. Before I go downstairs I stop by the girls' room for my own peace of mind to make sure they are still asleep. I close the door and make my way to the kitchen to grab a water from the fridge and find myself tiptoeing around the house, peaking around every corner and on high alert as if some intruder will pop out at any moment. Feeling silly, I shake the thought from my head before taking a few sips of water. Heading to the main floor bathroom, I prepare myself for what I may or may not find.

Taking a deep breath, I turn on the light so I can look at my reflection in the mirror. When my eyes adjust to the brightness, I notice my honey brown eyes look dark, sullen, and wide with lingering fright. I slowly move my hair out of the way. A couple of gray strands show through my chestnut hair, making me wonder if I should remove them. *Tomorrow's problem.* I think, and return my focus to my neck. I am sure I am going to have marks there, but all I see is my porcelain-colored skin void of any red marks, let alone bruises.

"Well, of course nothing is there, it was only a sleep paralysis induced dream," I say barely above a whisper, secretly relieved it really was simply a dream. It felt so real though, as if I were actually dying. *Oh well, guess this is what happens when you're stressed out, turning 30 next week, and your art career has been at a painful standstill for the last couple of years.* I take one last look in the mirror, satisfied there really are no marks on my skin, but make a note to dab concealer on my eyes in the morning. I turn out the light and head back to the kitchen to grab my water from the counter. Unfortunately, I am wide awake now so I walk into the living room to sit on the couch. Setting my water on the table, I reach for my sketch pad and start to draw what I saw so vividly, hoping it will help make sense of things. The smell of my charcoal pencil in my hand, produces a calming effect all on its own. As I touch the obsidian to the stark white paper, the evil intent of my attacker leaps off the page.

I hear the shower turn on from the upstairs, and grab my phone to check the time. Two hours have already passed. Feeling parched, I drink the rest of my untouched water and inspect my drawing as a whole. To my disappointment, nothing extraordinary stands out. A hooded figure, masked by darkness with an outstretched, gloved hand. Seeing it in front of me sends a jolt of fear down my spine as if I can feel the powerful gloved hand squeezing around my neck again. Threatening to end my life. Shaking the feeling away, I attempt to focus on the glove itself. It was soft, almost having a buttery feel like leather. I touch my neck absentmindedly, lost in the horrific memory of near death. I bring myself back to the present, knowing I should get breakfast started before Marc and the girls come downstairs. I give my sketchbook a final glance before locking the figure away between the pages.

I'm putting the food on plates when Marc walks in with the girls right behind him, sleep still present in their eyes. Seeing Marc in his crisp white dress shirt and the blue tie I love so much because it brings out his piercing blue eyes, I feel as attracted to him as the first day I met him on campus. He was a business major and I was an art major. *At least one of us was able to further their career.* I know he worked his ass off to get promoted VP in the company so he could provide for our family, but I can't help but feel a pang of jealousy that settles in the back of my mind.

The girls, however, are still in their pjs looking half asleep until they eye the food on the table, instantly waking them up a little.

"How are my girls doing on this glorious day?" he asks as he winks at me.

"We're good, Daddy, are you taking us to school today?" Annabelle says through a mouthful of eggs.

"I don't want to go to school," Adalaide whispers while looking down. She has always been more introverted than Anna, but luckily, Anna is able to bring her out of her shell on occasion.

My eyes find his, silently telling him to cheer up Ada, but he is already moving toward her.

"Unfortunately, I can't take you today, sweetie," he says to them, but Anna is already looking at Ada, giving her an encouraging smile.

"That's okay, Daddy," Ada says with a smile on her face now. "School actually sounds fun."

Marc picks her up lightning fast to twirl her around making her squeal with delight.

"That's the spirit, monkey! Now I can't take you girls to school, but… since it's your first day of first grade, how about I take my girls out for ice cream afterward?" he asks as he puts Ada back down. The girls cheer and giggle, they are always in the mood for ice cream.

―――

With the girls getting ready for their first day, I follow Marc to the door so I can get a kiss goodbye before he jogs to his car. He notices me waiting and gives me one final wave before backing out of the driveway, disappearing down the road.

"Girls, are you almost ready for your first day? I need pictures of you two so hurry and come down here." They run down the stairs. "Be careful," I yell, but they are already in the kitchen with backpacks on and ready. I'm so glad they decided to wear the matching yellow sundresses because they look absolutely adorable. I gather their long brown hair and tie it up with a yellow ribbon to match so I can see their faces better. Ada's freckles are a little more prominent on her face than Anna's are, but that would be the only difference between them and even then you have to look hard. They even lost the same tooth within the same week of each other, giving them the same toothy smile.

"Okay my Gemini stars, each of you hold this sign up and smile pretty for me." They love when I use the secret nickname I gave them, so we always have something among the three of us. Anna holds her sign up proudly and smiles her biggest smile while Ada holds hers slightly lower and only gives me a close-lipped grin.

"Come on, Ada." I say. "Please, for me, can you show me your pretty smile?"

"Okay, Mom, I'll try," she whispers as she changes her face to form a big smile. It doesn't quite meet her eyes, but it will do.

I snap the picture on my phone and quickly send it to their dad so he can see how adorable they look.

As we pull up in front of the school, Anna's eyes light up with excitement while Ada slowly sinks further into her seat.

"Come on, girls, I'll walk you to your classroom," I say hoping Ada will become less anxious. We walk in a line with me in the middle holding onto their tiny hands, Ada's grip so much tighter than Anna's. Their pony tails sway back and forth as they walk. Anna picks up the pace as we get closer, pulling my arm forward, while Ada pulls my other hand behind me. I give her a reassuring glance and squeeze her hand hoping to put her at ease. Up ahead their teacher stands outside the classroom door to greet everyone and seems to notice her hesitation because he walks over to us.

"Hi, I'm Mr. Young," he says with a full smile as he reaches his hand out to meet mine before kneeling down to greet the girls.

"Hi, I'm Autumn, Autumn Fowler and these are my girls, Ada and—"

"And I'm Anna," she says as she reaches her tiny hand out to shake his.

"Well, lovely to meet you three. What do you say you head on in and meet your other classmates," he says, gesturing for them to head into the classroom.

They do as he says and head toward the door, Anna pulling an unsure Ada along. I give her an encouraging smile before she disappears in the room.

"Thank you. Ada is pretty shy and nervous."

"That's okay, they are in good hands and I'm sure they will make lots of friends."

"Well, keep me posted on how they do, and thank you again." I give a small wave and turn to leave. My heart sinks the further I walk away from them, but I'm comforted knowing that they have each other.

Pulling into the driveway, I take the final sips of my coffee and head to the door. Putting one foot in front of the other and entering the empty house, the silence hits me. The memory of this morning's sleep paralysis dream comes racing back into my thoughts. I try to shake off my fears, but decide to put chores ahead of painting. I head upstairs to start the many loads of laundry that need to get done. After they are started, I go into the girl's room and do a quick tidy and make their beds. Standing in the middle of the room between their twin-size bed, I can't help but reminisce about when they were first brought home from the hospital, their tiny hands barely big enough to wrap around one of my fingers. Now, surrounded by the bubblegum pink walls that match their butterfly bedding, I realize how big they are getting. All of their dolls and stuffed animals wait, sitting at the small table posed and ready to have a tea party. I blink. I can't believe the girls are already starting first grade.

Before the girls, my art career was taking off, and my paintings were being sold at high end galleries. Since their arrival, I had to put my career on hold, but I think I'm finally ready to get back at it again. My studio beckons me to come inside. Obliging, I walk inside, but the atmosphere feels different, almost like someone has been in here, but nothing seems out of place. *Hmm that's weird, maybe I'm still feeling effects from this morning's nightmare.* I shake off the feeling, determined to create something. I choose various brushes to bring all the different textures of a landscape alive. I set my towels and water glass up before opening the window to reveal the beautiful scenery that is in my own backyard. We have a lovely lake with weeping willows surrounding it that are always so peaceful to look at. This will be a perfect first painting to get back in the swing of things. My brush is poised and ready to dip in the hunter green paint when I hear my cell phone ring. Annoyance runs through me. *Ugh, seriously?* I put the brush back down and go in search of my phone. I find it exactly where I left it on the kitchen counter.

"Hey," I mentally check the slight irritation coloring my voice.

"Hey, babe. You, okay? You sound a little off."

"Yeah, I'm fine, you caught me as I was about to start painting, is all."

"Oh, I'm sorry. I can keep it short. I only wanted to see how it went getting the girls to school on their first day. They looked so adorable holding up their signs."

"No, that's okay I *want* to talk to you," the heat rises in my cheeks at my earlier tone, "and yeah it was all good. I got them to their class. The teacher, Mr. Young, seems really nice and they went in okay, seemed a little excited even."

"Okay, good, that's good. I was a little worried about Ada this morning. She didn't seem like she was going to do okay."

"She was a little hesitant, but Anna really helped her," I say, forcing myself to be present in the conversation.

We talk for a bit longer until he says he has an important client calling and has to hang up. As soon as the phone call ends, another call comes through. *Why doesn't anyone want me to paint today?*

"Hello," I answer

"Hey, girlie! Just wanted to call and catch up," Liz says from the other line in her usual bubbly tone.

"Oh hey. Yeah, I just got the girls off to their first day of school and I was about to start painting," I tell her. Her bubbly personality is infectious, so my irritation is already gone.

"Wow! Nice. That was today?" she asks.

"Yep. I should really take the time to catch up on some sleep though," I tell her through a forced laugh.

"Why's that? Not sleeping too well?"

"No, not really." I'm definitely not ready to tell her about my sleep paralysis though.

"Okay, well you get some sleep then, okay? Talk more at your party. Love you!"

"Love you."

Putting the phone on silent, before anyone else can call me, I think about starting the painting, but all the unfinished chores cloud my mind and I am pressed for time. Disappointment radiates through me as I am forced to put off painting yet again. I'm upset that the fresh paint will dry and be wasted, but not enough to attempt to salvage it. I abandon my clean brush, turn the ringer back on my phone and leave my studio. *Maybe I can start painting tomorrow instead.*

Waiting in the air conditioned car, I take a moment to de-stress before my girls get out of school. I close my eyes, but am still plagued with thoughts from my nightmare. *Why now? What is the cause for this starting up again?* The more I question, the deeper I spiral. I pinch the bridge of my nose, forcing myself to put the thoughts aside. Opening my eyes, the bright yellow of the girls' dresses catch my eye as they walk out of the building. I can tell when they finally see our car, because they hold hands and break into a run, skidding to a stop before they wave at me through the window.

"Hey girls!" I say as I'm getting out of the car and pulling them into a big hug, "How was your first day; was it fun; did you make any new friends?"

"Yeah, it was super fun and our teacher is super nice!" Anna says with a big toothy smile on her face.

"Ada, how about you, sweetie?"

"Yeah, it was really fun. We made a new friend; her name is Sarah," she tells me as she glances toward Anna, wiping some of the loose hairs out of her face and tucking them behind her ear.

"That's awesome, well maybe you guys can have a playdate with Sarah sometime soon then," I tell them as I get them buckled in.

They both smile and bob their heads up and down, their pony tails swaying right along with their head. On our drive, we talk more about their day and what they did. I'm shocked when they inform me of their additional homework. *I don't remember having so much homework when I was in first grade.*

Once home, I make them a snack before dinner, and they set up at the kitchen table, eager to get their homework done so they can go upstairs and play. Luckily, their assignment doesn't take too long and they race upstairs. I can already hear them laughing while I start on dinner. Smiling to myself, I can't help thinking about how there is something about their laughter that always makes me feel wonderful and puts me at ease.

I hear the key in the lock before the door opens.

Marc is home.

"Perfect timing," I call out.

He comes over to me and wraps me in a big hug and kisses me on the top of my head. I close my eyes loving how intimate a single forehead kiss from him can feel. I lean back so our lips can meet, and he puts his hand in my hair to pull me in for an even deeper kiss.

"I missed you," he breathes into my lips before pulling back slightly to look at me, his hand still in my hair.

"I missed you too." I smile "Why don't you go get changed for dinner and send the girls down when you go up."

"Will do." He winks and gives me one more quick kiss and heads upstairs. Minutes later, I hear the pitter patter of the girls' feet rushing downstairs, followed by the heavier footfalls of their father. I load up the girls' plates with the spaghetti I made with extra meatballs, then serve myself and Marc. With mouths full of spaghetti, the girls tell Marc about their day at school, but mostly talk about their new friend Sarah, telling him I promised they could have a playdate with her soon. I only have to look at him and smile. He continues to listen intently, and agrees that Sarah sounds like a wonderful new friend. When we're all finished, he takes the plates to the sink, comes back, and whispers,

"I'll wash these when we get back, okay?"

"Okay," I say before he turns back around to face the girls.

"Hey! Who's ready for ice cream?" he yells with his arms wide open waiting for the girls to run into them.

"We are!" The girls scream with delight as they run into their dad's arms so he can pick them up and spin them around.

"Come on my little monkeys, go get in the car," he says moving toward the door so he can help them put their shoes on while I hurry behind them, locking the door as they jump in the car.

We head to our favorite ice cream shop, and as soon as we walk in, the sweet aroma of sugar overpowers our senses. The girls and I grab a table while Marc heads to the counter to place our orders. The girls each get a scoop of cookie dough peanut butter, he gets a mint chocolate chip, and I opt for a scoop of strawberry. We sit at a table near the back by the window and chat animatedly, bringing up the topic of the girls' starting piano lessons in a couple of weeks. The reminder makes them really excited and gives them something new and fun to look forward to. Once the final spoonful of ice cream is consumed, I take them to the bathroom so we can wash their sticky fingers and the mess they have all over their lips before we head back home.

The car is quiet. Anna is fast asleep when we get back and Ada is barely awake with her eyes fluttering open and closed every few seconds.

"I'm glad they had a fun first day of school." Marc whispers.

"So am I. I was worried for a minute about Ada, but I'm glad she has Anna to lean on." I grab his hand and squeeze it, "Thank you for taking them out for ice cream, it meant a lot since you couldn't be there on their first day."

"Of course! I had an unavoidable meeting, but I still wanted to make their night special." He smiles at their reflection in the rearview mirror.

Finally home, Marc carefully carries Ada up to bed while I carry Anna. As we tuck the covers around their sleepy bodies, Ada slightly opens her eyes.

"Don't forget the nightlight," she mumbles before drifting off to sleep again.

"Don't worry, sweetie, I won't. Goodnight, I love you," I kiss the top of her head and set the room a glow with their butterfly night light. With a final glance, I softly close the door behind us.

Once in our bedroom, Marc is already stripping down to his boxers and climbing into bed. Before I can join him, I go to the master bathroom to wash my face, put lotion on, and change into my night shirt. Finally sliding into the comfort of the sheets, I scoot close so he can pull me into his arms. I love feeling the warmth of his body on my back. Under the cover of darkness and comfort of my husband's arms, I confess my fears.

"I'm worried I'm going to have another terrifying dream tonight, the last one was really bad, and felt so real," I turn my head slightly over my shoulder to glance at him.

"I'm sure you won't, and if you do, try to remember to use your calming techniques to get out of it," he says as he starts running his hand through my hair. "And I'm right here if you need me. All you have to do is wake me up and I will help you the best I can."

"Okay, I'll try," I whisper, snuggling deeper into his embrace though deep down, the fear is almost crippling.

2

OPENING my eyes to overwhelming darkness, I start to panic. I try to calm myself and wait for my eyes to adjust, but still nothing. Off in the distance, I start to see a faint light. It seems so far away making me have to squint to get a better look at it. The light looks like a circle that seems to be growing bigger. I'm squinting hard trying to focus on bringing it into view, when I feel a headache coming on. My breathing becomes more rapid and I am not sure why unless my subconscious knows something I don't. I fear I will lose my mind in the darkness when suddenly, my vision snaps into focus and I can see the bright lights were coming from headlights. More of my surroundings start to come into focus and I realize there is a road in front of me with trees all around. I am sitting in a car, looking out through the windshield. I'm not sure how I got here; the car looks like my own, but why am I in my car on what seems like an abandoned road, and where am I going? Did I drive here in my sleep? I'm trying to wrap my head around what I'm seeing when I feel my hands grip the cool leather steering wheel, put the car in drive, and slam my foot on the gas. Before I know it, I'm speeding down the dark and twisting road with trees blurring by me on both sides. I know I am here, driving the car, yet it doesn't feel like me. A rush of confusion and panic threaten to overwhelm me, bringing on a panic attack. In the midst of my panic, I almost don't see the shadowy figure walking on the side of the road. Immediately something compels me to yank the steering wheel to the side. Gasping at the trajectory of the car, I try slamming my foot on the brakes, but it's like my brain isn't in control of my actions. I *will* myself to turn the steering wheel away, but that doesn't work either. A scream rises in the back of my throat, but it doesn't even have time to come out before I feel the impact the car makes with the figure.

The sound of bones crunching against metal and glass is sickening. He or she hits the hood of the car flying into the windshield cracking the glass on impact. I shut my eyes as tightly as I can, pressing myself against the seat and clutching the wheel until my knuckles turn white and cramp with pain. I hesitantly open one eye to peek at what I have done, but when I do, only blackness fields my vision. My eyes frantically move back and forth trying to adjust to the dark to no avail and unlike before, there is no light in the distance now. Feeling hysteria bubble up inside me, I frantically pinch myself hoping with all I have that this is a dream. As bruises form on my arm, I know I must be awake. Taking deep breaths to calm myself, tears run down my face and my breath shakes with each exhale.

I feel a cool breeze across my cheek.

I want to walk, but my legs are planted and feel heavy. When I look down, I feel something wet on my legs like they are submerged in water. My shoes and socks feel squishy and small waves are lapping against my thighs. Nothing here is making sense. I shut my eyes hoping once again that none of this is real and I will wake up soon, but I can still feel the water. Opening my eyes again, I expect to see blackness, but instead, there is finally a glimmer of light, almost as if it's moving in a dancing motion. When I look harder, it dawns on me that it's moonlight dancing on the waves of the water I am standing in. I look around me, hoping the surroundings will tell me where I am, but immediately regret doing so.

I can't hold my shock and terror in! I let out an ear shattering scream!

There is an older looking man under the water at my feet staring up at me with a vacant look in his eyes, and my hands are holding him under. I try to tear my hands away from him to help him, but they don't budge.

I feel the sickening satisfaction that he died at my hands.

Disgusted by my own thoughts, I hurl myself away from him with all my might. I am pushed back into darkness, only this time when I open my eyes, I'm in my bedroom and I can faintly hear Marc calling my name over and over again.

Autumn! Autumn! Autumn!

I focus on his voice and jolt up into his arms as he holds me whispering words of comfort. I am drenched in sweat and shaking so bad that he is having a hard time holding me.

"Autumn, babe, it's okay, you're okay, I'm right here. *Shhhh*. You had another sleep paralysis dream, it's okay."

I let him hold me as I try to convince my mind that what I witnessed was not real… but I know what I saw, and more importantly, how it made me feel.

"It was so real," I sob, I feel wetness on my face and reach up to touch my cheek, realizing I am crying.

"*Shhh*, babe, I'm right here you're okay, just breathe."

I listen to his voice and try to control my breathing when the girls come into my mind,

"Oh my God! Ada! Anna! Did I wake them up?" I ask in a rushed whisper.

"I don't think so. Are you okay if I go make sure they are still sleeping?" he asks as he's working on wiping the last of my tears away with his thumbs, cupping my face in his hands, while his own face is riddled with concern.

"Yes! Go, go," I grab his pillow so I can hold it tightly against my chest as a shield until he returns. I work on controlling my breathing, relieved when he comes back into the room so quickly.

"They are still sound asleep; I quietly called their names and they didn't even move. They must be really sound sleepers," he says with a hint of a laugh in his voice. I move to let him back in the bed and relinquish his pillow, moving my knees up to my chest and wrapping my arms tightly around them. *Ugh I'm never going to get any sleep.*

I rub my hands over my face. "Good, I'm glad I didn't wake them up."

Marc looks at me with a faint look of worry still creasing his brow, "Yeah, they're fine, are you okay though? This makes two nights in a row now." His eyes search my face, trying to make sure I'm okay.

"Yeah, it felt so real. I could have sworn I was actually there. Seriously, Marc, I was in the dark, in a car, and it felt like I hit somebody but had no control over anything." I let out a long shallow shaky breath before I can continue. "Then I was plunged back into darkness with only a glimmer of light. That's when I noticed the man. He was looking up at me from the water… dead." I decide it's for the best I don't tell him how it made me feel deep down. The idea I reveled in the man's death by my own hands is unfathomable. I'm disgusted at how I took pleasure in watching the life go out of his eyes. I shake the thought away before it makes me throw up. *Marc can never know. He too would be disgusted with me.*

Marc blows out a breath. "Wow, babe, that must have been really scary. I can't even imagine."

I stare off into the distance, taking deep breaths while he rubs his hands up and down my arms.

"Do you want to try and go back to sleep? Or do you need a minute?"

"I think I'll try to go back to sleep, I am really tired," I say, laying my head back on the pillow, but afraid to close my eyes for fear I will see the old man with the dead eyes again. I'm more afraid that it wasn't a dream at all. I'm afraid I may have murdered the man in cold blood… and liked it.

"Okay, well I'm right here if you need me again," he says as he starts to lay back down.

An hour has passed and I can hear Marc's deep breath as he gets back to sleep. Still staring into the darkness, I roll over and try a new position, close my eyes, praying for sleep to come, but it never does. Before I know it, his alarm is going off. He leans over to turn it off before coming back over to hug me.

"Good morning, did you end up getting back to sleep?" he asks through a yawn.

"No, I didn't," I say, disappointment coloring my voice.

"Oh, babe, I'm sorry, do you want me to go in a little late today and I can take the girls to school?"

"No, it's okay," I tell him as I rub my temples trying to fight off a headache. "I'll take a nap when I get back home from dropping them off."

"Okay, if you're sure." He leans over and gives me a quick kiss on the lips before he gets out of bed and heads for the shower

"I'm going to go start the coffee, okay?" I say as I get out of bed and pull my robe and slippers on.

"Okay, thanks babe."

I hold my growling stomach and ask, "Do you want any breakfast this morning? I am starving."

"Yes please, I'll have whatever you're having," he says from the shower.

"Scrambled eggs and bacon," I tell him. "Can you wake up the girls on your way down then?"

"Yes, no problem."

Being alone in the kitchen is calming for me and exactly what I need to refocus myself for the day. I busy myself getting the ingredients I need for breakfast when Marc rounds the corner and pours himself a cup of freshly brewed coffee.

"Are the girls awake?" I ask, cracking the eggs in a bowl.

"Yeah, they are slowly making their way downstairs," he says as he puts cream and sugar in his coffee. "Are you sure you're okay from last night? You looked really frightened."

"Yeah, I will be okay, still reeling, but after I drop the girls off, I'm going to come home and try and get some more sleep."

"Okay, babe, well I only want you to feel better. Two nights in a row of sleep paralysis seems to have really got to you."

"Yeah, the dreams both felt so real. It's going to take me a minute to get over them. I might end up taking the sleeping pills I got a while ago so I don't dream and I can sleep tonight. I don't know though," I say hoping I look and sound more relaxed.

I hear the girls coming downstairs and hurry to make the rest of breakfast while Marc moves to grab the plates and cups out of the cupboard.

"Okay, monkeys, who wants orange juice?"

"I do!" Anna yells while raising her hand high in the air.

"I want chocolate milk!" Ada says running to come sit down next to her sister.

"Okay! One order of orange juice and one chocolate milk coming up."

He pours the orange juice and sets it in front of Anna, and then goes to get the milk and Nesquik chocolate syrup from the fridge.

"I want it the special way you make it, Daddy." Ada says while fluttering her eyelashes so fast you could almost feel a breeze.

"Coming right up, monkey," he says smiling down at the milk in the cup.

He makes a show of twirling the Nesquik bottle in his hand and dumping it in the milk. When he's satisfied with the amount of chocolate, he waves a hand over it before putting the spoon in it to stir it all together.

"Here you go. Daddy's special chocolate milk." He dramatically bows before them making them erupt in giggles.

"You're silly Daddy," Ada says between her laughs. He gives her a wink and sits down beside them.

I'm plating everyone's eggs and bacon, only enjoying my own meal after everyone has dug in to theirs. Marc scarfs the food down and kisses the girls on the tops of their heads before coming over and giving me a kiss on the lips.

"I have to head out, I hope all my girls have a great day, I'll see you tonight, I love you!" he says grinning and waving as he heads out the door and leaving me alone to get the girls ready and off to school.

Something nags at me while I get ready to take a nap. Was my "dream" real? Or was it just a dream? Opening the door to my closet, I don't know what exactly I expect to find, but maybe it will help prove it was only a dream. Pushing every item of clothing to the side and going through each drawer thoroughly, I find nothing. I'm about to give up when I see them. Tucked in the corner under a blanket are my tennis shoes covered in mud and still wet. My hands fly to my mouth to cover my gasp, shaking my head. I buckle at the knees and hesitantly reach toward the shoes, hoping beyond hope, I'm imagining seeing them. With shaky hands, I bring the shoes closer to my face to inspect them. My new tennis shoes are sopping wet and caked in mud as if I stood in a muddy river bank or something. *It can't be. I'm not capable of something like this.* I feel hot tears fall from my eyes. *What have I done?* I pull my knees up and wrap my arms around them and cry. *I don't even remember putting my shoes in here and when could I have even done this?*

I can't stand to look at the shoes anymore and I can't exactly keep them in my closet. The meaning of them weighing so heavily on me, I feel as if I will be crushed. Disgusted, I throw them in the sink and begin to wash all of the mud and potential evidence away, not wanting to believe any of this is real or that I killed a man. For all I know, he is still alive. Better yet it was a dream. Besides, if my car was dented and the windshield cracked, Marc would have said something.

No, these wet muddy shoes don't mean anything.

After cleaning and rinsing the shoes of all traces of mud possible, I am even more tired and emotionally drained than before, making it much easier to pass out beneath my inviting covers.

Bang!

I sit straight up feeling a little bit disoriented. *What the hell?*

I cautiously put my robe on and slowly open up the door to peak into the hallway. My ears are straining to hear any other movement coming from downstairs, but there is nothing but eerie silence. I'm afraid to call out in case someone is in the house, so I punch in 9-1-1 on my phone, thumb at the ready to press the call button. I creep into the hallway and tip toe downstairs, careful to avoid all the spots that creak in the floorboards. I'm halfway down the stairs when it dawns on me that I should have grabbed the bat. *Ugh, stupid.* I get to the final step, and realize I have been holding my breath the whole time. Slowly and quickly as I can, I exhale and force myself to breathe as normally as possible. As I peek my head around the corner into the kitchen, I expect to see someone, but it's only an empty quiet space. Moving back toward the living room and down the hall toward my studio, our wedding photo catches my eye. It has a crack in the glass right down the middle and is hanging crooked. It's the least of my concerns, so I brush it off and continue on my hunt for a possible intruder.

With shaky hands, I grab the doorknob and open my studio door inches at a time until I can slip inside. Standing in my room, back against the door, I find my easel and canvas both on the floor and paint tubes thrown all around. Frightened at the reality of the situation, I sprint out of the room and run for the front door. I hope I can get out fast without the intruders noticing.

Outside, the dew on the grass soaks into my slippers. I clutch my robe tighter and book it for my neighbor's house, my phone pressed against my ear, praying for Marc to answer. In the light of day, I notice something on my arm. *Is that paint?* I slow down enough to inspect the substance. Yes, it is in fact paint streaked on my arm. *When did this happen?*

"Hey, babe, how's it going?" he asks brightly through the phone.

"I think someone was in our house, but now I'm not sure because I have paint on my arms and I don't know if it was me or not. I was so tired and… and I just don't know." It all comes out in a frantic rush. I'm not sure he heard a word I said.

"Babe, babe, slow down. What are you saying? Is there someone in the house? Or not? Did you call 9-1-1?"

I can hear the alarm in his voice, so I try to calm down and tell him exactly what happened.

"I don't know. I was sleeping, but heard a bang or thud coming from downstairs so I woke up and went to check it out and my easel, canvas, and paint were all on the floor. I was about to call 9-1-1, but I have paint streaks on my arms and hands so I'm not sure if it was me that did it while I was sleeping, like maybe I sleep walked? I don't know," I say running my hands through my hair and beginning to chew at my nails. Nothing about any of this is making sense, and I'm starting to not trust myself.

"Okay, is anything else out of order? Doors or windows open? Anything missing?"

"No, no, it was only my art supplies knocked over." My eyes scan the house. Half of me wants to see a figure walk by a window so I will know I'm not crazy.

"Okay, go to the neighbor's house, I'm going to call the police to be on the safe side so they can check things out and I'll meet you at home."

"I'm at their house now about to knock," I say, blowing out a breath.

"Good! I'll see you soon."

We hang up and I knock on their door, relieved when it's Patty who answers.

"Autumn, this is a surprise, what can I do for you?" she asks slightly confused as her eyes look me up and down no doubt thinking I must be crazy standing in front of her in a robe and slippers.

"Hey, can I come in? I think someone might have broken into the house, but I'm not sure. Marc is going to have the police take a look and I was hoping I could wait in here until they arrive."

"Oh, my *goodness!* Yes, yes come in, you poor thing," she says waving inside and locking the door behind me. She moves to the window checking if those are locked too as if the intruder might make this their next stop. She glances over to me, fear evident in her eyes, and I feel terrible for putting her in this position of distress.

"I'm sure it's nothing. I'm probably worried for no reason," I tell her in an attempt to calm her. Patty gives me a warm smile and reaches for my hands, giving them a light squeeze. We hear the police sirens before I see the lights. I give her a thankful smile and head to the door to wait outside and flag them over.

Two officers get out of their vehicle, one older who looks like he has seen some things in his day and the other young, a rookie maybe. Their faces don't give anything away as they calmly walk toward me.

"Thank you for coming. My husband is the one who called. We figured we would err on the side of caution. Be positive there wasn't actually an intruder."

"Ma'am, did you actually see anyone in the house?" the older officer asks gruffly

"No, I didn't, I... I heard a noise and came down to see my stuff on the floor in my studio." I stammer out, nervous they don't believe me.

"Okay, well we will check it out, be on the safe side and let you know what we find if anything," he says and signals to his partner to go around to the back of the house.

"Okay, thank you so much." I say.

Moments after they get into the house, Marc is rounding the corner and pulling up on the curb. He jumps out and runs over to me.

"Are you okay? Did they find anything?" he asks, looking at me before pulling me into his arms.

The police officer and his partner walk back out of the house and amble over to us.

"Well, I didn't see any sign of break-in and besides the room you told me about, nothing else seems to be out of place." His partner notices the paint on my arms and looks at me suspiciously. "Are you sure you didn't happen to knock everything over yourself?"

I feel my cheeks burning with embarrassment as Marc looks at me with a questioning expression.

"I'm... I'm not sure, I was upstairs in bed sleeping when I heard the crash... It wasn't me." But as I say the words, I realize I'm doubting myself more and more, and the police seem to pick up on that.

"What my partner means is, we have to ask all these questions to make sure we have all the information and will be able to rule things out," He says it professionally enough, like he's been through this many times, but his eyes tell me he doesn't entirely believe me. "Are you on any sort of medication, ma'am, that might make you a little fuzzy? Or perhaps you haven't been sleeping well and you might be confused?" the older officer asks, pulling a notebook out of his breast pocket. The younger officer, however, continues to stare me down.

"No. I mean, I used to take sleeping pills years ago. I was going to take one tonight because, yes, it's true I haven't been sleeping well, but I swear, I didn't take any this afternoon."

"Okay, well maybe you took one and don't remember doing it? Or maybe you were simply more tired than you think and don't remember making the mess yourself. In any case though, I'll ask around and see if any of your neighbors have seen anyone wandering around that they don't know."

"Thank you, officer!"

They go back to their cruiser and we watch them disappear down the road before I build the courage to face Marc.

"I swear, I don't think it was me. I don't know why I have paint on me, I wasn't even in that room today. I came straight home and went to bed." I don't tell him about the shoe incident.

"*Shhh* it's okay, let's get inside and have a look. There's no one in there now." His voice is calm as he says it, but I can see the hint of doubt on his face before he can shake it away.

We walk through the house and notice nothing else out of the ordinary, like the officer said. Marc helps me pick up my things in the studio, noticing the spilled paint is, in fact, the paint on my arms. *Maybe I did do it. I haven't had any sleep for the past two nights now.* Marc thankfully doesn't question me any more about it.

"I'm going to get cleaned up before we have to pick up the girls," I say, not being able to look him in the eyes.

"Sounds good, I'll meet you in the car then," he says, and abruptly turns on his heel and walks out the door.

Once in the car, he finally turns to me. "How about we order some pizza for dinner tonight," he asks as I put my seatbelt on, his voice is calm now, void of any judgment.

"Yes, I think that would be good," I say, pausing before saying my next thought. "I'm really sorry you had to leave work early for nothing."

"Are you kidding? Of course, I left. This is a huge deal. Your safety is my number one priority, Autumn. Let's not take the sleeping pills tonight though on the off chance you took them already and don't remember. Deal?"

I nod my head in agreement and angle myself toward the window, transfixed by the trees we pass, lost in my own thoughts.

As everyone eats their pizza, I zone out. Only the feeling of Marc's hand squeezing mine brings me back, reminding me I'm not alone. I put on my best smile and join in the conversation. Deep down though, I'm still scared and nervous about everything that happened. Between my dream and everything since, it's not looking too good.

Now that the girls are asleep, I decide it would be a good time to include Marc on my idea.

"We should look into getting a security system," I blurt out from the bathroom as I finish washing my face.

"Yeah, we could do that," he tells me. "I would feel a lot safer if we did, especially with you alone in the house for most of the day."

I climb in bed and feel his body heat radiating off of him. I already feel safer.

"I would too, let's do it." I let myself sink into the warmth of his body, and let my eyelids slowly close.

I'm awaken from my sleep with the tiniest of whispers.

"Mommy?" I force my eyes to open, still groggy, but I see Ada standing next to me.

"Hey, sweetie, what's wrong?" I ask as I sit up, fear hitting me in the chest.

"I'm really hot," she says in a sleep covered voice.

"Okay, sweetie, are you feeling sick?" I ask as I move the back of my hand to feel her forehead.

"No, just hot."

"Okay, come here and sit by the fan for a bit," I say as I walk over to the fan in the corner with her. "Feel better?" I move her hair away from her face and gather it in a bun, allowing the breeze to cool her faster.

"Yeah, that's better."

"Okay, go sit up by Daddy and I'm going to go turn the air on, okay?"

She mumbles okay and I set her on the bed in case she falls back asleep before heading downstairs to turn the air on. I flip the panel down and see the heat is set to 78 degrees. *What the hell? This was not set to this yesterday. It's one thing after the other, jeez.* I turn it back to air and set it to 68 degrees. When I get back upstairs, Marc is coming out of the girls' room.

"Did you put her back to bed?"

"Yeah, why was she in our bed?"

"She was hot and I put her in bed so I could turn on the air."

"Yeah, why is it so hot in here?" he asks, wiping the sweat off his brow.

"When I went to check, it was set to 78 degrees. You didn't set it to that for some reason, did you?

"Nope, not me. You know I'm always hot; I would have the air on all year long if I could."

"Hmm weird," I say mentally adding this to the ever-growing list of unexplained occurrences.

3

IN THE KITCHEN, finally alone. I enjoy some hot coffee and research security systems. I'm in the midst of making a pro/con list to determine which one would be the best for what we would need and fit our budget when I hear the doorbell ring. Downing the rest of my coffee, I walk over to the door wondering who could possibly be stopping by this early.

When I open the door, there's no one there.

Hmm that's weird, I swear I heard it ring.

I peek my head out and take one last look around before heading back to the counter to grab my phone and pick up where I left off with my research, but it's gone.

What the hell? I know I left it right here.

I look around the counter, on the floor, under the paper even, but still, nothing. I feel like I'm losing my mind. *Okay, just breathe.* I take a second look before searching the rest of the kitchen. Still not seeing it, I make my way to the living room where I spot it almost immediately. *How did it get over here?* The hairs on the back of my neck stick up and paranoia starts to set in. I quickly spin around expecting to see someone behind me, but no one is here but me.

I feel silly, but also unsettled so I sit with my back against a wall, having full view of both rooms and frantically search the security system, wishing it was already installed.

Ding dong.

Okay, I know I heard the doorbell this time. I hesitantly get up, phone clutched in my hands. I expect to find no one at the door again, but when I open it, I see my neighbor Patty standing before me. Exhaling a sigh of relief, my body relaxes and I tuck my phone in my back pocket.

"Hey Patty, did you happen to swing by a few minutes ago?" I ask as I move aside to let her in.

"Oh no, it's my first time here today. Why do you ask?" she says with a cautious look on her face.

"No, reason," I tell her, closing the door. "Can I get you a cup of coffee, or some iced tea maybe?"

"Iced tea would be great, thank you, it's a scorcher out there today," she says as she sits at the kitchen counter.

I grab two glasses out of the cabinet, fill it to the brim with my homemade iced tea and bring it over to her.

"What can I do for you Patty," I ask, sitting next to her and taking a sip of my iced tea.

"Oh, I was only wondering if they caught the intruder you had. It had me and Dave up all night worried." She reaches for her iced tea and practically downs the whole thing in one gulp.

"No, the cops said they found no sign of forced entry, but I haven't been sleeping too well so I think I may have overreacted to the situation and I made something of nothing. I feel really silly about the whole thing. I'm sorry for scaring you both."

"Oh! Well, that's great news. The cop asked us if we saw anyone out of the ordinary around and we both said no." She takes a final sip of her tea and I notice the striking contrast of her bright pink nail polish on her alabaster, aged spotted skin. Her matching skin tight, low cut tank top and short shorts are something I would be too embarrassed to wear. Patty is nearing her fifties now and tries to dress like she's a teenager. She still works out on the regular, so she can definitely pull it off though.

"Yeah, to be on the safe side, we are looking into getting an alarm system though."

"Oh, that will be nice as long as it doesn't go off all hours of the night and wake Dave and me. Our former neighbor, Carol, she had one and it malfunctioned all night long. We couldn't get a lick of sleep," she says as she waves her hand dramatically.

"Don't worry. We are doing our research to find a good one and get it installed right."

"Okay, well thank you for the iced tea, dear. I better be heading back," she says standing up.

"Okay, Patty, thank you for dropping by."

I walk her to the door and give a small wave before closing the door behind her. Checking the time on my phone I realize I need to eat some lunch before I have to go pick the girls up again. The fresh air calls to me and I decide to eat outside. That mixed with the sunshine is a sure fire way to clear my mind before I have to head out.

I pull up where all the parents are supposed to line up and notice Marc's car two vehicles ahead of mine. *Why is he here?* I turn the car off, head over to the driver's side window, and tap on the glass.

"What are you doing here?" he asks as he rolls down the window.

"What do you mean? I always pick the girls up." I am equally confused.

"Well, you texted me that I needed to pick the girls up today. You said you weren't feeling good and wanted to sleep."

"What? No, I didn't," I say as I reach for my phone, but sure enough there's a text to Marc sent from me only an hour ago asking him to pick the girls up. I immediately think of when my phone was misplaced and I couldn't find it.

Is someone messing with me, or did I text him and forget? I decide not to mention the possible mix up to him for fear of sounding crazy yet again.

"Ugh, I'm so sorry, I don't remember sending this at all. I was preoccupied with researching security systems, and Patty stopped by. It must have slipped my mind that I texted you." As I say the words, I can feel the blood rise to my cheeks giving away my embarrassment.

"It's okay, babe, not a big deal, we can start our night early since I'm already here." There's slight irritation in his voice, but he hides it well.

"Let's go grab a bite to eat and we can catch a movie after."

"Okay, sounds good. I'll follow you then," I tell him, trying to keep my voice light, but all I feel is guilt and worry that I'm losing my mind. I look up to see the girls running toward their dad's car.

"Daddy!" the girls scream in unison.

"Hey, monkeys! Who feels like eating dinner out?"

"Ooooo! Me! Me!" Ada says with delight.

"Yummy!" Anna says handing her backpack to her dad. "Can Sarah come with us and then have a tea party after? *Please?*" she asks, batting her eyes and fully sticking out her bottom lip. It's so adorable you will give her whatever she asks for.

Suddenly, we see a girl with cute blonde pigtails wearing a nice summer dress walking over to us with her mom. *This must be their friend Sarah.*

"I hear our girls planned a playdate for themselves," she says with a chuckle. "I'm Jeanie, nice to meet you." The fit woman extends her long, manicured hand toward us.

"Hi, yes," I say, shaking her hand. "Our Anna was just telling us about it." I look down at my smiling daughter before looking back up to Jeanie. "It's alright with us if it's alright with you. We were actually about to head out to dinner first, and then the girls can have their tea party at our house. I have a car seat in my car, so I can take her if you would like."

"Yes, that would be fine, I can pick her up around 6:30 then," Jeanie says as she runs her fingers through her daughter's pigtails. "Give me your number and address."

"Okay, that sounds good." We rattle off our phone numbers and our address before saying goodbye. Jeanie is a little more thorough and hands a list of every contact she has in case of an emergency. I tuck it in my purse and silently curse myself for not being a more prepared mother.

The girls decide to play rock paper scissors to see who gets to ride with Sarah. Ada ends up winning. I have a feeling Anna let her. *I guess it worked out after all that I "texted" Marc to pick them up.* Ada wants to ride with me so she and Sarah chat and periodically sing to the songs on the radio the whole way to the restaurant.

As we eat, the girls tell us about their next assignment they need to complete and how they made a new friend named Troy. He is friends with Sarah, so naturally, they are all friends now.

"Can we go play in the play area, Mommy?" Anna asks, clasping her hands in front of her and giving me her best please face, which prompts the other two to join in.

"Yeah, can we? Plleeaassee?" Ada and Sarah chime in.

"Sure, go ahead. Just for a little bit though."

"And stay in view," their dad adds.

"Yay!" they scream in unison before racing off to play. When they're playing, I decide now would be a good time to apologize again to Marc for the confusion.

"Ugh, I feel like I'm going crazy. Between the commotion yesterday, the thermostat, now not remembering that I texted you." I peek up to look at him, "I'm really sorry about everything. I hope it didn't get you in trouble or hinder your work too much."

"No, not at all, babe, it's fine, it was a slow day anyway. You need to get a good night's sleep, that's all," he says, but his words sound forced. "Should I be worried? You have been awfully forgetful lately."

I choose to ignore his tone. "Yeah, I know, you're probably right, I need to get some more sleep and everything will be fine. Hopefully, I can get it together by the time the girls start their lessons next week."

"It will be fine," he says breezily, "and if you need me to pick them up from their lessons to help out, I can do that too."

"I'll be fine to do it, thank you. You have been so amazing this past week. I really appreciate you being so understanding with all my crazy happening all at once."

His lips twitch in amusement.

"I like crazy, remember," he says with a glint in his eye, making me forget his tone and look at him. How lucky I am that he came into my life when he did, remembering how we first met.

I was a freshman at college, studying to be an art major at Illinois State University and he was a junior studying business. It was my first day on the quad, the warm sun beating down on me as I looked at each stone and brick building trying to figure out which was the right one for my art history course. I stood circling around looking at each building, feeling more lost and confused by the minute, when this handsome guy walked past me. Something about me must have caught his attention because he stopped and offered to help me get to my first class with minutes to spare. The handsome stranger even waited until my class was over to make sure I knew where I needed to go next. Something about him made me trust him and even though I had sworn off men, we exchanged numbers, hitting it off immediately. He was so charming, sweet, and of course, good looking. His athletic build, dark hair, and eyes as blue as the ocean made me practically swoon every time I looked at him. We began talking and seeing each other almost every day after that. When I was able to move out of the dorms and into an apartment, naturally we decided to live together.

The day I graduated with my bachelor's, and he with his master's, we were getting the standard cap and gown pictures when suddenly, he turned to me and got down on one knee to propose in front of everyone. It was like a dream come true!

I immediately said yes!

We were married a year later in June in a wonderful backyard ceremony with all of our closest family and friends. It wasn't much, but to me it was perfect.

The simplicity of my ivory dress with its sweetheart bodice, covered in lace, paired well with the sunflowers I had as my bouquet. Before I walked down the aisle, I remember not feeling nervous at all. My only feeling was the unbelievable certainty that I was meant to marry this man. When my dad walked me down the aisle, and I saw him standing there in his light gray tux, I looked into his eyes and knew he felt the same way. I didn't think our lives could get any better after marriage.

I was wrong.

One short year later, we welcomed our beautiful twin daughters into the world. Funny to think that we have been married for eight years already.

"What are you thinking?" he asks with a smile, bringing me back to the present.

"I was thinking about how lucky I am that you're in my life," I say blushing a little.

"I'm the lucky one," he says as he kisses my forehead, and tucks a stray hair behind my ear.

When we get home, we decide to indulge in a glass of wine. Moscato for me and Merlot for him. We hear the girls giggle every now and then upstairs while they have their tea party with Sarah.

"So, the girls start piano lessons next Wednesday at 3:30 till 5:30, so we will be home after you," I tell him as I sip my wine.

"That's okay, I can start on dinner and have it ready by time you guys get home."

"Okay, yeah, that would be great," he takes a big gulp of his wine. "So, do you have anything in mind for your big 3.0?"

"I don't know. Since it's on a Saturday, we could have the girls stay at my parents' house for the day and they can have a sleep over there while we go out with Freya, Ren, Liz, and their husbands. We could have a small party here?"

"That sounds like a good time to me." He downs the rest of his drink and signals toward mine. "Do you want a refill?"

"Yes, please, I will have one more I think."

I'm not quite sure if having alcohol is such a good idea when I am already having trouble sleeping and so forgetful, but the warm feeling it brings along with the slight buzz makes it worthwhile, even for a little bit. While Marc's in the kitchen refilling our glasses, the girls' laughter fills the space and I wish I could be that carefree again.

"What are you smiling at?" Marc asks. He stumbles a little in his walk back to me causing the wine to slosh in the glass.

"The girls, their laughter makes me happy," I grab my glass from him before he can spill it.

We're about done with our second glass when we hear the tiny foot falls running down the stairs.

"Mommy! Daddy! Can Sarah spend the night?" Anna asks as she's tugging on my arm.

"Yeah, can she?" Ada chimes in, equally as excited.

"I'm sorry girls, I'm afraid not. Her mom will be here soon to pick her up," I tell them. Seeing their faces drop, I quickly add, "Let's do it another time when it's been planned okay?"

"Why don't you girls finish up your tea party, maybe we can join you?" Marc asks. "I know I could use one of those cookies you bake so well."

They smile and say we can, but we have to hurry because Sarah is pulling the cookies out *right* now. We follow the girls up the stairs, Anna dragging me the whole way until we reach their room. I sit across from Anna, while Marc takes the seat next to me across from Ada. She carefully hands him the kids' teapot, afraid it will break if it were to be dropped.

"Here you go, Daddy, you have to pour everyone their tea."

"Okay, who wants their tea first? How about we start with Mommy?" He reaches for my tiny tea cup and pours the imaginary liquid inside.

"I would love some tea, thank you," I tell him, taking the cup back after he tells me it is full.

"The cookies are ready!" Sarah exclaims, handing the plate of freshly baked imaginary cookies to Ada. "Be careful though, they are still hot." Her cautious tone and furrowed brow are adorable.

"Here, Mommy, here is your cookie," Ada says. She proudly

puts the plate of cookies in front of me so I can choose one. "Don't forget to blow on it."

"Thank you, are these chocolate chip?" I ask Sarah.

"Yes," she giggles, "how did you know?" She sits down next to Ada.

"Oh easy, because they smell exactly like chocolate chip," I give her a wink and reach over to tickle her. Her fit of laughter is contagious for everyone.

The tap, tap on the door tells us that Sarah's mom has arrived and we head down to let her in. The girls walk slowly behind us trying to prolong the night.

"She is wonderful," We tell Jeanie. "Sarah is welcome here any time." The girls hug each other bye and Sarah moves to stand next to her mom.

"Thank you," she says. "Next time the girls can hang out at our place if you like."

"That would be nice, we will have to pencil something in." I tell her.

"Definitely, you have my number," she replies warmly.

She reaches down to grab Sarah's hand; with a final wave, they leave. I close the door behind them and it becomes the four of us again.

"Okay girls, time for your bath and bed."

"*Awww,* do we have to?" they both whine.

"Yes, I'm afraid you do, but what do you say I read you an extra story? Would you like that?" Marc asks them.

"Yeah!" They both yell. Anna turns on her heels and runs up the stairs to get ready for bed with Ada trailing right behind her.

Once they are all squeaky clean and in fresh jammies, they hold Marc to his promise of a story. After the fifth story, their eyes are drooping. They try with all their might to fight sleep, but its pull is too strong. He puts the book down and we hug and kiss them goodnight and slowly close their door. We hear the soft click of the door and turn to head to our room, anxious to feel the comfort of each other.

Marc reaches over to cup my head in his hand. He kisses me lightly at first before deepening it. We make love twice before we fall back against the sheets, breathing heavily, looking into each other's eyes, and I can't help but feel so much love from him. He rolls over, but keeps me in his arms so we are still lying together, me fitting perfectly against him.

"I love you." I whisper.

"I love you too," he nuzzles my neck and holds me tighter.

I don't want to break the spell we have between us right now but I need the darkness and security of being in his arms to discuss today's events and make sure he doesn't think I'm losing my mind.

"I was looking up security systems online and I think I found a few that could work for us if you would like to check them out."

"I can do that. Send me the links and I will look into them tomorrow."

I stay silent for a beat, content to listen to him breathe. I debate whether I should voice my concerns of forgetfulness, as well as how I secretly felt in my dreams. The forgetfulness is one thing to process, but I don't know how he will handle the sinister feeling I have. He could be afraid of me, or worse think that I was unfit to be around our children.

My muscles tense with what ifs. Feeling the shift in my body, Marc massages my neck, and kisses my shoulder with a featherlight touch.

"I know you're concerned with today, but you shouldn't be, you're probably exhausted from not sleeping well at all the past couple of nights, and I know you're stressed about turning thirty, which is really no big deal. Look at me, I'm two years into my thirties, and I'm doing fine," he teases. "You need your beauty rest." I know he is attempting to lighten the mood, but I want to correct him and confide in him. I wish I could voice all the other torments that have been plaguing my mind, but instead, I find myself saying the opposite of how I feel.

"Yeah," I sigh, "you're probably right, but I would feel better with the security system anyway." At the very least I will know if I'm leaving the house or not if I end up having another dream about murdering someone.

4

NEEDING something to distract my mind from everything, I'm hoping to get some painting done today while the girls are at school. Being in front of a blank canvas with a paintbrush in my hand allows me to de-stress and pour everything into my art. My works haven't been in a gallery setting in a long time and I want to get my talent back out there for the world to see. Even though Marc makes enough money for us to be more than comfortable, it's nice earning money on my own through my art.

I walk down to my studio, energized and excited to start on the landscape I had planned to make the day before. When I get close to the door, all my positive energy vanishes and I find myself hesitating to go inside.

Just breathe, no one is in there and everything has already been picked up, it's fine.

I reach out a shaky hand, my fingertips barely graze the knob. I take a deep breath, hold my head high and enter my studio. I walk directly to the curtains to let the morning light in and look at the calming lake. It looks so beautiful in the morning with the sun reflecting off the water and peeking through the weeping willow trees. Wanting some fresh air to come inside, I open the window all the way letting in the crisp, cool breeze. *Perfect.*

I take pleasure in the routine of picking out a blank canvas and gently rest it on the easel in front of me while I select a variety of paints and brushes so I can begin the process of bringing the beautiful landscape scenery to life. With furrowed brows, I focus on the colors making up my image — the beautiful, vibrant blues and greens of the sky and leaves to the weeping willow tree. I focus on the water, bringing in hints of white to try and capture the glint of the sun. My hand sweeps furiously across the canvas like it has a mind of its own, when suddenly, I'm brought out of my hypnotic like state with the sound of my cell phone ringing. I reach to answer it, and can't help but laugh at myself seeing all the paint that has somehow been smeared on my arm. *Ah the consequences of being an artist.*

"Hello," I say in an out of breath way, even though I am only painting.

"Hello, is this Mrs. Fowler," the voice asks, all full of business.

"Yes, it is, who's calling?" I ask as I put my brush in water so the paint doesn't dry out.

"Hi this is Karen Fitzpatrick, I'm the principal at the elementary school. I'm calling about Adalaide. She was sent to the nurse's office because she is not feeling well and is running a fever. We need you to come and pick her up."

"Oh my god, yes ok I will be right there. Is Anna feeling unwell too?"

"No, it's only Adalaide," she briskly informs me.

I hang up and abandon my painting. I decide to call Marc on my way over to let him know I'm going to pick up Ada from school early. When I arrive, I head into the school where Ada is waiting in the office for me.

"Are you ready to go home, Ada?" I ask. I kneel in front of her and put my hand to her warm forehead.

"Yeah," she whispers. "Is Anna coming with us?"

"No, we will pick her up once school is over," I tell her while I carry her in my arms to the car. Her cheeks are rosy and she lets out a small whimper. I move quickly to get her strapped in and rush to the driver's seat to head home.

I hate seeing my baby like this.

I glance at her through the rearview mirror. "Hey, sweetie, how are you feeling?"

"Not good, Mommy," she says barely above a whisper.

"Aww, I know, sweetie, Mommy's going to get you home and make you some chicken noodle soup and then tuck you into bed. How's that sound?"

Ada simply nods her head and closes her eyes. We get home in no time and I carry her inside, leaving her backpack in the car for now. I get her all set up and comfy on the couch and bring her the chicken soup to eat. She eats almost all of it while she watches her cartoons. Taking the final slurp of her soup, she hands the bowl out to me.

"Can I finish watching cartoons, Mommy?"

"Of course, sweety." I take the bowl to the kitchen and when I return, she is out like a light. She looks so comfortable so I leave her curled up where she is. I reach for the blanket on the other end of the couch, wrap it around her and kiss her softly on the forehead. It dawns on me that I left her backpack in the car. I grab my car keys off the counter, but on my way to the front door, I see her backpack out of the corner of my eye lying next to the door as if it has been there the whole time.

Huh? I guess I did bring it in after all.

I pick it up and set it on the bench so she can find it if she needs it. Turning back around, I feel my stomach start to gurgle and realize I haven't eaten yet. I return to the kitchen and make myself a late lunch before I have to wake Ada up and take her with me to go pick up her sister. I'm almost finished getting ready to go when my phone buzzes and I see Marc's name light up the screen.

"Hey, babe."

"Hey, how's our little trooper doing?" He asks.

"She's doing okay, got her some chicken soup and she's been sleeping on the couch since then. I was about to wake her up so we can go pick up Anna."

"Okay that's good, does she have any other symptoms so far?"

"No, just the fever. I'm hoping it will break later today."

"Okay, want me to pick up any medicine on my way home?"

"No, that's okay. I can grab it after I pick Anna up." I know he is eager to help, but it would be easier for me to get it.

We hang up and I load a sleeping Ada in the car and head out to get Anna. When we are all together and the medicine is bought, we go home so I can start on dinner for everyone, even though Ada insists she only wants the chicken soup again.

Everyone is eating at the table when Marc arrives and greets us with kisses on top our heads before walking over and kneeling next to Ada.

"How's my monkey feeling?" he asks, voice full of concern. He puts the back of his hand against her forehead, only taking it away when she pulls back.

"Meh, okay I guess." Ada says with a small shrug. "Mommy made me a special dinner, different from everyone else's."

I can't help but smile, thinking that she got the easiest dinner of everyone, but somehow, to her it's the best.

As the girls abandon their plates and head to the couch, I decide to pop in a movie. With them huddled in front of the tv, I wave Marc over to help me with the dishes.

"Did you get a chance to look into the alarm companies today?"

"Yea, I called a few places to get some quotes, and I think ADT is our best bet. They can have someone out here next Wednesday to get it all installed," he says as he finishes drying the plate in his hands before grabbing another.

"Okay, that sounds good. The girls have piano that same day too. Will that be a problem?"

"Nope, I scheduled it for early in the morning. Hopefully, it will give us the peace of mind we're looking for."

"I'm sure it will. It was probably me anyway and I simply don't remember doing it, or maybe I did it in my sleep or something." I chuckle, trying to make light of the situation and hide my insecurities.

"My, my what are we going to do with you?" he asks with mischief in his eyes. "Sleep paralysis with nightmares, and now sleep walking? I don't know, babe, you might have to sleep in the guest room and lock yourself in there at night."

"Oh yeah?" I say in mock seriousness. I grab a towel, twist it up, and playfully whip it at his legs a couple times.

"Okay, okay, truce," he raises his hands in defeat before his face breaks into a mischievous grin and he grabs the spray nozzle and gives it a light squeeze making a small amount of water come out to get me slightly wet, but not fully drenched.

"What the... I thought you said truce, mister." I say with a frown. I reach around him for a new towel to dry my face and hair.

"I know, but I couldn't help it." He has tears in his eyes from laughing so hard.

"Uh huh," I say laughing with him. "Well, I'm going to go change and you can finish up the dishes then."

I give him one last smirk before heading upstairs to get a dry shirt. When I come back down, the buttery smell of popcorn fills my nose, and I can feel my mouth start to water. Marc's already putting it in the bowl and heading toward the couch to watch the rest of the movie with the girls. I take a drink of water and sit between them, grabbing a handful of popcorn.

"Hey, sweetie, are you feeling any better?"

"A little, Mommy," Ada says as she reaches over to grab some of the popcorn.

When the movie ends, both the girls are already sound asleep. Setting the empty bowl on the table, I pick up Ada and he picks up Anna so we can carry them up to bed. Ada's deep rhythmic breathing is interrupted when I lay her down and she instinctively reaches for the comfort of her teddy bear. I lay the back of my hand against her forehead; it feels slightly warm still, but nowhere near as hot as earlier today, so hopefully the fever is breaking.

"Are you up for another movie, or are you too tired?" Marc whispers.

"I could watch another movie." I whisper back. "I don't feel tired at all."

A lie.

I am very tired, I simply want to prolong my going to sleep for fear of what might be in store. He wants to watch a thriller movie, but I prefer a comedy.

"My life feels like something out of a thriller movie right now, I could use a laugh," I tell him.

"Okay, you're right. Comedy it is," he says. I let him pick which comedy and we settle in with another bag of popcorn.

By the time the movie is over, we are both struggling to keep our eyes open as we slowly make our way up to the bedroom. The warmth of the room reminds me I need to check the thermostat. I pad down the stairs, feeling the cold wooden floor beneath my feet, hating that I forgot to put on my slippers. Before I can make it to the thermostat, a soft glow of light catches my eye coming from the living room.

Huh I thought I turned the tv off.

I walk over, seeing that the tv is still on. I look around for the remote so I can turn it off, but it's nowhere to be found.

Typical.

I walk over to the tv and turn it off manually, leaving me immersed in total darkness. The chill that runs through me makes me regret not turning on a light. The atmosphere is almost electric, as if someone is watching me. I spin around imagining I'm going to see someone standing behind me, but no one is there, at least I hope not. I mentally shake my thoughts away, quickly walk over to the kitchen light switch, and flood the room with a soft white light. Under the brightly lit room, I can't imagine shadows that aren't there. More at ease, I check the thermostat. Sure enough, it is set at the sixty-eight degrees like it should be. *Good, glad it's still working.*

Turning to go back into the kitchen, I swear I see a figure going across the living room. My heart rate accelerates and a rush of fear runs through me, freezing me in place.

Stop, just stop, you're acting like a scared child. There is nothing there but a trick of your mind.

I take a deep breath, and walk down to turn the other light on and look around to be sure. Of course, no one is there.

I am losing it.

I grab the abandoned glass of water from the counter and down it before turning the lights off and heading back upstairs. Marc is already fast asleep when I climb into bed next to him. The adrenaline coursing through me makes it impossible for me to sleep now. I turn on my bedside lamp, grab my book from the nightstand, and start reading. I'm about thirty pages in when my eyes start to feel heavy, and my eyelids begin to droop. Placing a bookmark in the book and reaching up to turn off the light, I notice it's already midnight. Sinking under the warm cocoon of covers, I drift to sleep with the steady sound of Marc's breathing next to me.

UNSTABLE

I feel like I only closed my eyes seconds ago when suddenly it's already time to get up again. I glance over to my nightstand to check the time.

Where did my book go?

I don't have time to think about it further; I need to get up and get the girls moving. Ada tells me she is feeling much better today, but to be safe, I check her temperature anyway.

"Yep, ninety-eight point six. Back to normal sweetie." *Thank god.*

Once they're off to their last day of school for the week, I head back home to eat breakfast and have some coffee before I take a nap. I can't seem to shake this grogginess. I set the alarm on my phone to make sure I get up in time to pick up the girls from school. As soon as my head hits my pillow, I fall asleep immediately.

My eyes slowly open; the room is slightly spinning. Rubbing the sleep out of my eyes, I sit up and realize how dizzy I am. The splitting headache that pulses deep in the base of my neck, spidering into my eyes, is not helping the situation either. *Ugh, maybe the nap was a bad idea after all.* I reach for my phone, unlocking it to see I have seventeen missed calls and twelve text messages.

What the fuck!?

Most of them are from Marc, so I tap to listen to the first voicemail.

"Autumn! Where are you? Why haven't you picked the girls up?" alarm heavy in his voice.

Oh my God! What time is it? I only looked at the phone long enough to see I had so many missed calls, I didn't even check the time. 3:30!

I'm forty minutes late from picking them up? No! That can't be right? I did not sleep that long!

I'm about to call the school when Marc's name pops up on my screen.

"Oh my God! I am *soo* sorry! I took a nap and didn't think I would sleep so long! I set an alarm and everything!" I tell him in a rush as I run downstairs still in my nightgown. My head is still pounding.

"Jesus, Autumn, why didn't you answer your phone!" irritation and anger are coming out of his voice in waves.

"I'm *sorry!* My alarm didn't go off and my phone was on silent, but I swear I had it set to ringer in case the school called about Ada again." My voice is shaking as I'm still trying to wake up. "I'm leaving right now to go get them!" I say grabbing my car keys about to rush out of the house.

"No! Don't bother, I'm already almost there," he snaps, making me wince at the harshness in his voice.

"Okay, Marc really, I don't know what happened," I manage to choke down the sob in my throat, but am betrayed by the tears that begin to form in my eyes and blur my vision.

He blows out a long breath before he continues.

"It's fine," he says, his voice still tight.

"Marc?"

"I have to go, I'm here now," He says followed by a click.

I sink to the floor and let the tears flow. Before I know it, I'm sobbing, which only makes my headache worse. I bury my head in my hands, putting pressure on my temples to alleviate the pain and work on slowing my breathing. Slowly picking myself off the floor, I wipe the last of my tears from my face and trudge upstairs. I wash my face and take something for the pain.

I can't believe I overslept! What is wrong with me, and why was my alarm turned off and phone set to silent? I was really tired; maybe I only thought I set the alarm, and maybe the ringer was still off from last night.

My thoughts swirl around every possibility, which brings my

headache back. I walk downstairs, more and more convinced I must be sleepwalking. What other explanation is there?

Shit! Dinner!

I grab my phone and decide to order a pizza. I am definitely not up to cooking and the last thing I want is to give Marc another reason to be mad. As I wait for the girls and the pizza to arrive, I collapse on the couch feeling completely defeated. Reaching over to grab the blanket, I uncover the book I was reading last night. With unsure hands, I reach for it, and gingerly pick it up, the fear and doubt worming its way back into my thoughts.

Startled by the door, I release the book and hurry to meet the girls at the front door.

"Girls! Mommy is so sorry I didn't pick you up today," I say. I rush to them and kneel down to hug them, but they wriggle out of my arms and run for the couch.

"They're upset as you can imagine," Marc says as he closes the door.

"I know, really I don't know what happened."

Running his hand through his hair, he lets out a shaky breath and then looks back to me.

"It's okay. When I got the call from the school that you hadn't shown up, I thought the worst, and then you wouldn't answer. I drove like a mad man to go get them. Luckily, their teacher Mr. Young stayed with them and kept them company."

"That's good, I just, I can't believe I did that," I say, trying to keep my tears of embarrassment at bay.

He finally reaches toward me and pulls me into a big hug.

"I'm really glad you're okay, but let's not do any more midday naps for a while, please."

I nod my head into his chest and sigh, before I pull back and tell him that I ordered a pizza for dinner. His lips twitch into a smile and he loosens a laugh.

"What? You don't want pizza?" I say looking at him quizzically?

"No, it's not that, it's… I ordered a pizza too," he says with a lazy grin on his face.

"Well, great minds think alike I suppose." I can't help the chuckle that escapes from me.

While Marc heads upstairs to change out of his dress clothes, I go to the living room where the girls are sitting on the couch. I kneel in front of them so I can look them both in the eyes to convey how sorry I am.

"Hey, my Gemini stars, Mommy is so *sorry* I wasn't there to pick you up today."

"You forgot about us!" Anna says with her face all scrunched up when she gets mad.

"Yeah, Mommy, you forgot about us." Ada says in a sad whisper as her eyes angle downward. She blinks and a tear slides down and drips off the tip of her nose, breaking my heart.

"Oh, my sweet girls, no, Mommy didn't forget about you! I—"

"Remember, girls, I told you Mommy had some car trouble. She couldn't get to you."

I look at him realizing that he covered for me and mouth *thank you* before turning my attention back to the girls.

"Yes, Mommy had some car trouble. But you know what, Mommy *also* ordered pizza for dinner, so you can have as much as you want and then we can go get some ice cream and have a movie marathon night since it's the weekend, how's that sound?"

Their faces soften and they blink at me before glancing at each other. I'm worried they are still upset with me until they look at me, this time with smiles on their faces.

"You mean we can stay up extra late tonight?" Anna says full of excitement, all trace of anger leaving her tiny body.

"Yes, I mean, unless you don't want to…" I say sarcastically as I look away and start to stand up.

"No! No! We want to!" they excitedly say in unison. They each get to their feet and jump up and down.

"Okay, okay," I say laughing. "Why don't you go get cleaned up before the pizza gets here?"

They zoom past me and almost knock their dad over trying to race upstairs as fast as they can.

"Thank you, I appreciate you telling them that," I say. I'm embarrassed he had to cover for me in the first place.

"Well, it was close to what I thought the truth was at the time, I pictured you being in an accident of some sort." He tries to hide the fear in his voice, but his eyes give him away.

"I'm sorry, it won't happen again I swear."

He pulls me into another embrace, holding me a tad too tightly. I bury my face into his shoulder, smelling his woodsy cologne I love so much. I feel so bad for scaring him. I make a silent promise to make it up to him.

The sound of the doorbell breaks us apart and we hear the girls running down the stairs screaming,

"Pizza!"

"Okay, girls, why don't you get some plates and napkins out and set the table so we can eat," I say as Marc moves around me to open the door.

We pay and tip the delivery guy and bring the first pizza in the house. Moments later, the second pizza arrives. We all eat way too much, but of course, the girls are still demanding the ice cream they were promised. *I'm not sure how they still have room for more.* We go to our favorite ice cream spot and get our usual. Instead of eating it there, we decide to get it to go. The girls have to start their movie marathon early enough so they will be able to stay awake for at least one or two of them.

When we get home, I tell the girls to get their pjs on in case they fall asleep, which they assure me they won't, but they still run up to put them on anyway. They return in their matching Elsa pajamas, each carrying their favorite blanket. As we get all cozy on the couch, Marc gets the popcorn and snacks ready. Searching through the abundance of kids' movies, the girls decide they want to start with *Moana*. This will be about the eighth time they have seen it, so of course they sing along to all of the songs. When the movie ends, the girls insist they are ready for their second movie, which they deem to be *Frozen*. I figured they would pick this one at some point. They are wearing the pjs after all. The third movie is an easy pick since naturally they have to watch the sequel. They sing along to all the songs while they dance around and pretend they too can shoot ice from their hands. As the night goes on, they stop singing along and stay curled up with all of the blankets. Sure enough, toward the end of *Frozen II* is when I see them start to close their eyes on and off.

"Hey girls, are you tired? Do you want to call it a night?" I ask.

"No… we can finish the movie, Mommy." Anna says, her voice full of sleep. Before she can hide it, she yawns and rubs her eyes.

"Yeah," Ada says through a yawn. "We can finish, we're not tired."

I stifle a laugh and look at Marc, who is also trying to hold a laugh in,

"Okay, if you're not tired, we can finish it."

We go back to watching the movie when Marc leans over and whispers,

"Happy Birthday, baby."

"Thank you." I smile and lean over to get a kiss. With everything that's been going on lately, I almost forgot it was my birthday. *Already thirty. How did that happen?*

Twenty minutes later we each have a girl in our arms taking them up to tuck them into their beds. Anna slightly wakes up and whispers,

"Is it morning, Mommy, did we make it?

"Almost sweetie, go back to sleep."

We finish tucking them in and then head to our room to get ready for bed as well.

"Let's hope next week will be better." I try to sound confident and calm, but my worry and anxiety slips out instead.

"I'm sure it will, babe. Sleep and a relaxing weekend for your birthday with no kids for a day should do the trick."

"What if it doesn't. What if I actually am going crazy?" I say it as a joke, but part of me deep down is starting to believe something is really wrong. "What if you *should* start locking me in the spare room so I can't sleepwalk?"

"We'll figure it out, let's work on taking it one day at a time."

We slide in bed and I send up a silent prayer, hoping he's right and that everything will work out. Oh, how I wish I had his optimism.

5

IT'S HERE... my thirtieth birthday. I know I should be excited, but I feel like it's all downhill from here. I always imagined my life and career would be totally put together and thriving by now, but instead, my art career has been placed on the back burner. Don't get me wrong, I absolutely love my Gemini stars and my amazing husband, but is it bad to wish for my art to be hanging in galleries and getting noticed like it was before? Not to mention being known for more than just a stay-at-home mom. I internally curse myself for being selfish, but can't help feeling insignificant. Not only do I not have a thriving career, but worse now, I also fear I'm losing my mind, or something dark inside me is trying to crawl its way to the surface. I'm sinking more and more into my consuming thoughts when the girls walk in the room. I instantly fix my face into a smile.

"Happy birthday, Mommy," they both say laughing and giggling, both running to jump on the bed so they can smother me in hugs.

"Thank you my Gemini stars!"

Moments later, Marc enters the room as well, carrying a tray full of food.

"Happy Birthday to you, happy birthday to you," Marc starts singing and the girls soon chime in with him, with their giggling, singsong voices.

When they are finished singing, I hug both my girls and reach out to take the bed tray holding a plate of eggs, bacon, and waffles complete with a coffee from my favorite coffee place.

"Oh, my! You guys were busy this morning! Thank you! It looks delicious!" I say with all the enthusiasm I can muster. I look lovingly to my girls and then my wonderful husband, trying to savor this moment.

"You're welcome, Mommy! We helped make the breakfast too. Try it, try it," Anna says, shoving the fork into my hands.

"Yes, they did, they were very good sous-chefs." Marc says as he sits on the end of the bed.

I take a bite of the warm, maple syrup covered waffle first, loving its fluffy sweetness.

"Mmmmm, that is good, you girls did a very good job!"

"Hurry so you can open your gifts, Mommy!" Ada demands. I assume she is moving to lean her head on my shoulder, but she snatches a piece of bacon instead.

"Yes ma'am," I say as I shove a big bite of food in my mouth. The girls giggle at my silliness, which is music to my ears. "Here, how about you girls help me finish this so I can get done faster?" I pass them the plate of food and they immediately oblige.

With every last bite eaten, they hold their cards out in front of me and demand that I open them first. I already know who made what card before I even open them. One is covered in glitter and hearts, which definitely screams Anna's personality, while the other one is more subtle, made in colored pencils and markers with a drawing on the front speaking more to Ada.

"Thank you, girls, I love them! You guys did a great job making these for me," I say. I pull them both into a big hug and kiss the tops of their heads.

"Alright, girls, why don't you go downstairs and start cleaning up while Mom gets ready."

They hop off the bed giggling and run downstairs. As I pull the covers off, and get out of bed, I step into Marc's arms for a hug, when he whispers,

"You can have your gift from me as soon as you come downstairs."

"*Ooo*, I wonder what it is," I say looking up at him before I pull away and head for the bathroom. "I'm going to shower and I'll be down in a few, okay?"

"Okay, I'll go get everything cleaned up."

I turn the water on and wait for it to get warm before I get undressed and step inside. Underneath the waterfall, feeling the hot water run on me not only wakes me up more, but also clears my stress away. I run my hands through my wet hair, *I can't believe I'm thirty today.* I do a quick wash of my hair and shave my legs today to feel semi-presentable. I stay in longer than I need to, letting the water run on my body for a beat longer. Once out, I feel refreshed and ready to take on the day, and I am really excited to see the gift my wonderful husband got me. *I wonder what it could possibly be.* When I finally get downstairs, there is no trace of the hurricane mess that was surely once in the kitchen from when they made breakfast, *Oh good.* The girls run up to me and each take my hand,

"Come on, Mommy, we're going to go get your present now," they say in unison as they pull me toward the front door.

"Okay, okay I'm coming," I say, barely having enough time to throw my shoes on before I'm pulled out of the house. I look back and see Marc locking up and running to catch up with us to help load up the girls.

"So, we're going to get my present?" I ask, looking at him, questionably.

"Yep," he says as he smiles back, not giving anything away as to what it might be.

I try to guess what it could be in my head. *Shopping spree; new car?* I laugh to myself, but then stop when a more daunting thought enters my brain. *What if he is taking me to an insane asylum?* I shake my head and put the ridiculous thought out of my mind. When I look up, I realize we turned into a parking lot with a little strip mall where there is a phone store. I know instantly, he's getting me a new phone. As if he can read my thoughts, he leans over and whispers,

"In case your old one was malfunctioning," he says with a wink.

I smile, and try to make it look convincing. I'm really grateful for the thought, but my insecurity is overwhelming. *What if it's not really the phone and it happens again with the new one. Then he will see that I am actually going crazy.*

"Oh, this is a great gift, thank you." Careful not to sound disappointed, I put every ounce of excitement I can muster into my voice. "I was wanting a new phone anyway."

Once we get inside though, I figure I might as well treat myself to the newest phone they have. *It is my birthday after all.* The salesperson introduces himself as Carter and leads us to the table with the newest phone, which ends up being really cool. He runs through all the features and everything it can do. Since he is good at up-selling, he points out the watch that goes along with it. There is a promotion going on, and before I go and keep the girls occupied, I give Marc a look that tells him to include the watch as well before leaving them to discuss the paperwork, cost, and what the monthly payments are.

"Do you like your present, Mommy?" Ada asks with her toothy smile.

"Yes sweetie, I really do,"

"When can we have phones, Mommy?" Anna asks, which piques Ada's interest. They both now wait impatiently for my response.

"When you're older my Gemini stars," I tell them.

"Yeah, but how *much* older?" Anna presses. I don't know the answer to the question, but luckily, I don't have to, because Marc calls us back over.

"We will talk about it with your dad later, okay?" I tell them as I reach for their hands. "Come on." They both nod in unison, but I know they will make sure we do, indeed, talk about it later.

I bring the girls back over and hand over my old phone so they can transfer all my contacts, photos, and apps onto the new phone. Then I listen to a rundown of how the watch works and what I need to do to sync it to my phone. It feels like we are in the store for ages, but I walk out with a brand-new phone and already wearing my watch on my wrist.

Worth it!

I can't wait to add more apps and text people using the watch now, making it easy to get ahold of people even if I misplace my phone. It has its very own alarm separate from the phone, so if my phone is off, hopefully the watch will still alert me. All good features for one tiny watch, but my favorite one would have to be the sleep tracker, something I definitely need help monitoring.

"Here, text me. I want to see it pop up on the watch," I tell Marc.

"Okay, will do, birthday girl." He smiles and pulls his phone out to text me.

Moments later, the notification pops up on the watch informing me that I have a new message from Marc. It reads, *Happy Birthday, Baby* 😊

"Thank you, babe, I love it!" I say texting him a smiley face back from the watch.

We head for home so we can get the girls all packed with their overnight bags to go to my parents' house for their sleepover. The girls tell us what they want to take to Grammy and Papa's house, which includes all their dolls and coloring books. Their bags are overflowing.

"Girls, you're only going for one night, you don't need all of your toys to go with you." I tell them laughing, and reach over to take some of the coloring books out.

"But, Mommy," the girls whine, "we *need* all of our stuff."

"Okay, you can each bring one doll, but let's leave your coloring books here because Grammy and Papa have a bunch at their house, okay?"

"Fine," they say glumly as they start to unpack all their coloring books and colored pencils.

"Thank you," I tell them.

I hear Marc downstairs rummaging around, hopefully getting things set up for when I come back from dropping the girls off. The timing is going to be tight since we spent a longer time at the phone store than we should have. All my friends will be here in no time to kick off the adult part of my birthday. The girls and I come downstairs, overnight bags in hand, and head for the door telling him I should be back in forty minutes or so.

The girls are singing to themselves to the songs on the radio, intermittently asking if we're almost there yet, when finally, we are. My parents come out of the house to greet them when I pull into the driveway.

"Hey, Mom. Hey, Dad." I say, getting the girls unbuckled and out of the car so they can run over to them.

"Hey hun, happy birthday!" Mom says before she focuses all her attention on the girls and kneels down to hug both of them at once.

"Look, Grammy, I brought my favorite doll, see, she's wearing a pink dress today just like me!" Anna says as she holds the doll up for Mom to look at it.

"Wow, very pretty, and what about you Ada, is your doll wearing a blue dress to match you too?"

"No, I kept her in her purple dress; it's her favorite color," Ada says as a matter of fact.

"Oh, I see, well that was very thoughtful of you. Why don't you guys run in and Papa will get you some fresh baked chocolate chip cookies."

"Cookies!" they yell and beeline for the front door.

"Not too many!" I yell after them, but I know they don't hear me or they don't want to.

Mom helps me grab their bags and we walk in after them to see that they are each already two cookies in. I give my mom a sideways glance silently asking her if she knows what she's in for. She gives me a knowing smile and pats my shoulder as she heads to put the bags in the spare room where the girls will be staying. Dad comes over and wishes me a happy birthday as he hands me a card.

"Don't spend it all in one place," he chuckles before going to sit in his favorite recliner.

I thank him and see my mom coming back into the kitchen so I can thank her too.

"Sorry to run out so fast, we had a busier morning than I thought, and my guests will be arriving, so..." I trail off, not wanting to come right out and tell her I need to leave now. Luckily, she gives me a knowing smile and hugs me before we head to the door.

"No worries hun, have a great birthday, what time will you be back tomorrow to pick them up again?"

"Whenever you need me to. I can come over early or in the afternoon, whatever works for you."

"Well, I was thinking we could take them for breakfast, so maybe you can pick them up around eleven then?" she asks as she stands in the doorway and I head to the car.

"That sounds perfect, Mom! And thanks again for watching them. We really appreciate it." I want to tell her more about what has been going on lately, since she is familiar with my sleep paralysis as well as my sleepwalking. It's always so clarifying to talk to my mom about my problems, but I'm running behind and it would take way longer than ten minutes to catch her up on everything crazy in my life.

"No problem, hun. It's always a joy when we get to watch them."

We smile and say our final goodbyes before I'm back on the road.

I get home and notice Ren's car in the driveway. I cut the ignition and run inside to greet her. She is sitting at the kitchen counter when she hears me come in. She twirls around and runs over to give me a big hug,

"Happy thirtieth!" she yells. "Are we doing a thirty flirty and thriving or is this going to be more of a dirty thirty." She chuckles and she hugs me.

"Well," I tell her, wrapping my arm through hers and walking to the backyard, "how about we start with a thirty flirty and thriving and see where we go from there." I wink.

"Okay, well I brought plenty of booze just in case." She laughs and then leans in to whisper in my ear. "I also brought some penis shaped suckers." She waggles her eyebrows up and down. My eyes go wide,

"Serenity! You didn't," I gasp in mock shock using her full name for emphasis, but I can't hold the act long before I start laughing, because I already know that's exactly in line with who she is.

"Of course, I did." She's still laughing as she walks over to get a drink from the cooler.

"Hey, grab me one of those to please," I say as I walk over to see how Marc is doing on the grill. He pulls me into a side hug and kisses me on the top of my head,

"Hey, babe, how'd the drop off go?" he asks as he's flipping the burgers over.

"Really good, sorry I'm a little late getting back." I'm staring at the burgers sizzling on the grill, mesmerized for a minute before he pulls me out of it.

"No worries, Ren and Glen got here early anyway." Speaking of Ren, she's walking toward me and tosses me the peach flavored hard seltzer.

"Thanks, I needed this," I say as I pop open the top and take a long drink, feeling the bubbles dance around in my mouth from the carbonation and the warming sensation of the alcohol.

"Whoa there, looks like we're already moving into the dirty thirty part of this party." She laughs. "Should I go get the penis shaped suckers now… or?"

"Oh hush, it's my birthday and I've had a rough week," I tell her as I down the rest of the drink and signal to Glen to bring me another one. Thankfully, he obliges.

I'm about finished with my second one when I hear Liz and Freya coming out of the back door.

"Happy Birthday!" they both say at once. They run towards me with their arms outstretched ready to pull me in for a group hug. The gift bags they have in their hands hit up against my back letting me know whatever is in them is large and heavy.

"Thanks, guys!" I pull back. "Food is almost ready and there's some beer and other drinks in the coolers over next to the patio chairs, and Ren brought plenty of other booze, too."

Carl and Ray are greeting Marc and Glen over by the grill, then head over to get themselves a beer from the cooler. The girls and I walk over after them, and they each grab a raspberry flavored hard seltzer, while I opt for a strawberry this time.

"Foods ready!" Marc yells.

"Oh good! I'm starved!" Ren says racing to grab a plate so she can be the first to dig in. Everyone stops what they are doing to stare at her with amusement. Feeling eyes on her, Ren turns toward us. "What?" she asked, her mouth already full of food. "I haven't eaten yet, okay?"

"Nothing, eat as much as you like." I tell her with a knowing smile. *I wonder if she plans to make the announcement tonight?*

Everyone else follows suit and loads up their plates as well before we migrate to the patio table. Marc goes over to the cooler and grabs us all another round of our preferred drink and we sit and catch up on everyone's lives.

"If anyone hasn't noticed already, I have not been drinking," Ren starts, then looks lovingly at Glen before continuing. "We're pregnant!" She beams and holds a hand to her stomach.

"Oh my God! Ren! Congratulations! I'm so happy for you guys!" Liz says rushing over to hug her.

"Thank you!"

"Yeah, you guys, that's awesome! Congrats!" Marc says. He eagerly moves to shake Glen's hand. Freya and Ray go over to offer their congrats as well.

"Sorry to hijack your party with my news," Ren says apologetically, "but I couldn't hold the news in any longer."

"Don't be! I'm glad you chose now to announce it! Seriously!"

After a few more congratulations, we break out the cornhole games and margarita maker. I make virgin ones for Ren, despite her protests of being fine with water. Luckily, we have two cornhole sets, so we can all play at once, girls against the guys. I have Ren on my team and we're playing against Marc and Glen, while Liz and Freya play against Carl and Ray. I throw the bean bag and for the life of me, I can't seem to get it anywhere near the hole, but Ren is doing pretty well, so we're only a few points behind. Liz and Freya, however, are crushing it. They are way ahead of their husbands and only need one more point to win.

"I don't know, Ren; I think our husbands might be cheating," I say as Glen puts yet another bean bag in the hole for three points.

"I think you just suck at this game," she says laughing

"Yeah, that could be true too," I muse. "I think I need another drink, maybe I will get better."

"I don't think that's how it works," Marc says laughing at me.

"Well, I don't know," I say incredulously. "Worth a shot though."

Marc ends up getting the final point they need making them the winners, and I look over seeing Liz and Freya cheering and rubbing it in their husbands faces that they won.

"Let's call it quits for now," Marc says and gives everyone a knowing glance. Before I know it, he takes off into the house. He appears moments later carrying a cake full of lit candles on top. He shields them with his hand so the wind doesn't blow them out. He sets it on the table in front of me, and my friends begin singing *Happy Birthday*. My cheeks burn from smiling so much and my face is flushed with all the alcohol in my system. I look around the table, and I feel so grateful to have these great people in my life.

"Go ahead, babe, make a wish and blow out the candles," he says, eyes bright with the flames dancing off of them.

I close my eyes making a big show of me thinking of a perfect wish, but what should I wish for? All I really want is for things to go back to normal and for me not to be crazy. I finally open my eyes and blow out all thirty candles in one huge breath, making everyone cheer,

"Wow, you still got them all in one breath, guess you're not so old after all," Liz jokes.

"Yeah, you're damn right I did," I say, laughing along with her.

"Here you go, babe, take the first piece," Marc says. He plops a giant piece of cake on a plate and slides it to me.

I eagerly grab my fork and dig in. The sweet taste of vanilla and chocolate touch my tongue. *So good!*

"Mmmmmm, this is delicious and you ordered it with the whipped frosting I love so much. Thank you!"

"Of course, babe." Marc smiles.

"It is really good," Freya says through a mouthful of cake. Everyone nods their heads in agreement

When we're all finished with the cake, I start grabbing the gifts my friends got me, so I can open them. I start with Ren's, and, as promised, she has the penis shaped suckers in there along with a dirty thirty shot glass and a thirty flirty and thriving wine tumbler. I put the gifts back in the bag, give her a hug, and thank her. Next, I move on to Liz's gift,

"My god, Liz, what did you put in here, a brick?" I ask. It's an effort to heave the present into my lap.

"Yeah, you know, I thought you could use a single brick for your front yard," she quips and rolls her eyes.

I mock her eye roll right back, rip out all of the tissue paper on top and reach in to pull out this heavy gift. The first box I pull out is a sound machine. *Useful.*

"You said you were having trouble sleeping," she says in defense when I look over to her with a raised eyebrow.

I put it aside and pull out the next box, which consists of bath bombs and facial masks.

"So, you can be more relaxed before you go to sleep," she says. "Pull out the last thing,"

I reach in and realize I need two hands to pull it out of the bag since it is quite heavy. When I finally get it out, I see that it's a weighted blanket. *No wonder it was so heavy.* I chuckle and give her a huge grin.

"Wow thank you, Liz, this is so thoughtful!" I say moving toward her to give her a hug.

"You're welcome, I figured you could use all the help you could get so you can sleep," she laughs.

"That she does," Marc says nodding his head while raising his bottle of beer as a salute.

"Okay, okay, open mine next," says Freya as she moves her gift in front of me.

I take out all of the tissue paper from the bag, reach in, and pull out two of my favorite bottles of Moscato, along with a wine glass that says, *Talk Thirty to Me*. I reach my hand in again and pull out the final gift: a gift card to my favorite coffee place. *Yum.*

"Awesome! Thank you, Freya! I love them!" I tell her, getting up to give her a hug.

"You're welcome… ya old lady." She laughs as she takes another sip of her margarita.

"Whoa… I think you've had way too much there," I laugh, "and who are you calling old? You're two years older than I am."

"Touché," she says, raising her cup in salute, causing everyone to erupt in carefree laughter. *Man, I really needed this.*

"Hey, I'm hungry again, who wants to order a pizza?" I ask.

"*Oooo* pizza," Ren and Liz say together.

"I'm always up for some pizza," Glen says.

"Alright, what does everyone want and I can call and have it delivered," Marc says.

We rattle off our orders, and everyone is in agreement with having plain cheese. To be safe, we also get one with pepperoni for the guys. The guy on the phone, Rick, says the pizza will take about forty-five minutes to get to us. While we're waiting, we start to clean up a little to make room and go back to chatting and having some more drinks.

"So, you're not sleeping, how come?" Ren asks, a little disappointed that I informed Liz and not her, but she tries to hide it.

I feel everyone's attention on me and I look to Marc for assurance, but his face is hard to decipher. I can't tell if he thinks I should tell them or not.

What the hell, might as well.

The liquid courage convinces me to come clean about everything. I have been dying to tell someone else to confirm I'm not crazy. I start from the beginning and divulge everything: the sleep paralysis mixed with the terrifying dream about murdering an old man in cold blood, as well as all the weird stuff happening in the house. They stay silent, their eyes fixed on me, so I continue. I briefly mention my forgetfulness, and sleepwalking, but of course I leave out the feelings of enjoyment I had from taking a life. When I'm done recapping, they're all staring at me, mouths slightly ajar and eyes wide with disbelief and shock. Suspicion? I can't really tell. Carl breaks the silence first.

"Wow, that's a lot," he says, running a hand through his hair exactly like Marc does. *Must be a guy thing.*

"Yeah, *honey*, why didn't you tell us sooner?" Ren chimes in with a look of worry on her face.

"Yeah, jeez Autumn, do you really think someone was in your house?" Liz asks with fear and a hint of skepticism lacing her voice.

"Forget someone in her house. You don't actually think you murdered anyone do you?" Ren asks although I can't tell if she's afraid *for* me or *of* me. Not knowing which sends shivers down my spine.

"I don't know, I don't know... I was hoping that confiding in you guys, would be able to... I don't know... help me feel less crazy about it," I say looking at each of them trying to see where they stand on the subject and wondering deep down if they do think I'm crazy.

A glimpse of fear flashes across Freya's face, but is gone almost as instantly. I wonder if I imagined it. In place of fear, her face is now pensive as she starts to bite her nails. I've known her long enough to know this is what she does when she's debating about telling someone something they don't want to hear.

"Spit it out, Freya, I can take it." I say. She flinches at my directness, but I can tell she is dying to tell me.

"It's probably nothing, but... I had this friend." She takes a deep breath before she continues. "She started forgetting where she put things, and forgetting when she would do tasks. Then she started having these hallucinations she thought were real. She couldn't tell what was real or not anymore." She looks down now nervous to continue, but Ray looks at her and squeezes her hand and urges her to keep going.

"Well... she ended up going to the doctor to get checked out and they found a tumor in her brain." Freya looks back up and quickly says, "But I'm sure what's happening with you isn't the same thing."

All I can do is stare at her in shock. I wanted to be told I wasn't crazy, but I didn't want this alternative to be the reason why. I hardly feel Marc come beside me and hold my hand trying to talk to me. I shake off the feeling of unease. I look toward him to try and ground myself.

"Babe, it's okay, it's probably not even the same thing. You're exhausted, and it's a lot to take in. Let's not think about it right now."

"Yeah, she's not saying you have the same diagnosis. I mean, the symptoms aren't even that similar," Liz says as she leans toward me and puts her hand on mine to reassure me. Nothing like the news of murder and a possible brain tumor to sober everyone up and kill the celebratory mood.

Suddenly, we hear the doorbell from inside the house, and everyone practically jumps out of their skin. Marc gives my shoulder a light reassuring squeeze before he gets up to answer the door. Until now I had forgotten all about ordering the pizza. I don't have an appetite anymore.

He comes back holding the pizza boxes in his hand and has some paper plates sitting on top of them. He sets them on the table and everyone starts grabbing for a plate and a slice of pizza. He puts a slice of cheese on a plate and puts it in front of me, asking me with his eyes if I'm okay. I give him a reassuring look and nod my head slightly, even though I'm anything but.

We all eat our pizza in silence for a while, letting our minds wander and try to forget the conversation of minutes ago. I'm still picking at my same slice when I excuse myself to the bathroom. Nobody objects. They all look at me with concern or pity, I can't tell. Once I'm in the bathroom, I close the door and stand over the sink looking at myself in the mirror. *Could I have a tumor in there? Is that what's happening to me?* I turn on the faucet and cup my hands under the cold water before splashing it across my flushed face. I do that a couple more times before I start to feel a calmness spread throughout me. I hear a light tap at the door so I turn the faucet off and pat my face dry.

"I'll be out in a minute," I call, trying to keep my voice as light and even as possible.

"Babe, it's me, can I come in?"

I move to unlock the door and step back so he can open it.

"Babe, it's okay, I'm sure there is nothing wrong with you. Why don't you come back out and enjoy the rest of your birthday?" he says as he moves to pull me in his arms.

"Yeah, you're probably right, I'm fine," I say, trying to convince myself more than him.

We walk back out to the patio where everyone is still eating their pizza, but stop and look up when they see me coming back out.

"Hey girlie, you okay, I didn't mean to worry you, especially not on your birthday. I'm awful. Can we pretend I didn't say anything?" Freya asks desperately.

"It's fine, I'm fine, don't worry about it. I'm glad you told me. In a way it kind of makes me feel better," I tell her. I hope my words have the reassuring tone I intend.

Sitting in awkward silence, we can all tell the night is pretty much over. What started out as a pretty great birthday has ended in disaster. Everyone switches to water in attempts to sober up. The forced conversation is almost unbearable, but better than discussing my impending brain tumor or whether or not I'm a murderer.

"The girls start their piano lessons this week," I blurt out.

"That's awesome! I took lessons when I was a kid and loved it. I'm sure they will too," Freya says, eating up the change of subject.

"Yeah, I did too, for a time. I only remember the beginning of one song now." I say with a forced chuckle.

"We are going on a cruise in a couple weeks to the Bahamas," Liz chimes in making us all hate her a tiny bit.

"Wow! That sounds amazing!" I tell her. "We haven't been on a vacation in, I don't know how long."

"Same here," Ren and Freya say at the same time, looking to their husbands accusingly. Even that topic doesn't last long before everyone falls silent again.

"So, Ren, when are you due?" Freya asks.

"We are due in late April! We find out the gender right before Thanksgiving!" she says unable to contain her excitement.

"That's awesome! What are you guys thinking it will be?" Liz asks.

"We don't care, as long as they are healthy," Ren says. "But I also would love for it to be a girl."

"I am more hoping for a boy," Glen chimes in.

"I vote boy," Ray says at the same time as Carl.

"Do you already have names picked out," Freya asks.

"Not yet, we are still looking and trying to narrow it down," Ren replies.

Not even the topic of an impending baby is enough to save the conversation and the awkward silence returns. I have no choice but to call it a night. Final wishes of happy birthday are called out to me as they leave and close the door behind them.

Lost in our own thoughts, Marc and I clean up the table and throw all the plates, empty cans, and bottles away in silence. All traces of festivities erased, the silence between us becomes unbearable.

"Marc?" I ask in a small hesitant voice.

"I know, babe," he says as he pulls me into a warm embrace.

"If I keep forgetting things or having any more realistic dreams where I can't tell if I'm dreaming or actually doing the stuff in my dream, can I please go get checked out?" I keep my face buried in his chest, scared he might judge me and think it's stupid.

"Of course, baby, I would never want that lingering over you. I would rather have peace of mind than unknowns. If you want, we can schedule you an appointment on Monday."

"No, I'm sure it's fine, I'll just wait and see for now, but thank you!" I say squeezing my arms tightly around him.

6

I AM DEFINITELY FEELING the effects of all the alcohol I consumed last night. I feel like death with this raging headache. *Should have switched to water sooner, ugh. Only thing I need now is lots of Tylenol, some food, and coffee. So thankful my parents have the girls until eleven.* Marc comes downstairs shortly after me holding his head as well, so I pass him the Tylenol before returning my attention back to my piping hot coffee.

"Thank you," he says through a yawn, "that was some get together last night."

"Yes, it was. I don't remember the last time we drank so much. Thank god we don't have to get the girls until later this afternoon," I say grabbing eggs and bacon out of the fridge making him wince.

"That's for sure, however, I might have mentioned to them that we could go swimming when we picked them up," he says, peering at me over his coffee mug.

"You didn't," I wince as the feeling of dread creeps up on me. "I thought we could have a nice relaxing day today; you know, movie day or something."

"Don't worry, babe, if you don't feel up to it, we can tell the girls no, or I can always take them myself."

"No, no it's fine," I say, rubbing my temples. "I'm definitely going to need a second cup of coffee, and about three more Tylenol."

Silence falls over us while we eat breakfast and drink our coffee. I wish I had an iced one instead. *I'll get one later anyway.*

"Do you want to head up and take a shower," he asks. The passion in his eyes, however, betrays his ulterior motives.

"Yeah, that would be nice," I say, getting up abruptly so he gets the hint I want to be alone. His curt nod tells me he does and I'm thankful for the space.

The shower takes longer than anticipated since I spend the majority of it letting the water fall on me, trying to wash away last night's drinking and conversation. I get out, realizing it's already time to leave and curse myself for taking so long.

"I'm so sorry! I didn't mean to take that long." I tell him.

"No worries, I can shower in the locker room before we swim."

I hurry to gather up the girls' swimsuits and towels so they can change when we get to the pool while Marc grabs the floaties, and goggles along with his swim trunks. I don't think I want to swim at all, but at the last minute, I decide to throw my bathing suit on under my clothes in case I want to enjoy the pool with my family. I grab a sketch book from my studio, figuring I can at least get some sketches done so I have ideas for other paintings.

When we arrive, the girls are already running out of the house with my parents in tow carrying their overnight bags.

"Mommy! Daddy!" they yell in unison.

I get out of the car and kneel in front of them bracing for the impact.

"*Oof,*" I say. "Hey, girls! Did you have fun at Grammy and Papa's house?"

"Yes, lots of fun," Anna says, stepping back out of my arms to be picked up by Marc.

"We got pancakes for breakfast," Ada tells me, staying in my arms so I can pick her up.

"So how was the birthday get together?" Mom asks. "You know you can leave these two with us more often. They are perfect little angels."

"Yeah, Mom, it was really good. And who? Not these two," I joke, "couldn't be." I tickle Ada till she laughs and squirms in my arms wanting to be put down. Before I do, I notice that Anna is also laughing like she is being tickled too, but she isn't. I set Ada in her car seat, buckle her all in, and turn back to Mom.

"Thanks again for watching them, Mom, we really needed that night off," I say with more truth than I originally thought.

"Oh hun, you know those two are always welcome over here. We love having them."

"Well, we might have to take you up on that then. Where's Dad by the way?" I ask, looking around for any sign of him.

"Oh, he's putting some cookies in to-go containers for the girls," she says and smiles.

"What are you saying about me?" Dad asks as he walks out with four containers.

"Oh my god, *Dad*! We do *not* need that many cookies," I say.

"Nonsense! We do need them," Marc says as he comes around the car to grab them.

"See?" Dad says with a smirk on his face as he hands the cookies over to him.

"Fine," I say, shaking my head.

When everything is all loaded up, we say our final goodbyes and head toward the pool.

The pool is fairly packed, but we manage to snag a few lawn chairs next to the four-foot end. We get everything all settled and I take the girls to change into their swimsuits while Marc watches our stuff, making sure no one else takes the chairs. We come out and the girls take off ahead of me to run to Marc, who is waiting with their floaties. The girls are so impatient, it takes longer than it should to secure them on to their tiny arms. After Marc slides the last floaty in place on Anna's arm, they race away heading for the water.

"Whoa there! Not so fast. I still need to put on *my* swim trunks, monkeys," he says, reaching to grab their hands.

"Hurry, Daddy!" Anna says as she grabs for her goggles.

"We want to go in now!" Ada says finishing Anna's sentence

While he's gone, I grab the sunscreen and generously apply it to their fair skin. They hardly sit still long enough, so it's lucky I finish as he comes back into view.

"Okay, monkeys, are you ready to get in?" he asks? "Oh, wait, can't forget goggles for myself."

"Yeah!" they scream with delight, heading toward the ladder.

"You going to hold down the fort here and guard the chairs babe?" he asks, "or do you want to come in with us?"

"I think I'll hold down the fort for a bit, maybe do some sketching," I say waving my sketchbook in the air.

"Okay… well if you change your mind," he says with a smile as he heads toward the pool hearing the girls demand for him to hurry.

I settle in one of the chairs, put my sunglasses on, and open my sketch book to a fresh page. I contemplate what to draw, but realize I have the perfect material right in front of me, the girls swimming. I look at them periodically while they swim around and get thrown up in the air by their dad. *I'm glad they are having so much fun.* When I have almost finished the sketch of them in the pool, the whistle gets blown. It's time for everyone to get out so the adults can swim if they like. The girls reluctantly get out, followed up by Marc. They pout the whole walk over to me.

"Hey girls, did you have fun?" I ask looking up at them and wrapping each of them up in a towel.

"Yeah… but when can we go back in?" Anna asks. She sits in her towel and stares at the pool.

"In a few minutes. It's a special time when adults get to swim by themselves," I say. "Perfect time for you guys to snack and let me reapply your sunscreen."

"Fiinneee," they both say at once.

I hand them each a water to drink while I put some more sunscreen on them.

"Did you bring any of Grammy's cookies with, Mommy?" Ada asks.

"No sweetie I didn't, but I have some granola bars if you're hungry,"

Before she can answer, the whistle blows again and they all but run out of my grasp.

"Girls wait, you need your floaties back on," I call.

"Okay, Mommy, but hurry," Anna says.

Marc helps Anna with hers, and I get Ada's on before they run off toward the pool. I settle back to open up my sketch book again, but decide I would like to cool off in the pool after all. I put the towels on each chair, the universal sign for everyone that they are taken, slip off my shorts, and head toward the pool. At first it feels cold, but as I get all the way in, it feels very refreshing.

"Mommy!" the girls say as they swim toward me. "You came in."

"I did," I say, closing the distance between us and hold one on each hip while we bob in the water.

Marc swims over and splashes us with water. "Hey, babe, glad you could join us."

"Hey!" they scream in unison, wiping water from their eyes.

They wriggle out of my arms and start to splash the water right back at their dad.

"Get him," I yell playfully, splashing water in his face.

It's three against one in our splash war. Marc doesn't stand a chance and proceeds to wave his invisible white flag.

"We win!" they squeal with delight.

"You sure did, monkeys," Marc says, pulling them both in for a hug. We swim around for a while longer and go through two more adult swim periods before deciding we have had enough of the pool. I help the girls dry off and change while Marc gathers up our belongings.

"Here, I'll start loading up, you change into some dry clothes," I tell Marc, already reaching for the towels and floaties.

"Thanks, babe." He gives me a swift kiss on the cheek and disappears into the locker room. He is already jogging toward us before I even get to the car. *Must be nice to dry off and change so quickly.*

"Alright, who wants hot dogs on the grill when we get home?" Marc asks.

"We do!" the girls yell in unison.

Everyone is worn out by the time we get home. As Marc works on preparing the food, the girls plop on the couch and watch cartoons. I move to my recliner and reach for the book I've been reading, hoping to get at least halfway through.

I don't. *Maybe later.*

With the food in front of me, I realize how hungry I was after I take the first mouth-watering bite. I devour the whole thing in record time, and I'm not the only one.

"So, do you girls have any homework you need to get done?" I ask when we are finished eating.

"Yeah, but it's only one thing though." Anna says.

"Well, go ahead and get to work on it." Marc chimes in.

They reluctantly go get their assignments and Marc agrees to help them so I can get some painting done.

I am ready to finish my landscape. I gather all my paints, but when I sit in front of my canvas, I drop everything to the floor gasping. My hands fly up to my mouth. The beautiful canvas I was working on has three black paint swipes running down the length of the canvas.

"Marc! Girls! Can you come in here?" I struggle to keep my voice calm, but internally, I am anything but. I gather my composure as I hear them run down the hallway.

"Yeah, babe, what's up?" he says looking at me with questioning eyes that have a slight bit of concern in them. I turn the canvas around for him to see.

"Did any of you come into my studio and paint these black lines on my canvas?" My voice comes out calm and steady, which is good because I don't want to scare the girls.

Marc's brows crease with confusion, "No, wasn't me"

"Girls? Did you do this? It's okay if you did. Mommy won't be mad, I promise. I only want to know the truth."

They look toward each other before looking back to me, confusion also on their small faces.

"You did it, Mommy," Anna says. I reel back at the accusation. My blood runs cold and shivers shoot down my spine.

"What do you mean... I did it?" It takes an enormous amount of effort to keep my voice even as I look at the two of them. "When did you see Mommy do this?"

"Umm. A few nights ago?" she says timidly. The question appears in her eyes, asking if she's in trouble. "I was thirsty and... I came down to get some water and I saw you go in there, so I went to ask you to tuck me back in." She finishes, not being able to look me in the eye.

My heart breaks. I don't remember the encounter, "Honey it's okay, Mommy isn't mad," I say sweetly and kneeling down to brush her hair behind her ears. "Go ahead and tell me what you saw." She meets my gaze with more confidence now that she knows I'm not mad at her.

"I saw you, Mommy. You were in here holding the paintbrush, painting. I tried to talk to you, but you told me to go back to bed," she says with a shrug, "so I did."

I look to Marc and let him see the fear in my eyes before looking back to the girls. I set the canvas back on the easel and kneel down to pull them into a hug.

"Okay. Thank you for reminding Mommy, I must have forgotten," I say with a warm smile. I am trying as hard as I can to hide my growing anxiety. "Go ahead and finish your homework, okay."

They run back out of the room, leaving Marc and me alone.

"Marc, I don't remember doing this," I say in a frantic, hushed whisper.

"Shhh, babe, it's okay, you were probably just sleepwalking or something," he says as he pulls me into a hug. "I hear you get up in the middle of the night sometimes, but I didn't think anything of it since you always come back to bed and seem fine."

"Maybe we should call and make an appointment for me, check everything out, just in case," I try to relax in his arms, but I feel like I'm going crazy. I want to be able to remember what happened.

"Okay, babe, if that's what you want to do, we can, but I don't see any harm in you sleepwalking. Why don't you go watch some tv with the girls and have a cup of chamomile tea?"

"That sounds good," I head toward the couch, grateful to Marc for bringing me my tea and doing what he can to keep me relaxed.

The tea is long cold. I haven't taken more than two sips. My mind is too fixated on the black lines on my canvas. The girls have long finished their homework and are now playing upstairs, while I zone out in front of the tv. The gurgling sounds my stomach makes tell me it must be close to dinner time.

Ding Dong.

I am brought out of my never-ending thoughts for the moment. *Who could that be?*

"I decided to order take out for dinner… hope that's okay." Marc says.

I'm hit once again with how much I love him. "Thank you, that means a lot."

We eat in silence on the couch while the girls start a movie. Everyone seems engrossed in the movie and is almost done with their food, but I have barely touched mine. I am still shaken, wondering what on earth would possess me to paint black lines on my landscape in the first place.

Well, you were sleeping and you had painting on your mind, so maybe you thought you were painting a masterpiece when in reality you painted three black lines. Nothing makes sense and I am nowhere near a resolution.

7

MY MIND IS STILL on last night's canvas incident and I am nowhere near figuring it out or remembering what happened. Hoping to turn my focus to something else, I turn on the tv while I drink my second cup of coffee. *Luckily Marc is making my doctor's appointment today, I don't know how much more of this I can take. I need answers, good or bad.*

I turn on the news. Pushing away my thoughts, I make myself cozy on the couch underneath my favorite blanket, drinking my now lukewarm coffee. They are finishing up the weather report for the week when a breaking news banner flashes at the bottom of the screen, catching my attention.

"The body found in Sugar Creek last night has now been identified as sixty-year-old Ken Woo."

I move to the edge of the couch. I don't even hear the rest because I am looking at the picture on the screen. Seeing his face, I drop the remainder of my coffee on the floor; I don't hear the crash when it lands.

What the hell?

I'm frozen in place. The picture staring back at me has the same face, and same eyes as in my nightmare.

That can't be right.

When I can finally move again, I realize I have coffee all over the floor and my socks. I don't bother cleaning it up. Instead, I frantically grab my phone. My hands are shaking so badly, it takes me three attempts to type in Marc's number. When it finally goes through and starts to ring, I push the phone against my ear, willing him to pick up.

"Pick up, pick up, pick up," I whisper frantically over and over.

He finally picks up on the fourth ring. *Thank god.*

"Hey, babe, what's up?" he answers coolly.

"It's him... the same guy... he's... he's... dead!" I stammer out the words, finding it impossible to even explain what is going on since I don't understand it myself.

"Whoa, whoa, babe, slow down," he says in a rush. "Who's dead? What are you talking about?" He's frantic on the phone, now fully invested in the conversation.

"The guy... from my nightmare!" I tell him.

"Babe, you need to calm down, breathe, and then tell me what's going on." He struggles to keep his voice even, and patient.

I take a few deep breaths and move to sit down, pinching my nose between my fingers before I continue.

"The man, the one I saw myself murdering in my dream, hitting him with the car and then holding him underwater, he's on tv... as a real person. He's dead," I say as calmly and slowly as possible, trying to give him as much detail as I can.

"What do you mean?" he asks, his voice full of confusion.

"You know, the sleep paralysis dream!" I shout, willing him to get on the same page as me and remember. "That same guy I saw myself murdering in my dream? Well, he is the same guy they are showing on tv right now! They found him in the river!"

I'm trying to stay calm, but I feel hot tears running down my face. The flash of my muddy shoes enters my thoughts. Bringing my hand to my mouth, I manage to stifle the strangled sob that threatens to come out.

It was me! I did this! Why else would my tennis shoes be caked in mud? I was there! My thoughts are damning and I feel the walls start to close in on me.

"Babe, it's okay. Take a breath. Is there any way you're projecting your dream onto this tragedy because they are similar?" he asks in a calm, careful voice. "I know how upset you were yesterday when you found out you sleepwalked. You're probably still feeling it and trying to see something in this that isn't there."

I try to focus on what he is saying to me instead of the muddy tennis shoes I got rid of. That last part of what he said really hurt, but maybe he has a point.

No, I know what I saw, don't I? Did I sleepwalk into some mud instead, and that's how the shoes got ruined? I'm starting to doubt myself a little. I wipe the tears from my face as I try to calm down.

"Babe? Are you still there?" he asks.

"Yeah... I'm here, I'm just... He just... He looks exactly like the man I saw in my dream, Marc, I'm really freaking out here." I stop myself before I can voice my next fear that suddenly infiltrated my mind.

What if it wasn't a dream? What if I was sleep-driving and actually killed this man? I already had the feeling of liking the way it felt to kill him, oh my god no! No! I did not. Could not do this! I shake my thoughts away. *This is insane. There was no damage to the car and you're not capable of something like that, besides, he was found in the river. They didn't mention anything about his being hit by a car first. Did they?*

Before I can spiral any further with my thoughts, I need to get more information about the man they found, how he died, and when.

"Babe, do you need me to come home?"

I can hear the concern in his voice, but I don't want to be a burden to him and keep making him miss parts of work.

"No, it's fine. I'm fine, I just..." I stop because frankly I don't know what I need. "You're probably right, it's nothing."

"Babe, I have to go, I'm getting called into a meeting okay, but I'll call you afterward."

We hang up and all I can do is sit in a state of shock as more tears continue to flow down my cheeks. When I can finally get up and look around, I remember I still have my spilled coffee mess to clean up. I pick up the big pieces of broken mug first before wiping the coffee up with a paper towel. With all the coffee cleaned up, I have nothing else to preoccupy my mind, so I walk around the house in a daze. I decide to start some laundry. I'm on autopilot, going through the motions, when I hear the door downstairs open. I freeze, cursing myself for leaving my phone downstairs, but remembering I can also make phone calls from my watch. I type in 9-1-1 and get ready to hit call, when I hear a familiar voice.

"Babe? Are you here?" Marc calls from downstairs.

Oh, thank god.

I clear 9-1-1 from the watch and run downstairs to greet him, but mentally wrack my brain. *What time is it; did I miss picking up the girls again?* A glance at my watch tells me he is simply home early.

"Oh my god, you scared me!" I say. "What are you doing here?"

He sets his briefcase down, and begins to loosen his tie, "I came home early,"

"But... what are you doing here, I told you I was fine... you didn't need to come home." I say, guilt heavy in every word. I have to look away from him so he doesn't see the apprehension on my face.

"I know, but you sounded really anxious on the phone, and I

wanted to be here for you," he says with a sly smirk, looking back toward me, "and… I took the rest of the week off too."

"What? Why? You didn't have to do that," I grind out. *Great, he thinks I'm not sane enough to be left alone.*

"It's fine, babe. I had some vacation time and figured now would be the perfect time to use it. Besides, the alarm system is getting installed on Wednesday and the girls are starting piano lessons the same day. I figured it would be easier on you if I were home to help with everything." His embrace is reassuring, but his body feels rigid. I ignore it and melt into him, my tears flowing freely against his shirt.

"Thank you, I really appreciate it," I say between sniffles. "Did you happen to make the appointment yet? I think I really want to go now."

"I did, yes. They can get you in this Friday at ten," he says as he rubs his hands up and down my arms.

"Thank you."

"Of course, babe."

He makes me some food while I sit on the couch with the tv off. I don't want to chance seeing the dead man's face again.

"Here we are. Some food should help you feel a little better." The sandwich looks unappetizing, but I smile and eat it anyway.

"Thank you."

He devours his sandwich, glancing at me between bites. "Why don't you go upstairs when you're finished and get some rest, I can pick the girls up today."

"That would be wonderful, thank you, I could use a nap." I leave the rest of the sandwich and head upstairs. "Goodnight."

"Sweet dreams babe."

In the privacy of my bedroom, I prepare myself to do some digging. How can I sleep if sleep is the root problem of all this?

I set my pillows up to give me a nice backrest so I can sit up in bed to do research on what might be wrong with me. I'm not quite ready to look up details about Ken Woo, who I may or may not have murdered. Instead, I focus on figuring out what is wrong with me. This ends up being a bad idea since I get dragged down a rabbit hole. Sleep paralysis and sleepwalking are possible signs of sleep deprivation or interrupted sleep. The forgetfulness, however, can also be the result of sleep deprivation *or* a brain tumor, like Freya was telling me. The hallucinations, or vivid dreams, can also be a symptom of sleep paralysis or brain tumor as well.

Ugh what a mess.

All the symptoms I'm experiencing can all be linked from one extreme to another. There is no definitive answer. *Of course, why would it be simple.* My mind is reeling with the information overload when I hear the front door open. The girls are talking to Marc downstairs.

They're home already, jeez. Still feeling dazed, I close all the tabs on my phone and run down to greet them.

The time with them goes by in a blur, and I hope they don't pick up on my inner turmoil. The last thing I want to do is to worry them.

As the night goes on and the girls are long asleep in their beds, I notice that Marc hasn't even brought up the events of today. I don't want to be the first to bring it up either. It feels like the largest elephant in the room pushing us farther apart. If he is feeling the same way, he never lets it show. I wait until I hear his breathing start to slow and become deeper, telling me he is fast asleep. Slowly moving the covers off, I climb out of bed, and head into the bathroom, closing the door softly behind me. I put a towel down on the cold tile, and lower myself onto it, sitting cross legged. Immersed in the dark, blue light emanates from my phone. I take a deep breath before typing the name of the dead man in Sugar Creek into the search bar. Multiple articles appear. I choose the first one on the list:

Local Man Found in Sugar Creek. I take a deep breath before I read the article.

> A sixty-year-old man identified as Ken Woo was found in Sugar Creek, Bloomington, IL. His death has been ruled a homicide. Mr. Woo's cause of death was drowning, but he suffered from other injuries consistent with a hit and run. The coroner has set the time of death to be at least six days ago between the hours of 10 pm and 5 am. Local police are in search of a suspect. If anyone has information, they are asked to inform their local police department. Mr. Woo was the Head of Pediatrics at the Children's Hospital of Illinois, and leaves behind a wife and two sons…

My eyes are wide as I read the rest of the article. I realize I'm squeezing my phone so tightly that my hand is starting to cramp. I go back up to the part about how and when he died, reading it over and over again.

Homicide.
Hit and run.
Drowned.
Six days ago. The same time I had the dream.

I stare at his picture and I am positive it is the face I saw underwater. *What does this mean? Did I do this? I have never seen or heard of this man before; what possible reason could I have to kill him?*

Before I can rationalize my thoughts, an anxiety attack threatens to overwhelm me. I try to slow my breathing and ground myself by rubbing my hand against the softness of the towel and then touching the cold smooth tile. My eyes are closed; the phone is off; I'm in complete darkness. My breathing is coming easier and my chest doesn't feel as tight anymore. Now would be a good time to call it quits on looking at this article and try and get some sleep. I crawl back into bed, slowly so I don't wake up Marc and worry him.

When I pull the comforter around me and lay my head against my pillow, the pull of sleep is strong. I don't fight it.

In my dreams, I keep replaying the nightmare I had over and over again with different scenarios. Me killing him; me watching someone else kill him; me being psychic and the police thanking me for helping them find who really killed him, and so on. I toss and turn for most of the night and barely sleep at all. The only consolation is I don't have sleep paralysis or any new nightmares. I'm also fairly sure I did not sleepwalk, but then again, I didn't think I had the last time either. I'm not entirely sure I can really trust myself.

8

THE NEXT DAY passes me in a blur. With Marc being home to help take the kids to school and pick them up, I hardly get out of bed to do anything besides eat and say hi to the girls when they come home. It's only been a day, but I feel like I have been isolated for weeks. Marc's eying me more than usual. Is that worry or annoyance behind those intense glances? Now that it's Wednesday, I'm hoping things will turn around with the added sense of security the alarm system will bring. *Or maybe it will be the damning evidence that puts me away.*

Marc's constant presence must have a positive effect on me though: my mind is clearer and my sleepwalking has all but ceased. On the surface, I'm more myself, but underneath I'm closed off. I hide in the bedroom, convincing myself more than anyone I need to catch up on sleep. That's not the reality though. If I were to be honest with myself, I simply don't have the courage to face anyone.

But I have to.

When Marc comes back home from dropping the girls off, I

make my way downstairs to get some coffee and breakfast so I can shower before the alarm company arrives.

"Hey, babe, how are you feeling this morning?" he asks.

"I'm fine," The hostility in my voice takes me by surprise.

"Did you get any sleep last night?" he asks cautiously

"Yeah... a little, more than I have been at least."

"That's good I'm glad," He sounds truly genuine, and I feel lousy for having an attitude.

After I finish my breakfast, I put the dishes in the sink and head upstairs.

Fully naked, I open the shower door, and extend my hand out to feel the warmth of the cascading water. I sense his presence before I feel him put his hand on my hip while the other brushes my hair aside to kiss my neck.

"Want some company?" he asks into my neck, giving me goosebumps.

I suck in a breath and bite my lip in anticipation. I really want to say yes, but I find myself hesitating.

"Sorry, I think I would prefer to be alone this time," I tell him in a small voice.

He takes his hand away and steps back leaving me chilled.

I turn to look at him, "You're not mad, are you?" I ask in an uncertain voice.

"No babe... I'm not mad... I'm just wondering when all this moping is going to end and I'm going to get my wife back," he barks. He flings his hands out and gestures toward me.

His words are like a slap in the face. I give him an incredulous look, covering myself with a towel.

"*Shit*," he mutters under his breath. "I'm sorry, that came out wrong." He moves toward me again with his arms outstretched. "Babe really, it's fine, I'm honestly just frustrated. I'm sorry. That was a dumb thing to say. I swear I didn't mean it."

"It's fine," I say, ducking my head. I discard the towel and disappear into the shower before my tears start running down my face.

It's only when I hear him leave that I let my tears fall from my eyes, mixing with the water as they run down my face. I know I have to hurry before the alarm company arrives, so I try to push down my feelings and pull myself together. I promise myself I will be more present today with the girls and my husband.

Staring at my bare self in the mirror, fresh and new, I'm ready to uphold my promise.

I'm going to the doctor on Friday anyway. No use worrying about something until I have to. With new found confidence I get dressed and walk downstairs right as Marc lets the guys from the alarm company in the house. I make myself scarce while they do their thing and head to my studio. I need to assess the damage, the three black lines I allegedly painted, has done to my landscape piece.

Standing in front of the canvas, the three black lines taunt me. I can't bear to look at them any longer.

I set it aside and put a fresh canvas on the easel so I can start a brand new painting. I pull my sketchbook for inspiration and find it in the drawing of my girls swimming. The pure joy on their sun kissed faces is exactly what my heart needs right now. With a smile on my face for the first time in a while, I start my painting. I'm focused on getting the complex color of the water perfect to bring out the fluidity of the waves they made with their splashing. It takes me a moment to hear the knocking on the door, no doubt coming from Marc. He doesn't wait for me to answer before he lets himself inside.

"Babe, they're finished and going to give us a demonstration on how everything works, okay," he says. His apprehension radiates off of him as he waits for me.

"Okay, I'll be right there, just let me clean my brushes off," I know he can sense my happiness radiating off of me.

He gives me one last look, nods his head, and then heads back down the hall. When I come out, I hear them in the living room waiting for me so they can start. They explain to us how the alarm code works and have us choose the code we want to use to arm and disarm the system. We decide on the girls' birthday of course. Then they show us the sensors at every entrance to the house including the windows, which makes me feel more secure. Finally, they show us the cameras installed at the front and back doors.

When everything is said and done, we barely have enough time to see them out the door before having to head out to make it on time to pick the girls up. From there, we head straight to Mrs. Lang's house. The girls are giddy the whole way in anticipation of their first lesson.

Pulling up to the house, the first impression is how charming it looks. The house is a decent sized cottage with magnificent evergreen trees on either side. The whole scene is brought together by the cobblestone walkway leading up to the beautiful front door that has a large lion head knocker. *Wow, this looks like a painting Thomas Kinkade would do.*

I am still admiring everything when I feel the girls take my hand so we can walk up to the door together. The girls are standing in front of us, nervously waiting to start their lessons. Before I even get a chance to grab the knocker, the door opens and a sweet looking old lady opens the door wearing a flowery apron. She is exactly how I pictured she would look.

"Come in, come in. You must be Mr. and Mrs. Fowler. You can call me Mrs. Lang," the old woman says, addressing us before she looks down toward the girls. "And you must be Annabell and Adalaide. Excuse me if I don't know who is who just yet." Her kind eyes glance between them.

"Hi, yes this is Annabell," I say gesturing toward Anna. "And this is Adalaide. But you can call them Anna and Ada if you'd like." Her smile is warm as she welcomes us inside.

Inside the cozy house is a wonderful wood fireplace on the left-hand side, practically begging to be lit for the winter. In the center is a beautiful mahogany grand piano with open windows behind it, commanding the attention of the room.

"Wow, your piano is beautiful," Marc says. "Is that what the girls will practice on?"

"Thank you, dear, and yes this is the very one," she says proudly. She shuffles towards the kitchen, removing her apron, and returns with a plate of cookies.

"I hope you don't mind, I made extra," she says, gesturing for us to help ourselves.

"Thank you, that is very thoughtful of you." I reply.

"Here you are, girls. Would you like a cookie before we get started?" Mrs. Lang asks.

They look to Marc and me for permission before they each grab one. They delicately nibble the gooey cookie as they look around the house.

"So, I have the parents sit through the first session to make sure the girls listen to all the directions. If they can, then for the rest of the lessons, it's better for them to come alone, so they won't be distracted," She leads us to the comfy looking couch near the fireplace. "Make yourselves at home."

"Thank you," we reply.

"Okay, girls, who would like to go first today?" she asks.

The girls look toward each other. Then Anna stands up and walks toward Mrs. Lang,

"I will," Anna says confidently, looking up toward Mrs. Lang.

"Okay, dear. Are you Anna or Ada?" she asks as she leads her toward the piano.

"I'm Anna," she says and takes a seat on the bench.

They start the lesson with the basics, Anna on the bench and Mrs. Lang in a chair next to her. They go over how to sit properly with her back straight, how to place her hands on the keys, and even what the pedals do, though she won't be using them for the first few lessons. Once Anna is seated properly, her hands and arms poised correctly over the keys, Mrs. Lang walks her through how to play a few notes, which she calls the C scale. Mrs. Lang plays first, then has Anna repeat what she did. I think Anna is doing great and she looks like she is really enjoying it. I can only hope Ada likes it as much as her sister when it's her turn.

After thirty minutes, they switch and Ada learns the same things. She plays as well, if not better than her sister.

"Well, the girls did excellent, I'm sensing some raw talent in there." Mrs. Lang smiles as she walks over to us.

"That's great," Marc and I say together, smiling at each other and then at the girls. I am beyond proud of them.

"So, for every lesson, they can come in on their own and take the whole hour apiece. You may wait outside in your car or run any errands you have during that time," Mrs. Lang says. "Also, I will provide the books for them in the next lesson." She looks toward the girls. "You girls must practice every day. If I can tell that you have been practicing, we can discuss learning harder songs." This earns an excited look from them.

Mrs. Lang glances back to us, "Do you have a piano at home for them to practice on?"

"No, not right now but we can get one. What do you recommend?" Marc asks.

"Well, since they're beginners, you can start with an upright, or even a baby grand, whatever will fit best in your house. If that won't work, you can get them a keyboard, but I don't usually recommend it unless it's a last resort," she says.

"No worries, we will get them a piano to practice on," he stands taller carrying himself with pride.

"Okay then. Well, that's all for today. Same time next week, and you can either pay weekly or pay for the whole month, whichever you would like," Mrs. Lang says as she walks us to the door.

"Okay, thank you so much. We will discuss it and let you know next week," he says as we head out of the house.

The girls talk excitedly the whole ride home about taking lessons, how much they liked their teacher, and the biggest one, when the new piano is arriving. We tell them we will have to shop around for one and see. We also need to find a spot to put it as well.

When we arrive home, they run inside and start telling us all the spots that the piano would fit perfectly, only less than half of which are suitable options.

"Why don't you girls start on your homework while I get dinner going?" I tell them.

"Okay, Mommy." They sprint to get their backpacks and return with assignments in hand.

"I have a few phone calls I have to make for work, they won't take long." Marc says. He kisses me on the cheek and steps outside.

Dinner smells delicious. I'm about to finish up when a thought pops in my head. *Did I put my paints away?*

I crack the backdoor and poke my head out to get Marc's attention. "Can you finish the food? I have to check something in my studio."

He cover's the phone with his hand, "I'll be done in a second."

As promised, he comes right in to take over.

I head down the hallway to my studio. When I step inside, the air feels different. I hesitantly walk toward my easel and take a deep breath before peeking my head around to glance at my canvas, praying nothing is wrong with this one.

Oh good, exactly how I left it, and I remembered to put my paints away too. I pivot to leave when I notice something out of the corner of my eye. The ruined landscape is now propped up on the drying rack. Walking over to get a closer look I see that not only are there no black lines on it, but it's also completely finished.

What the fuck? I know I didn't finish it.

I reach out to touch it and yank my fingers away quickly. Shock courses through me. The painting is still wet!

"No! That is not possible!" I say in disbelief. I fixate on the mix of greens and blue on my fingertips and my fingerprint in the corner where I touched it, proof that it's real. My breath is coming faster now. My mind starts to swarm with thoughts. The walls are closing in on me. I force myself to take a few calming breaths and think.

Okay, calm down, maybe you decided to finish it.

Just breathe, Autumn.

I scrub the paint from my fingertips with a discarded rag. Satisfied that every trace of paint is gone, I back away from the painting slowly before sprinting out of the room. As I make my way to the kitchen, I stop a few feet out of sight, and run my hands over my face and pinch the bridge of my nose to keep from sobbing. Only once I feel more in control do I finish walking the rest of the way in. Marc is already bringing the food to the table where the girls are waiting.

"Did you girls wash up before you sat down?" I ask, trying to keep my voice even and as normal as possible. I pretend nothing is wrong.

They bob their heads up and down and wait for dad to put the food on their plates. I sit down, a mask of neutrality in place, and wait for Marc to pass the food over to me.

Marc doesn't suspect anything. His face is relaxed as he enjoys easy conversation with the girls. I can't tell him about the painting.

He wants the old, unburdened, not crazy Autumn back, so that's who I will try to be.

I'm alone in the dark.

The cool breeze of the night air rustles my hair.

Everything seems quiet. *Where am I, why am I outside?* I inspect my surroundings, hoping to get a glimpse of Marc, but he's nowhere to be found. Through the bushes I'm standing in, I see a house in front of me, but it is not familiar in the slightest.

Did I sleepwalk here?

Without warning, my legs propel me forward, crouching under a window. I wait a beat, looking around to make sure no one is around before I slink toward the back door. My heart is pounding in my chest. I reach out and pick the lock of the door, almost too easily. My breath catches in my chest, and to my horror, I realize I'm wearing black leather gloves. The same ones from my dream.

No! This can't be!

I don't want to go into the house, but something inside me pushes me through the door. Once inside, I tiptoe around various pieces of furniture in the dark until I reach a hallway with a door all the way at the end. I walk down the mysterious hallway, and notice the pictures hanging on the wall. They are snapshots of people I don't know, and I wonder again, what I'm doing here. Deep down, I fear I already know.

With the door now in front of me, I extend my gloved hand out and slowly turn the knob, inching the door open ever so slowly until the space is big enough for me to slip inside the room. Inside, I see a bed with what looks like an older woman sleeping.

Where the hell am I? Who is this?

I want to panic, but there is an eerie calmness over me. I know exactly what I'm here to do and it... excites me. Instead of retreating, my legs betray me and saunter closer to the bed. Sound asleep in that bed and unaware of my presence is an old woman. I'm standing directly over her.

Wake up!

Don't wake up!

I can feel my heart trying to beat out of my chest. Is it from nerves or excitement? I can't tell. Something heavy is now clutched in my left hand, and I reluctantly glance down to see what it is.

A butcher knife.

Exactly like the ones I have in my house.

I know exactly what I am here to do and I feel... excitement. Anticipation courses through me like electricity. The light from a lamppost outside catches the knife at exactly the right angle, putting a glare on the shiny steel. I raise my arm and with no hesitation, and run the steel blade across the old woman's throat. I am positively thrilled by the color of the bright crimson liquid that is left behind. The old woman startles me when her eyes snap open, her hands instinctively fling to her neck, frantically trying to stop the bleeding. Confusion and fear are evident in her eyes as she realizes I am not here to help her.

Call 9-1-1.

I don't listen to my thoughts. I *want* to watch the blood gush from her throat, knowing she will bleed out soon. I relish in the foreboding look in her eyes, pleading with me to help her... but I don't. The moment seems to last for an eternity and I savor every last second of it until finally, her eyes glaze over. She releases her final breath, and her hand falls limp against the pillow.

I'm flung back into blackness. My eyes open and I'm in my bed, sweat soaked. I try to sit up, but I can't move. I scan the room with my eyes since my head is immobile. I try to speak, but nothing comes out. Movement catches my eye by the door. A black figure slinks in the shadows, but I know it's only a hallucination caused by sleep paralysis. I close my eyes and focus on my calming techniques so the paralysis will pass and allow me to move again. It takes a few minutes, but I can finally start to move my toes and fingertips. When the rest of my body follows suit, I open my eyes and the figure I saw in the corner moments ago… is gone. I bolt out of bed and run to the bathroom with mere seconds to spare as I fling the toilet seat up and throw up, disgusted with myself.

I kneel on the cool smooth tile, holding my long hair back. I throw up once more. Unable to do anything else, I sit for a while, comforted by the coolness of the tile. I take a few more deep breaths to regain my composure so I can confidently get to a standing position. I close the door so I don't wake Marc, surprised that I haven't already. I lock the door for good measure and then turn on the light. Under the harsh fluorescents of the bathroom, my skin looks pale. My red-rimmed eyes are puffy and weary. The honey brown hue of my eyes now appears almost black. I plant my palms on either side of the sink and search my face looking for any sign that what I saw was real.

I refuse to believe I could have ever had those thoughts or feelings. I reach for the faucet with my shaky hands and turn it on, cupping the cold water in my palms. I splash it on my face a few times hoping it will soothe me and make the nausea disappear. I cleanse my mouth of the lingering bile and take a few more shakey breaths. *In through the nose; out through the mouth. It was just a dream; it was just a dream.*

Wasn't it?

My watch catches my eye. "That's it! My watch tracks my steps."

My hopes are shattered when the number of steps tracked shows over five thousand. There's no way it should be that high, I was home, asleep. I can't contain the tears.

I'm a murderer.

Numb, I pick myself off the floor and return to bed. Sensing my presence, Marc rolls to face me in his sleep. I want to wake him more than anything, but he looks so peaceful. I wouldn't know what exactly to tell him anyway. *Besides, you're supposed to be normal, Autumn.* I pray for a dreamless sleep so I can leave the horrible thoughts behind me.

9

ON FRIDAY, I'm all but counting down the minutes until I can go and see the doctor to get my scans done. At this point, I'm hoping for a tumor of some kind that can explain everything. I had been so busy waiting to get to this day, I don't realize Marc has noticed a change in me until he clears his throat in the car and looks at me with concern and hesitation, his tell-tale sign that he's about to bring up a difficult topic. I know better than to ask what it is, so I simply wait until he works up the nerve to start. The seconds tick by and he continues to stare out the windshield. I fidget in my seat becoming more uncomfortable until the warmth of his hand intertwines with mine. I begin to think he has changed his mind until he grabs my hand,

"So..." he begins, stealing a glance in my direction. "I noticed you have been having more issues when you sleep, and you seem really distant with, not only me, but the girls as well."

Shit!

I glance over at him and wince.

I was going to come up with a lie or brush off his concerns, but find myself saying the truth instead.

"I didn't know you were awake when it happened." I pause, focusing on our intertwined hands. "I honestly thought I was keeping it together under the surface and you couldn't tell anything was wrong," I say barely above a whisper. "And I wanted to be back to the normal Autumn you said you wanted."

"Oh, babe, I told you I didn't mean that. I always want you to come to me with problems. I never want you to feel like you can't or that you are alone in what you are feeling. I was awake, but figured you wanted your space since you closed the door to the bathroom," he says. His eyes are still fixed on the road but he continues to sneak glances toward me every now and then. "And babe, you're not very good at hiding your feelings when things are upsetting you, even the girls asked me about it." I snap my head to look at him, my eyes wide with concern.

"You didn't tell them, did you?" The panic drips off every word.

"No, of course I didn't. I told them you were having a hard time sleeping, nothing more." He gives a closed lip grin before the grimace comes back across his face. "Tell me the truth, what's happening."

I hesitate before I'm able to continue.

"I'm scared you will think differently of me if I tell you everything," I say, not able to meet his eyes.

"Babe, I would never think differently of you," he says, giving my hand a light squeeze. "I love you. You can tell me anything, you know that."

"Okay, here it goes," I say and I take a deep breath, ready to give him the *Cliff Notes* version of everything. "I feel like I am going insane. The painting with the three black lines I don't remember painting, well it was repainted as if nothing ever happened. It was still wet when we got back from the girl's piano lesson." I pause before going on. "And last night I had a gruesome dream of murdering an old lady in her sleep."

I can't bring myself to say out loud how the act of murdering two people secretly made me feel. He would have me committed for sure, or take the girls away in fear that I couldn't be trusted around them.

"I checked my watch though and it had tracked steps as if I was walking all night instead of being in bed." I put my head in my hands and take deep breaths. The car jerks to the side of the road before he shifts it into park. I brace myself for what his reaction is going to be, what he will say.

"Oh my God! Babe! Why didn't you tell me?" he asks. The intensity in his voice makes me look at him. Hurt flashes across his face, but it's gone in an instant, masked by something else I can't decipher. *Fear? Compassion?* "That sounds so awful and scary, I would have wanted to be there for you."

"I know, I'm sorry, I just… I just didn't know how to tell you, I'm really worried…" I hesitate and bite my lip. *Should I tell him more?*

He looks at me with patience and urges me to say whatever it is on my mind. I avert my eyes, too ashamed to look him in the eyes when I reveal my biggest fear.

"I'm… I'm starting to think that maybe, it's me doing it somehow, like in my sleep or something." My words come out in an unhurried whisper.

He reaches his hand across to place it under my chin and pulls my face up, urging me to look at him.

"Babe…" he says in a calm, even voice, his eyes searching mine, "you can't really believe you are actually committing these murders, can you? That's impossible. I would know if you left the bed and didn't come back for hours at a time. Besides, we have the alarm system now. It's brand new, you're still getting the hang of how to punch in the code. I'm sure you wouldn't be able to do it in your sleep. I would know if you were sleepwalking. How about we check the security cameras to see if you left the house at night, how does that sound?"

Of course! The security system! Why didn't I remember that sooner? We can check the cameras and see if I left the house at all! Ugh, I could have checked them right away instead of wondering for two days.

"I would like to check the cameras to see but, if it's not really me, I'm afraid something is wrong with me, like a tumor or something."

"Of course, babe, but that's not the only other alternative. You have sleep paralysis episodes, and sleepwalking that explains almost everything. Even the forgetfulness since you're probably sleep deprived." He says it sweetly and full of patience.

"I know. You're probably right." I sigh. His eyes flick to the time on the dash and starts to pull back onto the road so we can make it to the doctor's appointment on time.

"Besides, we should find out something within a few days after you have your scans. Let's not get ahead of ourselves with worry unless we have to." He glances over, teeth flashing, as he brings my hand to his lips and kisses the back of it, temporarily melting my worries away.

When we pull into the parking lot, I feel like a tremendous weight has been lifted off my shoulders since confiding in my husband. We are a team, and with him by my side, I can handle anything. We walk in the office hand in hand, no longer dreading the scans or what the doctor has to say.

Sensing how I feel, Marc whispers in my ear, "We can handle whatever we find out, together."

After signing in and waiting in the waiting room, the doctor finally calls me back so I can change into the hospital gown before being led to the MRI machine. They hand me ear plugs before putting a face cage over my head and telling me to lie very still. When they are behind the glass, they inform me that when they start, it's going to be loud and I should remain still and relaxed. The nurses slide me into the intimidating magnetic machine where a loud intermittent banging noise fills the space. Luckily, the ear plugs help muffle it.

When I'm finished, they help me back to my room so I can change. Marc is brought in followed by the doctor so we can discuss the reason for my visit. We inform the doctor about my medical history, including my sleep paralysis induced nightmares, sleep-walking, and finally the forgetfulness. I divulge a few detailed examples to him and I'm afraid the doctor is going to commit me to the psych ward on the spot. Fortunately, he believes what Marc has been saying this whole time, sleep deprivation, which can cause all the symptoms I'm experiencing. He truly believes it's the most likely diagnosis for everything.

"So, not a brain tumor then?" I force my tone to portray pure curiosity and concern, instead of hope.

"Well, we will let you know the results of the MRI tomorrow, but I strongly believe the imaging will be clear of anything alarming," the doctor says. "In the meantime, I'm going to prescribe an antidepressant, which can be used to help regulate your sleep cycle. If the episodes continue however, we should think about getting you into a sleep study to monitor you further and verify there isn't another underlying sleep disorder"

"Okay, what are the side effects of this drug?" I ask, nervous about taking an antidepressant.

Marc, sensing my fear and hesitation, places a hand on the small of my back.

"Some of the side effects can include dizziness, drowsiness, headache, etc.," the doctor says nonchalantly. "If you start experiencing any of these don't hesitate to call and we can reevaluate keeping you on it or switching you to a different one."

I chew my lip, digesting the information, "Okay,"

"Let's start off by taking one a day right before bed," the doctor says.

"I can do that," I say. He nods and leaves the room.

We check out at the front desk and rush to fill my prescription before we have to go pick up the girls from school.

"Thank you for taking so many days off of work lately," I say when we're in the car. "I really appreciate not having to do all this alone."

He looks over at me and smiles, one hand on the steering wheel, the other interlacing in mine.

"Of course, babe, I'm always here for you, whatever you need."

My heart does a flip, elated to have a loving, understanding husband. The feeling gets spoiled however, when I notice something off about his expression. I quickly shake it from my thoughts. *You're looking for things that aren't there.*

"I love you," I tell him, a heartbeat later.

"I love you too."

One of the side effects the doctor mentioned comes into my mind. "What if I experience a bad side effect? I'm already tired and forgetful. What if I become even drowsier throughout the day? I don't want to take a nap and not wake up in time to get the girls from school again."

"I don't think you will babe, and if you do, we will cross that bridge when we get to it. If it will make you feel better while you're getting used to them, we can see if your parents can pick the girls up. That way, if you are sleeping, they will still be picked up from school. From there, they can call me if you aren't able to get them and I can on my way home."

"I think I would prefer that; I can call them tomorrow and see if they would be okay with it starting on Monday. Good thing I will be trying them over the weekend, maybe I won't even need to call them if I don't have any side effects though."

"Well, if you do, I can always go in later to work and drop them off before I leave, that won't be an issue either," he says, though I can tell he is lying about it.

We get the girls from school and head home and all I can think about is checking the footage from the security cameras and hoping these pills work so I can finally have some sleep.

I breeze past Marc anxious to see the footage. The girls run upstairs to play. I am stopped in my tracks when his hand circles my wrist.

"Not so fast. I think you should practice arming and disarming the alarm," he says.

"Fine." I disarm it first and then arm it with no problems. "See, I know how to do it."

"I'm just making sure," he says. "Come on, let's get started on dinner."

"I thought we were going to check the footage?" I blurt out.

"We will, when the girls are asleep." I roll my eyes in protest, but follow him anyway.

The night seems to drag out of spite, but finally, it's time to get the girls tucked in and head to check the footage. We look back to Wednesday, the night I dreamt of the second potential victim. I stand behind Marc chewing on my nails, anxious to see anything out of the ordinary.

Static. The entire day is nothing but static.

"What's wrong? Why isn't it working?" I ask, apprehension clouding my mind.

"Well, my best guess is they weren't online yet, but that doesn't make sense, considering we have all of the video recordings from Thursday and today. Maybe it was only a glitch since it got set up that day. No worries, it's working now," he says.

How can he be so casual? He knows how important this is!

I nod and try to hide my disappointment. This was supposed to be the end of it. The thing that puts my mind to rest. Though, a lack of an answer, could be the actual answer. *Could I have somehow disabled the video feed?*

Choosing not to entertain my thoughts, we head upstairs and I get a glass of water from the bathroom sink. I say a silent prayer and pop the pill in my mouth feeling it slide all the way down my throat. I walk over to my side of the bed, and pull back the covers, anxious for this to kick in.

"Did you take your pill already?" Marc asks, joining me in bed.

"Yep, now let's hope that it works," I say optimistically.

"I'm sure it will, babe, the only way to find out though is to sleep," he leans over to press an intimate kiss to my temple. "Goodnight, baby."

"Goodnight."

I turn off my side of the light and lie back on my pillow, looking up at the ceiling. With a heavy sigh, I close my eyes.

Light peeks through the windows, interrupting my sleep. *I did it, I slept and didn't have a single dream.* I open my eyes to look over to see if Marc is still in bed. Nope, he must be downstairs with the girls already. I slowly sit up and feel my head spin. *Ugh*, I bring my hand to my head hoping to steady it. *Welp, one side effect is already making an appearance.* I sit until some of the dizziness passes and I can go to the bathroom to get dressed. When it does, I stand up, but immediately get another wave combined with some nausea. I wobble on my feet, but manage to balance myself enough to get to the bathroom.

Ugh this sucks. Fortunately, the cool damp cloth eliminates my dizzy spell and nausea. I test my balance and when I'm satisfied I won't tumble or be sick again, I go downstairs. The smell of coffee hits me first, followed by bacon. My stomach growls in anticipation of food. I walk into the kitchen and desperately pour myself a cup of coffee, but don't see any bacon.

"Good morning, sleepy head, we were wondering when you were going to join us," Marc says from the couch.

"What do you mean?" I say looking at him while I add my cream and sugar.

"I mean it's almost 11:30," he says with a chuckle.

"Yeah, Mommy, you were asleep for a while. Dad said we had to be very quiet so we didn't wake you," Anna says. "But now that you're awake, can we turn the tv up louder?"

She doesn't bother waiting for me to respond before grabbing for the remote and turning it up, probably louder than is needed. The noise brings the pounding in my head back with a vengeance.

"Sweetie, can you turn it down a little please, it doesn't have to be as low as it was, but please, turn it down a little for Mommy," I say, wincing in pain.

Catching a glimpse of me, Marc hurries to my side, his eyebrows knitted together in concern.

"Babe? What's going on? Are you okay?" he asks, putting a hand on my shoulder and leaning his head down so he can look me in the eyes.

"Yeah, I'll be okay, I already had some dizziness, nausea, and now somewhat of a headache," I say with a small smile spreading across my face, "but... I slept really well."

"Well, I'm glad to hear about the good sleep, but I'm sorry you're already feeling some side effects," he says, empathy evident in his voice. "If it continues into next week, we will call the doctor and see about switching."

"That's okay, it's nothing I can't handle," I say, waving him off. "However, if I'm going to sleep this long, I will definitely need you to drop the girls off at school until I can get adjusted."

"Yeah, no problem," he says. A hint of annoyance flashes across his face and is gone in an instant.

After I finish my breakfast, I take a shower while he makes lunch for the girls. With the water as hot as I can stand, I let it cascade over me like a waterfall. I lean my head back and let the pressure ease my pounding headache. I run my fingers through my wet hair a few times trying to rub away the headache and anxiety before it consumes me. I'm hesitant to leave the safety of the shower where my problems don't exist and step back out into a world where I will be forced to face them. Eventually, I sigh as I turn the water off and step out into the cold harsh air, making the tension in my body, and headache immediately start to surface again. I'm about to get dressed when I hear footsteps coming down the hallway.

"Hey, babe, is everything okay in here?" Marc asks as he peeks his head in the door.

"Yeah, everything's fine, I'm almost done, getting dressed now," I yell from the walk-in closet.

He leans up against the door frame, his eyes traveling the length of my body before landing on my face, "Okay, I'm just making sure, you've been up here for a while."

"I know, I'm sorry, I lost track of how long I was in there."

"I figured. I wanted to make sure you were okay. The girls are watching tv now, but they were asking about going to look at pianos today." His eyes study me, gauging my reaction. "I know you're not feeling the best today so I told them I would ask, and if not, we can go next weekend or something."

I look away, battling the pros and cons in my head. I really hate letting the girls down, but I also really wanted a lazy day. I turn back toward him and answer hesitantly.

"Well, I don't know if I'm really up to it today, but I would hate to let them down, and they are going to need one so they can practice. If that's what they want to do, maybe you could take them without me?" I ask, hoping I don't seem like a horrible mother for not wanting to go out today.

"I could take them, if that's what you want, or we could always go next weekend or something."

"Well, maybe next weekend then, when I get used to these pills," I say, relieved we are on the same page.

My relief turns to dread when we get downstairs and the girls run over with the biggest smiles across their faces wondering if we're going to get ready and leave to shop for a piano. Marc steps in to give them the disappointing news so I don't have to.

"Not today, monkeys, but we can go next weekend when Mommy's feeling better okay?" he asks, ushering them back into the living room.

"Why, Daddy? Can't *you* take us?" Anna asks, disappointment heavy in her words.

"Can't we just go today, Mommy?" Ada says, looking up to me with her best please face. I almost cave right then and there, but I don't.

"I am so sorry, sweetie; Mommy isn't really feeling up to it today," I tell her hoping they both can see how sorry I truly am.

"I promise, we will go next weekend. What do you say?" Marc asks.

Silently, they nod their head yes and sulk back to the living room, leaving me heartbroken and full of guilt. I look to Marc for reassurance, but he is already turning away from me mumbling that he is going to go for a run.

Since when does he run? I don't bother questioning him right now; instead, I focus my attention on my girls when he leaves.

"Hey, my Gemini stars, Mommy is really sorry we can't go today like you wanted," I say as I kneel in front of them. "How about Mommy paints your nails instead, what do you think?"

"Yeah! I want pink!" Anna says excitedly.

"And I want purple," Ada says with a big smile on her face. Their excitement is enough to make my guilt dissipate.

"Alright, let's do it," I tell them.

"We want to paint *your* nails too, Mommy. They should be red," they say at the same time.

"Okay!" I tell them, astonished by their bold color choice for me. "Quick, go get all the supplies and meet me back down here." They run to gather everything, and before I know it, we are ready for our home manicures.

They are almost done painting my nails when Marc finally comes back home from his run. Instead of acknowledging us, he heads straight upstairs no doubt to take a shower. The girls' faces fall in disappointment. They wanted to show off their freshly painted nails. I ignore my bubbling anger and focus on distracting them.

"Hey Gemini stars, why don't you watch some cartoons, I'm going to go talk to Daddy for a second okay?"

"Okay, Mommy," they respond in unison, while Anna reaches for the remote.

I focus on controlling my anger with every step I take, but one look at him brings it bubbling to the surface again.

"So, how was your run?" I ask, busying myself with folding the girls' clothes.

"It was fine," he says, not offering up any more information.

"When did you start running?" I'm aware of my harsh questioning tone, but I don't care.

"I don't know, a few weeks ago I guess." I can tell by his vague answers, I'm not going to get much else out of him, so I decide to drop it. I'm still seething, but I remind myself that I haven't been completely forthcoming about my true feelings in my dreams, either.

10

MY SYMPTOMS ARE the same waking up today and I slept in until almost noon again. The only bright side is that I had another night of good sleep with no nightmares. I cautiously get out of bed, keeping the dizziness at bay, when I hear music coming from downstairs. *It sounds like a piano, but how can that be?* I shrug into my robe and head down to see what's going on. When I get downstairs the girls are in the living room on the floor huddled around something I can't see, but it sounds like a keyboard.

"Hey girls, what do you have there?" I ask them. I have to side step around them to get a better look.

"Daddy took us to the store today so we could get a keyboard to practice on until we get the real piano," Ada says, still pushing random keys that sound good together.

"Well, that was very nice of him," I tell them as Marc emerges from the backyard.

"Hey, babe, glad to see you're up, the girls and I got up early today so we could go get that. I left you a note in case you woke up before we got back, but obviously you didn't," he chuckles. "I was about to take the burgers and brats off of the grill, did you want some or are you going to eat breakfast?"

I fix my face into neutrality to hide my annoyance, "I came down to see what the music was. I'm going to take a shower, I'll come down after and have some eggs or something, and coffee, can't forget the coffee."

I stalk back into the bedroom, fuming with every step. *I can't believe he took them to get the keyboard without me.* I strip off my robe and get in the shower, not waiting for it to get warm. *I wanted us all to go together so I could see the excitement on their faces. I need to start setting an alarm for myself so I can make sure I don't keep waking up this late.*

Through the clarity of the water, I feel silly for being angry. I should be happy that they have something to practice on. When the anger subsides, it is soon replaced by anxiety when I remember I should be getting my MRI results soon. Since taking the pills I am more convinced that all I needed was, in fact, some good old fashion sleep. Even so, a nagging thought keeps plaguing my thoughts. Regardless of desperately trying to put it out of my mind. *Will the lady I supposedly killed in my dreams appear on the news as well?*

My wrinkled fingertips alert me that I have been in here longer than I intended, letting my thoughts spin out of control. I reluctantly turn off the water, and emerge in a steam filled room. I wipe the mirror so I can see myself clearly. I'm not totally convinced I know who is staring back at me.

When I get back downstairs Anna is playing the keyboard now while Ada watches. It sounds like the scales they learned at their lesson. *I'm excited for them to get their first book so they can learn a few songs.*

Marc eyes me cautiously, "You were in there a while, everything okay?"

I wave him off and start a fresh pot of coffee, "Yeah, lost track of time in there that's all."

"Well, do you want me to whip you up some pancakes? I made them for the girls this morning," he says.

"No, that's okay, I feel like having an omelet today," I say. I start preparing all the ingredients.

"Okay, well here let me make it for you," he is already beside me attempting to grab the spatula from me.

I spin out of his reach, "It's okay, I can make it myself,"

"Okay, if you're sure," he says, gazing at me pensively before shaking his head and wandering back in the living room. "Oh, and before I forget, the girls are asking when they can have another playdate with Sarah,"

"I don't know, we will have to get in touch with Jeanie and see when they are free. She did say that they could have one at her place next time though, maybe we take her up on it."

"Yeah, we could do that. I can ask her tomorrow."

"I think I'm going to eat in my studio today," I tell him. The sound of the keyboard is already giving me a headache.

"Okay, we will be here," he says casually while the girls continue to play. *If these side effects don't get better in a week, I'll ask to change prescriptions, or maybe I'll ask the doctor tomorrow when they call about my results.*

The silence is exactly what I need. I set my food and coffee down at my table and open up my curtains so I can enjoy the day. *Maybe after I'm finished and my headache is gone, the girls and I can go outside for a walk. I think the fresh air will do me good.* I contemplate finishing up the painting of the girls, but decide against it, wanting to spend some time with my Gemini stars.

My headache subsides. The quiet mixed with eating helps tremendously.

The girls are still playing the keyboard when I come back in the room, so I hope they will want to go.

"Hey girls, would you like to go for a walk? We could go to the park and play for a while before dinner," I ask lightheartedly.

"Yeah! I want to go down the big slide!" Anna says. She abandons the keyboard and jumps up and down in anticipation.

"I want you to push me on the swings, Mommy," Ada says equally excitedly.

"We can do whatever you want there!" I say, beaming. Their blitheness is contagious, and I can't help but pull them into a hug, "Okay go grab a warm coat and your tennis shoes."

They run upstairs to get ready while I stand up and hold my head, waiting for the dizzy spell that abruptly hit me, to pass. Thankfully, it does.

Marc notices and looks at me apprehensively, "You sure you want to go to the park today?"

I brush off his concerns and slip on my new tennis shoes, "Yeah, it will be fun. Besides, I could use the fresh air and a normal day with my wonderful family." I kiss him on the lips, catching him off guard.

When everyone is ready, we head out to the park, the girls clasp hands and skip in front of us.

"Don't get too far ahead, girls," I call out to them. They hear me and slow their pace instantly.

Luckily, the park isn't too crowded today. *Thank god.* Anna immediately takes off toward the big slide, while Ada runs to the swing set.

"Come on, Mommy, push me!" Ada yells. She impatiently waits for me to catch up. The sun changes her eyes to an amber gold. They are bright with excitement.

"Coming, sweetie," I tell her. My words come out breathless. *I need to be in better shape.* I call over my shoulder to Marc, "I'll push her on the swing and you look out for Anna, deal?"

"Deal," he says, jogging after Anna.

When I reach the swings, I start pushing Ada back and forth, the squeakiness of the chains getting louder and louder the higher she goes. I don't even have to see her face to know that she is beaming from ear to ear, enjoying every minute of flying through the air.

"Do the underdog, Mommy, the underdog!" she says gleefully.

"Okay, but hold on tight, okay?"

She says okay and I call out, "One…two…" When I reach three, I push her up as high as I can and run under her, making her squeal with delight.

"Again, again!" she demands through her fits of laughter.

"Hang on, sweetie, Mommy needs a minute." I laugh and wait until she slows down again. She makes me do the underdog three more times. *I should have gone with Anna to the slides instead. I am out of breath.*

The girls run around a while longer while Marc and I sit on a bench and watch them play on the colorful jungle set. They run across the bridge, swing from the monkey bars and zip down every slide. It's like they are made of energy that never goes away. I'm thankful to be sitting so I can catch my breath. I am so exhausted and sore. My knee brushes up against Marc's and I realize I have forgotten how nice it is to sit beside my husband and enjoy each other's company. He must feel the same way because his arm reaches above my head, draping across my shoulders to pull me closer to him.

"I'm sorry we went without you to get the keyboard. I should have woken you up, but I knew you needed the sleep."

"That's okay, I understand, and yes, I do need the sleep, but I also want to be present with you guys and not sleep the day away, or have these headaches and dizzy spells," I tell him as I rest my head on his shoulder.

"I know, babe, but it's only been a couple of days. You undoubtedly will have to get used to them or find something that works for you. Besides, your results will be in soon and that could tell us something completely new," his tone is positive, but we both know the new information could consist of my having some sort of brain tumor.

The comfortable silence consumes us, content to watch the girls play. After a while, they abruptly stop playing and run over to us, declaring that they are tired and absolutely dying of hunger.

"Okay, okay monkeys, we're coming." Marc chuckles.

"We want piggy back rides!" they both say at the same time. My muscles refuse and I groan internally, but find myself obliging.

"Okay, let's go then," I say.

Ada leaps onto his back, while Anna carefully climbs onto mine, aware of my sore muscles. The short distance has never felt so far. My knees shake with effort and my lungs burn, but I made it! Anna slides off my back and trails after Ada to the living room. The only thing on my mind is collapsing onto the couch. My relief is short lived when I realize we still need to make dinner.

Marc leans toward me and whispers in my ear. "Don't worry, I already ordered food when we were walking back, why don't you go upstairs and rest until it arrives. Should be around an hour," he says

I sag into his arms and kiss him, "This is why I love you,"

"I know," he says with a wink. He lets me go but not before slapping my ass on my way up the stairs.

My body hits the bed and it feels like I have sunk into a cloud. My muscles relax and the pull of sleep is stronger than ever. *I'll close my eyes, just for a minute.*

Waking up to the hunger pains in my stomach, I head downstairs, wondering why Marc never came to wake me.

"Hey, there you are, I just put the girls to bed, and your food is in the fridge, I couldn't get you to wake up, so I figured I would let you sleep," he says getting up from the couch, seeming startled to see me. "I was about to head to bed myself."

"Oh, okay," I say hesitantly. "That's fine. I think I will have some food though; I'm starving."

"I'll wait with you until you're finished then," He tells me, though I get the sinking feeling he doesn't want to.

"No, that's okay, I'll just eat and come back up when I'm done," I tell him, letting him off the hook.

"Okay, if you're sure," he says as he walks by me to give me a kiss on the temple before quickly heading upstairs.

I stare at the empty space where he was moments ago and a feeling I can't quite identify starts to take root in my thoughts. I'm not entirely sure if I'm trying to see something that isn't there, but I suddenly have a horrible feeling that Marc didn't think I was going to wake up at all the rest of the night. Shock was etched into his features. He tried to hide it, but it was there.

Maybe he figured the pills make me sleep longer like I have been every morning. I try to rationalize and brush the thought away. *You're just being paranoid, Autumn, get a grip.* With my food warmed, I settle in to satisfy my hunger. I eat in silence, and feel stupid for even thinking that, but in my gut, I feel like I'm right.

11

ON MONDAY, as promised, Marc takes the girls to school. Good thing because I didn't wake up until almost 10am, which is slightly better than the 11:30 I was getting up at over the weekend. Luckily though, my sleep has been much better, no more sleepwalking, that I'm aware of, and definitely no more nightmares.

Thank god!

The nausea and dizziness are non-existent today at least. I grow weary, anticipating a call from the hospital with the results of my MRI. The wait drags and with every passing second, I'm convinced it's bad news. I need to occupy myself so I don't go crazy–when the vibration of my phone halts my thoughts.

"Hello," I say a little too eagerly.

"Hello, is this Autumn Fowler?"

"Yes, this is she."

"We have the results of your MRI here and am happy to report that everything looks normal," the voice on the other line says.

"Wow, that's great news, thanks," I say flatly before hanging up.

I don't know why I'm upset about such great news. *Who actually hopes for a tumor in their brain?* I was hoping one sure thing would be wrong, something we could fix. Looks like I will be on antidepressants for the rest of my life. *Figures*, I turn on the tv to get some background noise while I let the news soak in. I text Marc that I'm awake and able to pick the girls up from school instead of having my parents do it. I purposefully leave out the part about my results, however. I'm not sure why I don't tell him; maybe I'm afraid of his reaction? Who knows, but after my feelings last night, I know I'm not ready. I'm so lost in my own thoughts that I almost miss what the news anchor says. I reluctantly turn the volume up, and rewind so I can hear the whole report.

I know I heard the word "murder." I hope I'm wrong.

"An elderly woman identified as fifty-three-year-old Gwen Frost was found dead in her bed early this morning. The widow has been living alone since the death of her husband two years ago. Her granddaughter hadn't heard from her in a few days and went over to check on her. The woman's cause of death was exsanguination. Her throat had been cut. The police have ruled this a homicide. If anyone has any information, please call your local police department."

When they finish with the report, it is followed up with her picture on the screen. To anyone else she might be a sweet old lady — a stranger— but to me, I see a woman I murdered in cold blood. My jaw drops open and I have to reach for the back of the chair to steady myself. I am *one hundred percent* sure this time. This woman, Gwen Frost, is the woman I dreamt of killing.

I lower myself to the floor, covering my face with my hands. *What is happening to me? What have I done?* I'm frozen in place. I don't shed a single tear. I simply sit. I'm in shock.

Did I do this in my sleep? Am I somehow psychic? The last thought seems a bit of a stretch, but is preferable to the first. *Do the police have any leads, should I turn myself in? Should I wait until they bust down my door to arrest me in front of my family? Good thing my dad is retired. I would hate to have to be arrested by my own father.*

I'm spiraling. It's only when my phone vibrates in my hand do I come out of my state of shock. It's Marc. I'm not ready to speak to anyone right now. I'll text him instead. The message is short and concise: *Can't pick up girls, feeling sicker.* I text my mom next and make sure she will be able to pick them up instead. They reply back simultaneously, him with a worried face emoji, followed by saying he will swing by my parents' house on his way home and get them. My mom says it won't be a problem. When I know the girls are taken care of, I call my friend Ren and ask if I can come over to talk. She is the only friend I have who believes in psychics and is into true crime, so I know she won't judge me.

Even if it is me committing these horrendous acts of murder, she will know what to do. If she takes me in to the police, at least I won't be alone. I almost chicken out as her name appears on the screen, but I close my eyes, take a deep breath and call. The sound of the phone ringing while I wait for her to pick up is almost unbearable. What seems like fifty rings later, she finally answers.

"Hey girl, what's up?" she asks, sounding out of breath.

"Not much. Hey, I'm in serious need of some real talk. Are you free if I come over?" I ask in a rush before I can lose my nerve about confiding in her.

"Yeah, sure sweetie, I just finished my workout. I'll shower really quick and be ready by the time you get here."

"Okay, thanks, see you in a bit."

I grab my purse, arm the alarm, and head out the door in a rush, eager to get to her house. My driving is a little on the erratic side and I pray I don't get pulled over because I might end up confessing to murder.

After twenty-three years of friendship, I don't even bother knocking when I arrive. Instead, I use the key she gave me and let myself in, calling for her when I do. She rounds the corner to greet me. As soon as I see her, I fall apart. Tears spring from my eyes, flow down my face, and I collapse into her arms.

"Oh my God! Autumn, sweetie, what's *wrong?*" she asks as she catches me, her voice full of concern and confusion. "Is it the girls? Are they okay? Marc? What is it?"

I'm choking back sobs, but manage to shake my head to let her know that he and the girls are fine. She pulls me close and walks me to the couch holding me against her while she whispers soothing words in my ear, and waits for me to calm down enough to talk to her. I focus on her hand running through my hair, and the smell of the lavender soap. With my breathing smoother and no fresh tears threatening to leak out, I pull away from her embrace. I give her an apologetic look and wipe my hands across my face, clearing it of all the tears. She's looking at me full of worry with her eyebrows knitted together, but she waits until I start to speak before she says anything.

I don't know where to begin, so I start at the beginning and leave nothing out. I'm even bold enough to include the unbearable thoughts about how it really felt to murder those poor people, not realizing how good it feels to get off of my chest. To her credit, she listens to me patiently and doesn't say a word until I'm finished. The only reactions she has are the faces she makes upon hearing the gruesome details of each dream. When I have divulged every last detail, she stares at me with bulging eyes. Waiting for her to speak is agonizing.

"Okay, let me get this straight. You're dreaming about killing people only to find out those people are actually dead now?" she asks in a slightly higher pitched voice, with her hands raised in front of her. "And you liked doing it?"

"Among the other things... yes," I say wincing slightly. "Do you think I'm crazy?"

She bites her lip as she ponders the question for a beat.

"I don't think you're crazy... but sweetie, this is a lot. I mean like a lot, a lot."

I hang my head in shame. "I know."

"And you say your tennis shoes were muddy as well, and you don't know how they got that way?" her brows twitch together, deep in thought, processing.

"Yes, I cleaned them, but I don't know if that was the right thing to do or not." I sigh. She reaches for my hand trying to comfort me, but I can see the idea forming in her eyes.

"What? What is it?" I ask in a rush, desperate for any theories.

"Well, it's definitely not the same, but I was thinking of the time in high school... you remember... the sleepover incident?" she hesitantly asks, her eyes trying to gauge my reaction.

I look at her confused not knowing what she is talking about. "What do you mean? What sleepover incident?"

Her eyes look at me in disbelief. "You honestly don't remember? It was like, a big deal, Autumn," she says as she lets go of my hand and stands from the couch. "We were at Freya's house for a sleepover, back when we were friends with Laura. Remember?" She pauses to see if anything is ringing a bell, which it is not, before she continues. "Okay... Well you and Laura had a huge fight about Chris. She wasn't supposed to come to the sleepover, but she did anyway, knowing it would get under your skin. Anyway, things were tense but fine, and we went to sleep. We were awakened by Laura screaming because you were holding a knife trying to stab her. It was only when we got the knife away from you that we realized you were sleepwalking. You honestly don't remember that?"

"What? No! Of course I don't remember that! Are you being

serious right now?" I ask. I am on my feet, pacing in front of her. "Fuck."

"Hey, it was a long time ago. Nothing happened or became of it, but it does kind of sound a little similar to the last murder you saw," she says in a small voice. "But, look, I know you; you would never do anything like that, okay? You're a good person, besides, what does Marc think about all this? Does he notice you leaving in the middle of the night or anything? I mean, I would think that if it was you, someone would notice if you got up and left your house in the middle of the night."

"He knows, yes, only, not about the second victim being found, or my feelings toward it. He thinks I'm projecting my dreams onto these people, drawing parallels between them, not that I'm actually dreaming of these real-life people that have been murdered." I tell her.

"Well, he could have a point there," she says.

"Yeah, you're probably right," I say. In my heart though, I know these are real people.

"Hey, you could become a fortune teller," She laughs a little trying to lighten the mood, but it doesn't work. Now I have something else to worry over, the incident from high school, which I have no recollection of happening. *At least she doesn't run screaming from me...*

"I'm sorry to unload all of this on you. You don't need my drama. You should only be worrying about growing that beautiful baby," I tell her ashamed that I brought all this darkness on her.

"Sweetie, no. I'm your friend and I am always here for you no matter what. Okay?" Her compassionate eyes search mine.

"Thanks, Ren. I know you are." I tell her, wrapping my arms around her for a hug. "Anyway, enough heavy. Let's talk about you now."

"Well, these food cravings are insane." She laughs. "I never used to like pickles, and now, I can't get enough, especially when I pair them with ice cream."

"*Eww.* What?" I say wrinkling my nose, "That sounds awful."

"I know, it's crazy." She laughs, absentmindedly rubbing her stomach. "We're almost done with the nursery. Do you want to see it?"

"Yes! Of course I do!" She takes my hand and leads me to what used to be their guest bedroom. It's a beautiful combination of modern neutrality.

"We couldn't wait to find out what we were having, so I went with a neutral theme," she says proudly.

"It's perfect," I tell her. "Well, I should get going. Thank you again for listening to my outrageous story."

"Anytime. Hey, if you do have another dream, call me and describe it to me. That way if it is on the news later as a real person, I can be your witness that you aren't projecting."

"That would be great!" I tell her and head for the door. I like the idea, but also worry that if I'm right, like I know I am, she really will run screaming. As we say our goodbyes, I can't help but feel a little relieved. She took my news better than I could have hoped.

Glancing at my front door, I notice it is slightly ajar. A burst of fear shoots through me like electricity. *I know I closed the door before I left.* I immediately have 9-1-1 typed in, ready to call as I slowly approach the house. I know it's stupid and I should immediately get back in my car, drive away, and call the police. After what happened last time though, I don't want to sound like the girl who "cried intruder." The security alarm isn't sounding, so it's turned off, which could mean either whoever is inside somehow disarmed it, or, more likely, in my rush to get to Ren's house, I not only neglected to arm the alarm, but also didn't latch the door all the way.

I slip inside the house, slowly closing the door behind me.

The house is silent.

I wait a few minutes, my ears straining to catch any sound out of the ordinary, but I hear nothing. I reset the alarm and do a quick check of the house to be sure. Only after I come out of the final room, satisfied no one is here, do I start to relax a little.

Functioning on autopilot, I'm lost in my thoughts, while I make dinner. I don't even hear someone approaching me from behind and when I feel arms wrap around me, I gasp and jump, turning around ready to defend myself.

"Sorry babe, I didn't mean to scare you," Marc chuckles. "I just got home. I said your name a few times. I thought you heard me."

"It's okay. I'm feeling a little jumpy today is all," I say, my heart rate slowing as I wrap my arms around his waist, nuzzling his chest. I feel silly for my reaction.

"Okay, well dinner looks amazing. I wasn't sure you would be up to make anything tonight," he says. To my dismay, he lets me go. Instead, he works on setting the table.

"Yeah, it has been a rough day," I say, deciding not to tell him about the door incident, and working to make my face as neutral as possible.

We eat dinner in relative silence, Marc and the girls doing most of the talking.

"We have a playdate with Sarah tomorrow, Mommy. Sarah's mom said we could come over," Anna says with a mouthful of food. I look at Marc for confirmation, and he gives me a slight nod.

"That's great, girls," I say with a forced smile. I feel bad for not having more energy to hide my burdens from my girls. I can tell they are aware that something is wrong, even if they don't know exactly what it is.

"Hey, are you girls excited to shop for pianos this weekend?" I ask, hoping to lighten the mood and distract them from my own inner turmoil. Hearing the word "piano" makes them perk up instantly and has them grinning from ear to ear, which leads to an animated conversation on whether they want an upright or a baby grand. I'm grateful they are doing most of the talking and I can plaster on a smile. Marc catches my eye while they are still discussing what kind of piano and color they want, and I know immediately, he knows something is wrong, and he is not falling for my act of distraction.

Great, I wonder if I should tell him. He didn't believe me the first time.

I give him a confused look and furrow my brows pretending I don't know why he's looking at me like that. He gives me one final knowing glance before turning his attention back to the girls. I ignore him and take the dishes to the sink to wash while the girls and Marc start looking for places the piano could go, realistically. While they are distracted, I let my mind wander again. I vaguely hear him tell me he is going to get the girls ready for bed, and find myself nodding in acknowledgement. I'm only brought back to the present when I sense someone standing behind me. I turn almost expecting someone else to be there, but find Marc looking at me with not only concern, but also with a slight bit of anger. I fix a smile on my face, shut off the water, and turn to him trying to pretend nothing is wrong.

"Hey, girls all tucked in? I'm all finished here if you want to head up to bed ourselves, I'm wiped," I say lightheartedly.

"Babe… just stop… I know you well enough to know something is off with you today. What aren't you telling me? We tell each other everything," he says, all traces of anger diminished, leaving pure concern in his voice.

"I know." I say lowering my head looking down at the floor, my mask slipping from my face. "I didn't want you to worry. I thought I could handle it myself."

"Babe, what is it? Another bad dream?" he asks, taking a small step toward me, cupping my face in his hands gingerly coaxing me to look at him.

"I'm worried you won't believe me."

"Babe, you can tell me anything, you know that. Whatever it is we can figure it out," he says with a hint of urgency in his voice.

Without a word, I walk away from him and grab a bottle of wine from the fridge. I get two glasses and walk into the living room. Pouring two full glasses I look back to where he stands in the kitchen full of apprehension before deciding to join me. I hand him a glass and take a big sip of my own.

I take a shuddering breath, then another gulp before I begin.

"The woman, from my second nightmare. I dreamt I slit her throat in her own bed, well that same woman was on the news today. Dead. She's real and was killed the same way I dreamt she was..." another gulp. "Marc..." another gulp, "I think I might actually be killing these people."

Neither of us says a word. The silence between us becomes daunting. He brings his untouched glass of wine to his parted lips and downs the whole thing. He pours himself one more, downing it before he can look at me.

"*Shit,* Autumn, you can't honestly believe it's you doing all this can you?" he asks with disbelief written all over his face and running a hand through his hair. "Why didn't you tell me?"

"I didn't want you to worry, and you already thought I was projecting my dream into reality with the first murder," I tell him in a rush. "I talked to Ren, and she said that if it happens again, I should describe the face I see and everything about it. If it is on the news, you guys can believe me."

"So, you talked to Ren about all this already?" he says with obvious hurt in his eyes, mixed with something else I can't decipher.

"Well, I tried talking to you and I didn't feel that you believed me, you actually kind of blew me off," I say defensively.

"Blew you off? *Blew you off?*" He gets up and starts to pace in front of me, anger and annoyance radiating off of him. "I took you to get your MRI scans done to see if anything was wrong. We got a damn security system installed for fuck's sake! I took time off work to help you out. I leave later for work to drop the girls off and now pick them up from your parents! You think that's blowing you off? Seriously, Autumn!" His hands are shaking with pent up rage as he tries to calm himself.

I wince at his words knowing he is right; he has done all those things for me. I feel ashamed now that I thought I was completely alone. I get up from the couch, noticing the slight buzz I have, but manage to not waver on my feet as I approach him. I rest the palm of my hand on the center of his chest.

"Look, I'm sorry. That was the wrong thing to say. I know you have done everything to try and make me comfortable and secure with everything going on," I say hoping to catch his eyes. He keeps his eyes fixed on something in the distance refusing to look at me. I cautiously move my hand toward his face, and coax him to meet my eyes. "I'm really, really sorry. I didn't mean for it to sound how it sounded. All I meant was, I felt that way when you said I was projecting my dreams into real life events."

He clenches his jaw and gives me a piercing look, his icy eyes searching mine. Finally, his eyes grow soft again and he lets out a long, exasperated breath and shakes his head.

"I shouldn't have dismissed your dreams; I want you to feel like you can tell me what's bothering you," he says with a tender tone. "You have to admit though, it does sound kind of crazy. I don't think it's you though. Seems absurd to me that you would be capable of something so horrendous as murder." He pauses before looking at me again. "I really do think the doctor is on to something though, babe, with the whole sleep deprivation. As far as the people in your dreams, I don't have an answer, but if you do have another nightmare like those again, please tell me everything about it, every last detail, especially what they look like. If it ends up happening in real life, well, we can cross that bridge when we come to it. How does that sound?" His arms pull me into a warm embrace, as he strokes my hair.

"That sounds good, thank you," I say against his chest.

I reluctantly pull away, and start cleaning up the wine glasses and the empty wine bottle. I can feel Marc's eyes on me, and I know he is still worried about all the unexplained things. It's definitely going to have to be a larger conversation, preferably for another day when we're not buzzed. I'm glad we were able to clear the air. He knows everything now, well almost. I feel like we are on the same team and can overcome anything, together. I angle my body toward him and he is still standing, watching me. The look is unsettling but before I can say anything, a look of compassion slips onto his face.

"Let's get up to bed. I think we both could use a good night's sleep; don't forget to take your pills though," he tells me as he walks past me and heads up the stairs.

"I won't." I tell him, but when I get upstairs, I already know I won't be taking them tonight. I feel bad for lying to him, but I can't seem to shake the feeling that he isn't being one hundred percent honest with me either. About what, I'm not sure.

12

TO MY EXTREME DISAPPOINTMENT, I didn't get any sleep last night. Pure exhaustion is heavy in every muscle, and I have to put a great deal of effort into small movements. *Maybe I should have taken the pills.* I manage to pull myself out of bed and go through the motions of getting ready. Marc is surprised when I come downstairs while he is finishing up breakfast.

"Hey, I didn't think you would be awake this early. Are you getting used to the pills now?" he asks as he downs the rest of his coffee, moving to pour a cup for me.

"Yeah, I didn't think I would either, but I didn't get much sleep last night. I'm not sure why," I say, taking the coffee mug from him and adding cream and sugar to my liking. "If you want, I can take the girls to school today since I'm up."

"That's okay, babe, I can continue to take them. If you didn't get much sleep, you should take a nap later." He starts making breakfast for the girls, humming a tune I can't place. *Someone is chipper this morning.*

I agree, but I decide to wake the girls up and hang out with them before they have to go to school. They are beyond excited to eat breakfast with me today, demanding we have pancakes in addition to what their dad is already making. He hides his annoyance before the girls can see it.

"Order of pancakes, coming up," he says. The girls beam with excitement.

"I'm glad you get to have breakfast with us today, Mommy," Ada says.

"Me too! Good call on the pancakes, it sounds delicious. And what makes pancakes better?"

"Warm syrup!" they yell.

"Exactly," I tell them. Of course with syrup comes a very sticky mess, almost making them late for school. Seeing them this morning is a reminder that I need to pull myself together, and be their responsible mom again. Realistic dreams and sleepwalking be damned.

My first act of responsibility will be to clean the sticky syrup off the table, *one small step*. Once the table is devoid of all syrup, I get myself clean and prepare to conquer the rest of the day. I run over the list I made in my head like a mantra: clean house, do laundry, finish painting... My mantra stops short as I walk past the hall mirror and do a double take. I don't recognize my reflection. My hair doesn't look as shiny or voluminous as it usually does. My eyes are dark, with big circles underneath and puffy; not even my skin looks the same, it's pale and dry. *My god I really need to get this sleep and everything under control.* I take one last long look in the mirror before sighing and deciding to add it to my mantra. Clean house, do laundry, finish painting, and self-care.

I throw on my comfiest sweatpants and loose-fitting t-shirt, no sense being uncomfortable while cleaning. With my hair up in a messy bun, I begin gathering all of the laundry, starting with lights since I know I am down to my last pair of underwear. The rest of the cleaning goes by in a blur. I am a woman on a mission. The more I clean, the better I start to feel, loving when the house starts to smell fresh again. A sense of accomplishment fills me but I am utterly exhausted. Physically and mentally drained, I decide it best to skip working on my painting. My creative juices are not flowing the way I would like. Instead of heading straight to the bed, I push myself to do my three-step face wash routine. To have an extra soothing aspect, I follow it up with some calming lotion.

"Comfy bed here I come," I say to myself.

Not wanting a repeat of the last time, I set five separate alarms on my phone and on my watch as well. *There, now I can't oversleep.*

It feels like no time has passed, yet I wake up. I stand up to get out of bed, but I can't see anything around me no matter how much I squint and rub my eyes. I feel warmth on my skin, like sunlight shining on me. I open my eyes and find myself bathed in sunlight. I look around and see that I am in someone else's house.

Again.

No, no… no… not again!

I shut my eyes, willing myself to wake up, hoping this is a dream, but when I open them again, I'm still in the same foreign house. I feel my legs propelling me forward, moving slowly through the house, trying not to make a single sound. I focus on taking in my surroundings and commit as much detail as I can to memory, older style home, outdated, family pictures adorn every empty space on the walls. My heart is racing as I creep through the house on silent feet. My eyes wander down to my hands, and a chill courses through me. I'm wearing all black with what looks like the same black leather gloves I had on before.

Not only am I wearing the same gloves, but I'm also holding the same knife I have seen in my previous dream. My hand wraps around the hilt, its familiar weight, a comfort in my hand. The sun peeking through the windows glints off the menacing steel blade. My blood runs cold with fear and excitement all at once. When I look up, I find myself entering what looks like a bright welcoming kitchen bathed in warm sunlight with a smell of freshly baked cookies. I notice a woman standing at the kitchen sink in a lovely sundress with an apron tied across her back. She's facing forward so she hasn't noticed me yet.

I want to call out and warn her. Tell her to turn around and run, but I don't.

Her melodic humming fills the space. *What tune is that? Why does it sound so familiar?*

She hasn't heard me yet and I find myself closing the distance between us. I see her reflection in the window, and try to commit her face to memory: kind eyes, dark complexioned, possibly Mexican, gray and black hair. Her eyes catch my movement in the reflection lurking behind her. Her eyes widen with fright.

It's too late.

My movements are quick and calculated. I plunge the knife into her back while my other arm wraps around her throat. A small scream escapes her lips, but before she can continue, I bring the knife up to her throat and slide it quickly across. The metallic scent of blood fills my nose, as it soaks into my sleeve. Her body goes limp in my arms and she crumples to the floor, dead. I look up to the window and am horrified, yet proud when my own reflection stares back at me, eyes black with hatred, cold and malicious. I wink at myself before stepping over this poor woman's body and head to the kitchen table. The chocolate chip cookies are waiting for someone to eat them. So I oblige.

With my gloves still on, I pick one up and bring it to my mouth. It tastes good, still warm and gooey, exactly the way I like them with the right amount of chocolate chips. I shut my eyes, part of me not wanting to believe I could commit anything so callous and completely void of remorse. I have the faint taste of the chocolate chip cookie in my mouth before I find myself in darkness again.

A pulling sensation brings me back to my own house and bed. When I manage to wake up, I am drenched in sweat, and unable to move. I breathe in short erratic breaths, replaying everything I saw, committing it to memory. I try to slow my breathing and calm down enough so my body can move again. It takes a few minutes, but I can finally move my limbs again, however, when I bring my hand up to wipe the sweat off my face, I freeze in horror. Clear as day, a swipe of blood covers my hand. Panicked, and not wanting to believe my eyes, I jump out of bed and run to the bathroom to inspect the red substance.

Please be paint.

With trembling hands, I inspect the substance under the harsh fluorescents.

Not paint.

It has a reddish-brown color to it and carries a distinct coppery smell.

I feel the bile rise in my throat. I turn toward the toilet ready for it all to come out, dry heaving instead until my stomach hurts. I can't rinse the blood off fast enough. I gaze at everything but the red stained water as it goes down the drain, the mere sight of it unsettles me. Once the water runs clear again and every spec has been washed clean, I brace myself against the sink and splash some cold water onto my face so my initial shock and horror can subside.

Relax Autumn, it's probably nothing. You probably got some paint on you and you don't remember, that's all, but I know, deep down, that what I had on my hand was not paint. I take a couple of final deep breaths before I leave the bathroom, grabbing my phone so I can relay everything to Ren, which should be easy since the whole thing is burned into my memory. I notice the time. The girls are out of school already and will be home soon.

Ugh, seriously?? I set a fucking alarm!

Instead of calling, my curiosity gets the better of me. Sure enough, all the alarms I had set on my phone have been turned off. Next, I check the alarms on my watch and see that those have also been deactivated, but the more concerning thing I notice with my watch is the step count — way higher than it should be. Feeling shaky and off balance I try to rationalize everything in my head.

Okay, okay, think, you walked around the house in your sleep and decided to turn off all of your alarms and got into some paint... yeah that's it.

What even is reality anymore?

I need to call Marc to come home, then ask my parents to pick up the girls and keep them for dinner. I am way too unstable right now to drive or focus. I pick up my phone with trembling hands and type Marc's number, chewing my lips as I listen to the ring — once, twice, three times. I'm afraid he isn't going to pick up at all. My heart starts to sink, but I am met with overwhelming relief when I hear him say hello on the other end. *Thank god.* I'm about to greet him back but the words get caught in my throat and a sob makes its way out instead.

"Babe? Is that you? What's going on?" I can hear the concern and fear in his voice.

All I can do is cry on the phone as he listens to me, knowing the worst thing must have come true... and it did.

"Did you... did you have another dream?" There's hesitation in his voice and when he mentions the dream, it's all I can do to keep my composure long enough to allow small *"yes"* to escape my lips

"I'm coming home... I'll be there as soon as I can, okay? Try to stay calm."

I let out a small, hiccuped *"okay,"* and end the call. I sink to the floor, the tears flowing so fast as my sobs rack my shoulders. Utterly defeated and alone, I lie on the floor in the fetal position. I have never felt more broken and alone. Tears silently stream down my face and I make no move to wipe them away. I find it hard to believe I have been here long enough for him to be home already, but he's opening the front door and calling my name. Even though I know I should let him know where I am. I don't. I don't even attempt to move, nor do I utter a single word. I'm simply too emotionally drained. Eventually, I hear his footsteps embarking up the stairs and know I will soon be found. The relief inside me when I see him standing in the doorway is unbelievable.

"Oh baby, come here it's okay," he says as he walks toward me and scoops me up in his arms in one swift motion and carries me back to bed. He holds me until the tears stop running down my face and I can tell him every painful detail about my latest dream... if that's what it was.

My head is against his chest and his arms are wrapped tightly around me. I begin to tell him every horrendous thing I did in my dream. The words freely flow out of me, almost as if saying them out loud has the ability to make them some made up story and not reality. Once I start, I don't stop until I get to the very end, even including the paint or blood on my arm when I woke up. I wish I had left it so he could see it and be able to convince me that it *was* paint, and my eyes were simply playing tricks on me.

Marc takes a deep breath and stays silent, processing everything I told him. While I wait for him to tell me his thoughts, I push into his chest and listen to the steady rhythm of his heartbeat. I breathe in time with him and find myself in a sort of relaxed state. When he finally answers, his voice is calm and reassuring,

"Okay, babe, first of all I am truly, truly sorry you had to experience that. I can't imagine how scary and traumatic it must have been for you. Second, you gave me all the details, but let's try not to get too alarmed at the reality until it becomes one. And third, if, and only if it does become a reality, will we discuss the possibility of what the red mark on your hand was. I honestly don't believe you could sleepwalk and not remember it, but more importantly that you could murder someone in cold blood while you were sleepwalking and not remember it." He says the words I want to hear, but his tone is not convincing. His hand runs comforting strokes through my hair and I find myself nodding along with everything, willing myself to believe his words.

"Maybe we could look at the footage again to see if I left the house. And you're right, I will try not to get ahead of myself... but my last two dreams... I know I didn't tell you the details before they were on the news... but Marc, I swear to you it was the exact same. Everything that was reported, I lived it so to speak. I knew everything that happened before the news even uttered a word." I whisper the last part, knowing how I must sound... guilty.

He stops midway down my hair and pulls back to meet my eyes, staring deep into my soul.

What is he searching for? Does he think he will be able to tell if his wife is a cold-blooded serial killer? I search his eyes for an answer and come up empty.

"I know with a hundred percent certainty that you, Autumn Fowler, are not capable of anything you see yourself doing in your dreams, but if it will make you feel better, we will check the footage for sure. We got them for peace of mind, right?"

A flash of something crosses his face, but it is gone in an instant before I can tell what it was. However, he sounds so confident, I'm not sure how he can know me with such certainty and not be the slightest bit afraid of me, or at the very least, afraid for our daughters' sake. I mentally shudder at the thought of ever compromising their safety. I shake my head not wanting to dwell on what I may or may not have seen, and bring myself back to reality.

He pulls up the footage, and I tell him the time I went to sleep so he knows exactly when to look.

Ice chills my veins.

Once again, the video feed is static, as if it had been turned off right at the perfect time I would need it to prove my innocence.

"What the hell?" Marc mutters under his breath.

"Why isn't it working? What's wrong with it?" I ask. Panic drips off my every word.

"I don't know, maybe it stopped working? You didn't somehow turn it off, did you?"

"What? No!" I all but scream out in defense.

"Okay, well, the rest of the day is recorded… I guess I can call and ask the company what they think could be wrong with it."

"Yeah… do that." I say curtly. I know I should check my tone, but I'm scared and I don't like being accused. *He's probably right though. I must have turned them off.* The silence between us grows and I can't bear it any longer.

"When do we have to pick the girls up from my parents' house?" I ask.

"Well, the girls are at Sarah's house now for their playdate, and your parents are going to pick them up from there. I talked it over with them and they said it would be alright with them if they stayed at their house for the rest of the week, into the weekend if necessary. The only thing I will need to do now is drop off some clothes and things if we decide to go that route." He searches my face, trying to gauge how I'm going to react.

The news catches me off guard. At first, I'm angry. He revealed my troubles to my parents without consulting me. But the fact he wants my daughters to stay away from me for a week means he must think, on some level, that I'm guilty. However, the thought of traumatizing the girls or worse, hurting them is horrifying.

God forbid I am committing these murders, I don't want them in the same house even if I know I could never hurt them. I thought I knew I could never commit a murder… let alone three, but here we are.

"Thank you, that would be a big help, and I think it would be for the best, at least until we know about my latest nightmare and I get adjusted to my medication," I tell him.

He has a small look of shock on his face, probably expecting more of a fight, but in the end, I have to admit it is a good idea and the girls' safety and mental welfare have to come first.

"Okay, well I'll start packing some of the girls' things, and we can take everything over to them. We pick up some Chinese for dinner on our way home," I tell him before walking out and heading to the girl's room to grab outfits for them to wear for the rest of the week. I can barely hear Marc downstairs talking on the phone with my mom, I presume. No doubt he's letting her know our decision.

Guilt and sadness overcome me when I think about the girls staying with my parents for so long.

We head out knowing we will get there after they get back from Sarah's house. Pulling into the driveway is harder than I anticipated knowing I won't be taking my girls home with me. With a final deep breath, we head to the door. Marc's hand encloses mine for comfort and I squeeze back in silent answer. No one comes out to greet us this time, so we knock on the door and wait to be let in. A heartbeat later, mom answers the door holding a dish towel. Worry and confusion are written all over her face as she steps aside to let us come in with the girls' belongings. They are coloring at the coffee table in the living room, refusing to acknowledge us. Marc and my parents venture into the other room so I can have a moment with them to explain.

"Hey, my sweeties, we brought you some clothes and stuff so you can stay here for the rest of the week with Grammy and Papa.

Won't that be exciting?" I ask, kneeling down to their level, pulling my lips into a convincing smile.

They simply look at each other and continue to color, but Anna answers without looking up to me.

"Are we staying here forever, Mommy, like you don't want us anymore."

My heart shatters into a million pieces. "Honey, no! Of course not! You're my Gemini stars! Mommy is having a rough time right now and wants to be all better for you girls. While I do that Grammy and Papa are going to look after you. It's only going to be for the rest of the week, maybe the weekend. I will call you every day and you will be back home before you know it. Besides, you will have fun. Think of all the cookies you're going to get to eat." The mention of cookies does the trick and their frown turns into a mischievous grin, and I know they have taken advantage of the never ending batches of cookies their grandmother makes.

"Okay, Mommy, I guess it will be fun," Ada says.

"Yeah, we do love cookies," Anna chimes in.

They start talking animatedly about their day, playing at Sarah's house, every trace of disappointment vanishes from their tiny round faces. I sit with them a while longer before Marc comes over and I get up to go speak to Mom outside.

"Autumn, tell me what's going on. Marc says you were having a hard time sleeping or something. I know there is more to the story. Tell me. Are you okay?" The worry lines in her brow are deep and prominent as she searches my face trying to find the answer. The concern on her face and in her eyes ages her and I hate that I am the cause.

"Marc is right, Mom, I haven't really been sleeping. I'm having sleep paralysis again. I'm sleepwalking, and having horrible, horrible nightmares as well. The doctor prescribed an antidepressant that is supposed to help me with my sleep deprivation, but it makes me drowsy." I leave out all the other details. *Now is not the time or place, besides, it would take too long to explain.*

"Yeah, that's kind of what he said too. Well, I hope everything gets better for you, and of course the girls are welcome here anytime. We love looking after them," she grabs my hand and leans in close to me, her eyes full of insight. "I know there's more to this than you're saying, so when you're ready… I will be here to listen, okay Bug." Having her call me my childhood nickname as she holds my hand almost brings me to tears. I avert my eyes so she can't see, but know I'm not fooling her.

"Thanks, Mom, I really appreciate it. I will tell you everything soon. Maybe I can come over for lunch one day while the girls are at school and tell you and Dad."

"I would like that very much, Bug. Now come on, let's get back inside. I'm sure you guys are starving. Do you want me to heat you up some leftovers?"

"No, that's okay, we're going to grab some takeout and eat at home."

She pats my shoulder and we head back inside to say our goodbyes to the girls. Leaving them breaks my heart and I know I'm taking my pills again tonight. I will get whatever this is under control for my daughters' sake.

13

THE DIZZINESS HITS me like a freight train; it's practically unbearable to sit up. I do my best to get my bearings and when I do, I notice that Marc is still lying next to me, sleeping. *Oh my god, what time is it?*

"Marc! Hey, get up you're going to be late for work," I say, shoving his shoulder until he rolls over and opens his eyes.

"Fuck! What time is it?" he bolts up right searching for his phone. He looks groggy and uncoordinated.

"It's eight now, so not horrible, you could still make it, and you'll only be a little late." I try to sound reassuring, but the nausea and crippling vertigo leave my words falling short.

"*Ugh,* wait, I took this day off," he says, rubbing sleep out of his eyes. "I thought you would need me just in case… well you know, if something came up on the news."

"Oh, thank you," I tell him, taken aback by his action, "That really means a lot. Are you sure it won't be a problem?" I lean back so I can look into his eyes.

"Yes, babe, I'm sure, it's all good we have the whole day… but I do have to go back tomorrow… and I'm not sure how much longer I can go in late, so you might have to start taking the girls to school again when we take them back from your parents," he tells me. The guilt on his face is apparent, so I change the subject.

"Well, since we're up, how about I make us a big breakfast after I take some Tylenol. This dizziness is brutal." I get out of bed, test my balance, and make sure the room stops spinning before I make any sudden movements.

"That would be awesome, thank you," he says as he gets out of bed, following me downstairs. "If you feel too bad though, I can always get breakfast going, it's not a problem."

"No, I got it, besides, I like making breakfast." I give him a quick kiss.

"I'll get the coffee started," he tells me through a yawn.

"Thanks."

It feels like old times, the two of us having breakfast together. It's nice. I want to savor every minute of having him here this morning, especially if the body of my "latest victim" is found. It's a weight lifted from my shoulders to have him next to me for support. Blissfully happy, and in sync with each other, we decide to take our good moods to the bedroom.

As we untangle from each other, I realize how much I missed this. Us together. Seeing him smile, and staring at his wonderfully toned body, I can't help but run my fingers along his abs, feeling him tremble under my touch.

"That was amazing," he says as if reading my mind.

"I couldn't agree more," I tell him as I lean in for another kiss. *This feels like the first step in getting us back to how we were before.*

We reluctantly leave the bed and head back downstairs, leaving the safety of each other. The reason he stayed home in the first place creeps back into my thoughts. He gives me an encouraging nod and I turn the news on. While I'm snuggled in the crook of his arm, I realize I've almost forgotten how good he smells and how well we fit together. Feeling relaxed and happy, I tilt my head up towards him,

"Let's turn the channel, pick a movie to wa—" I stop short when I see the expression on his face and I whip my head toward the tv, my expression immediately mimicking his. We stare wide eyed at the breaking news banner displayed across the bottom of the screen. I hold my breath as he reaches for the remote to turn the volume up, afraid we might miss any detail.

"Another female victim was found yesterday afternoon by her husband, Alex Sanchez, when he returned home from playing golf. The victim has been identified as 65-year-old Carol Sanchez. Mrs. Sanchez was found dead on her kitchen floor with fatal stab wounds to her back and throat."

After they show her picture on the screen, I gasp and hold my hands against my mouth. Marc reaches for the remote to turn the tv off. He stands motionless with his back facing me, unmoving. When he finally turns around, his face is pale white, and looks haunted. He shakes his head and runs his fingers through his hair with shaky fingers.

"Autumn, please don't tell me this is what the woman from your dream looked like," he says clearly hoping for my answer to be no — it's all some joke. But all I can do is look at him with angst and he knows immediately.

This woman is exactly who I saw.

"Maybe it's not the same person... there has to be a reasonable explanation for all of this, right? I mean I know you're not capable of something like this, maybe you're... I don't know... psychic or something... maybe you happened to see the breaking news before they aired it."

I can tell he is grasping at straws to try and make sense of everything, to form some different explanation to show his wife and mother of his children isn't, in fact, a serial killer. Wanting to make him feel better, I go along with his explanation.

"You're right. We need more information. Let's do some digging, and find out more about these people and the details of how they died… There could be an explanation we can't see," I walk into his arms, but am stunned when he pulls away from me.

It's an invisible slap to the face.

He's afraid of me.

"Are you sure you want more information? I mean what little we do know seems pretty damning on its own." Seeing the hurt in my eyes makes him walk back his words. "I just don't want this to become an obsession, or for you to have any more reason to think you could have done this."

I try to swallow my hurt feelings so I can assure him that I will only do a little digging on the three victims and will stop when it's time for us to pick up the girls this weekend. But there is a real possibility I will be going to jail for these murders. Having a deadline to stop looking into everything seems like a good compromise and he agrees. I decide to get a head start before he can change his mind, and grab my laptop to start researching. Marc opts to sit on the couch next to me, and zone out in front of the tv, obviously changing the channel to sports instead of the news. So far, I haven't found anything new besides what was already stated on the news.

I discover the second victim, Gwen Frost, used to be a nurse back in the day, and that her husband passed away two years prior from natural causes. Nothing shady about his death. No obvious clues jump out about who she is, so I move on to see if there is anything else the victims might have in common regarding how they died… besides me.

Ken Woo was run down and then drowned. However, the second and third victims were both elderly women who were stabbed while in their homes. Gwen Frost was in her sleep. And the last woman, Carol Sanchez, died in broad daylight. Nothing about the victims makes sense to me. The only other connection I can find between them is that both Ken and Gwen worked in a hospital setting, he in pediatrics and she as a nurse. But they worked in different hospitals.

None of this makes sense. The only consolation I have is the fact that I don't know, nor have I ever heard of any of these people. My eyes burn, and a persisting pain in my head is getting worse. I have to close my laptop.

"Find anything useful?" he asks, pausing the new show he has started to watch.

"No, only more questions." I tell him, massaging away a headache. "I think I need some food or something; my head is starting to hurt and my stomach is growling."

"Yeah, I was wondering when you might get hungry. Want me to get take out?" he asks.

"That sounds good, thank you. I'm going to lie down here and close my eyes for a moment." I set my computer on the coffee table and reach for a blanket to cover my legs.

I am awakened from my cat nap by the sounds of Marc coming home and the smell of food filling the room.

"You awake?" he whispers.

"Yep, it smells good, I'm starving." I want to eat on the couch, but my aching back needs to sit in a real chair. The tension between us is evident. My whole body is on edge. I want to find out more information and get to the reason I am seeing myself as a killer. *You're going to make yourself crazy, going around in circles like this.* I can't take the sound of my own thoughts anymore so I cut my meal a little short. The girls should be home with Mom for the day.

I think I'll call and check in with them.

I grab for the phone and tell Marc I'm going to call my mom and see if she got them to their piano lessons okay. He barely acknowledges me while he picks at his food. Needing some privacy, I take my phone call to another room and close the door behind me. My mom finally picks up on the fourth ring sounding out of breath.

"Mom? Are you okay? You sound out of breath," I say, concerned it was a mistake for letting her take the girls for so long.

"Oh yes, yes I'm fine. The girls and I were playing a little game of tag outside while we wait for dinner to arrive," she says. The sound of her glass filling with water comes through the phone before she greedily gulps it down.

"Mom! You were supposed to take them to piano lessons today! They had to be there at 3:30," I tell her, but I can only be mad at myself. It's my fault they are there in the first place.

"Honey, what are you talking about? You called me earlier and told me that it was canceled today."

I'm taken aback by the news, "What? No, I didn't."

"Honey, are you feeling okay?" The concern in her voice is clear as day.

I never called Mom today to cancel the girls' lesson. Did I?

"Autumn, are you still there?"

"Yes. I'm here… Are you sure I called you? Maybe it was Marc."

"Yes, I'm sure. Honey, are you not sleeping well again?"

"Yeah, no, it's fine. Must have just slipped my mind. No worries." I force an airy tone, but my mind is reeling. *I do not remember calling her.*

"Okay, if you're sure." Her tone is skeptical, but accepting. "The girls would like to say hi. Hang on; here they are."

"Hi, Mommy!" The cheerfulness in their voice sets me at ease if only for a moment.

"Hi, my Gemini stars!"

"Are you doing better, Mommy?" Ada asks in almost a whisper.

"Yeah, sweetie, almost." Tears threaten to fall, but I hold them at bay.

"Will we be going to lessons next week, Mommy?" Anna asks in a cute, demanding way.

"Yes, sweetie, I promise." My voice falters slightly. *How can I not remember canceling this week?*

Marc must have known I would be talking to the girls because he opens the door and waves to me. He wants to talk to them next. I reluctantly say my goodbyes and hand the phone over to him. Since he is using my phone, I gesture to him that I need to make a call with his. He simply nods his okay.

Good, because I need to call Mrs. Lang and smooth over any confusion.

The conversation goes as well as can be expected. To my dismay, I never called her to cancel their lesson. She gracefully accepts my sincere apologies and my offer to pay her for her time. We are to have them there next week and call for cancellations in the future. I release a huge sigh of relief and let myself collapse on the couch to wind down for a second. Marc, finished talking with the girls, hesitantly sits next to me. We look at each other for a moment trying to read what the other is thinking, or who should react first. I don't want to bring up my forgetfulness with canceling the girls' lesson, but maybe he will remember me doing it? I continue to go back and forth in my head trying to decide.

In the end, he caves first, solidifying my decision to not bring it up. He pulls me into a slow, careful embrace. Smelling his familiar cologne, and knowing what it feels like to be in his arms, makes me release the breath I am holding and crumple into him. I am grateful the tension between us has lifted, at least momentarily. Not wanting to break the spell, we stay like this for what feels like forever until he clears his throat to break the silence.

"How about we have a little date night tonight? What do you say? We can go catch a movie and then go out to eat at that restaurant you like so much. That Italian place, how's that sound?"

I'm not sure what I expected him to say, but it definitely wasn't that, however I am so grateful.

"That sounds wonderful," I tell him sincerely. I kiss him. It's a hesitant, quick kiss, but when he returns it, I know we will be okay.

We check some showtimes and see what is playing and end up choosing a nice light romantic comedy to distract us from all the heaviness in our minds. Wanting to make it feel as much like a date as possible, I do a quick comb through my hair, apply some mascara and lip gloss, and put on my form fitting jeans and a nice blouse. I am determined to have a normal, fun date night with my husband. My heart flutters when he makes a cat call whistle and twirls me into his arms, dipping me by surprise, followed by a kiss. It brings a smile to my lips. I love when he catches me off guard with his actions. It's like the events of today never happened.

"What was that for?"

"You just look so damn good," he says as he looks me up and down.

"Oh stop." I laugh. "Come on, let's go."

He grabs my hand and opens the door, setting the alarm to the house on our way out. Heading to the theater, I realize how excited I am for our mini date night.

When we arrive and open the door of the theater, it's like walking into a whole new world. I'm instantly slammed with the smell of buttered popcorn, along with the *Pop! Pop! Pop!* The kernels make as they turn into light fluffy, crunchy morsels. Getting our tickets is my favorite part. You can hold onto the ticket stubs and always remember this moment in time. In the distance I can hear parts of different movies when people open the various theater doors.

"I will need a large popcorn," I tell Marc when we get up to the concession line.

"All for yourself?" he asks.

"As a matter of fact, yes," I say, putting my hands on my hips, daring him to laugh at me. I know for a fact I won't eat it all, but I love having the option.

To his credit, he only lets a small smile cross his lips. He obliges and orders two large popcorns with two large drinks. He orders his with extra butter, *ewww*, and mine with no butter.

The movie is a great idea. My thoughts are more relaxed and I haven't considered the murders or my nightmares throughout the whole thing, but as we start to leave, the uncertainty and anxiety creep back in. Marc instinctively reaches for my hand as we walk towards our car. A silent comfort. I tilt my head back and take in the wonderful weather and feel the light warm breeze across my face. Forever the gentleman, he opens my door for me. Before I can get in, I have a prickling sensation of someone watching me. I whip my head around, scanning the parking lot for anyone or thing out of the ordinary, but there's only a quiet, empty parking lot.

"What are you looking for?" he asks, following my line of sight. I glance back at him and for a split second, recognition crosses his face.

Is there someone out here?

His mask of neutrality is back in place in an instant. I question if I even saw anything at all.

"Nothing… just got a weird feeling I was being watched is all, but I don't see anyone," I tell him as I get into the car and let him close the door.

"No one out here but us babe. I think you're still a little worked up from everything that happened today," he tells me as we back out and head to the restaurant.

I nod my head and turn to look out my window, scanning the parking lot one last time before it's out of view.

No one was there, but I can't seem to shake the feeling there was.

You're just worked up like Marc said, it's nothing.

By the time we reach the restaurant I have convinced myself that the feeling was all in my head, and I'm beyond ready to have a nice meal with my husband and a semblance of a normal night. There's a line at the door and they let us know the wait is going to be about thirty minutes.

"That's fine," he says and proceeds to give his name and number so we can be texted when a table is ready. Instead of going back to our car, we sit on one of the benches outside and enjoy the lovely night. The breeze is wonderful, lightly caressing our skin, keeping us the perfect temperature while we wait. I lean back against his chest while he puts a comforting arm around me. No words need to be said.

Now this is the comfortable silence I prefer, instead of one filled with tension. I close my eyes to focus on how peaceful this moment is. The vibration of the phone interrupts the moment, but it is a welcomed one. *I am starving.*

The hostess shows us to our table in one of the back corners. *Perfect.* We sit down and start with a glass of wine and a nice appetizer. Our conversations stay in a safe zone of the kids, his work, and how much fun we're having. When our main course arrives, the conversation falters ever so slightly when I mention having a goodnight sleep, making us both freeze. We know the reason I might not. Shaking it off, he gives a curt nod and tells me I will and quickly changes the subject back to the girls.

"I wonder if they are having a good time at your parents' house? They are probably getting fed a lot of cookies," he says with a glint in his eye.

"Oh, I'm sure of it," I say. "My mom is probably making them a different kind of cookie every night; tonight I predict they had snickerdoodles," I say.

"Speaking of cookies, do you think you have room for dessert?" he asks. He picks up the dessert menu.

"You know I always have room for dessert," I tell him, taking the menu away from him. *Hmmm let's see... yes, they have it.* "I will have the crème brûlée." *My favorite.*

"I thought you would say that." He chuckles. "And I will have the brownie a la mode."

We flag down our waiter, place our dessert orders, and go back to talking about the girls. We stop when we see the waiter heading toward us with our delicious looking desserts.

"Oh my god, this looks great," I tell him, staring at the browned sugary top of my crème brûlée. I lightly tap the top of the caramelized sugar with my spoon, getting such satisfaction when it breaks and reveals the custard. I scoop a huge spoonful and take a bite.

"*Mmmm*, so, so good!" I say rolling my eyes back.

"Clearly. Would you and your dessert like a room to yourselves?" Marc teases.

"Oh hush."

I finish mine long after Marc has finished his. The bloat in my stomach betrays me, but it is totally worth it. Only one more thing could make this a perfect mini date night, going to bed with my wonderful husband, resolidifying our bond and connection despite all of the turmoil around us.

14

MUSIC FILLS the entire house with an upbeat rhythm. It lifts my spirits and awakens a happiness I haven't felt in a while. I sing at the top of my lungs, dance like nobody's watching, because no one is, and decide I should look as amazing on the outside as I feel on the inside. I put on the cutest outfit I can find (not too fancy), focus extra time blow drying and straightening my hair, and put on a full face of makeup, choosing bold colors for my eyeshadow. I admire myself in the mirror: a whole new me. Thanks to the concealer, my dark circles are gone and I look as refreshed and alive as I feel. I look way too good to be cooped up in the house today, I deserve to be seen. With that thought in mind, I reach out to my friends and ask if they are free for brunch. Freya and Ren inform me they are busy today, *bummer*, however, Liz says she is free and can meet me in ten minutes.

Our usual brunch place? She texts.

See you there. I respond.

I assume I will arrive before her, however, as I pull in the parking lot, I notice her car. *She must already be inside.* I walk in, scanning the tables and booths, and see her in one of the booths near the back at the same time she spots me and stands to flag me over.

"Hey, girlie. You are looking fantastic today! What's the occasion?" she asks as we hug.

"I felt like making an effort today is all," I say.

"Well, that's good to hear. How are you? It feels like forever since your birthday party," she says, taking a sip of her coffee. "I ordered you a coffee by the way; your usual, hope that's okay."

"Perfect! Thank you, and I know, I know, things have been a little stressful at home," I tell her, not really wanting to get into it and dampen my good mood.

"I heard... Ren filled us in on everything you guys talked about." She eyes me cautiously as she puts her coffee mug down.

"Of course, she did..." I say. I take a sip of my coffee, not surprised in the least. "Well, yes, it was very stressful, and it happened again... I didn't get a chance to tell her the last one, but Marc knows," I say as the waitress comes around with our food order. "I'm trying not to think about it though; it's probably nothing, and I need to get myself back on track so when we pick the girls up from my parents' house, everything will be back to normal." I know she has way more questions and she plans to pull the answers out of me whether I like it or not.

"Of course, I understand that... it's just... it all seems so strange," she chews on her lip, deep in thought. "I mean... maybe you're psychic or something."

I give her a weary look hoping she will change the subject. *If one more person tells me I must be psychic...*

"I'm sorry, I know you don't want to talk about it... all you have to know is we are all here for you," I nod appreciatively, but refuse to say anything and focus on my food, eating a few bites in silence. *Maybe brunch was a bad idea after all.*

"So, how are the girls' lessons coming along?" She asks.

"They missed yesterday's lesson due to miscommunication, but Marc and I got them a keyboard to practice on until we can get them a real one this weekend," I inform her, relieved she isn't pursuing the former topic. Overall, I'm glad I am getting some friend time in. It's much needed.

"Well, that's exciting! I'm sure the girls would love to have a real piano to practice on." Her words are pleasant enough, but I can tell she still wants to talk about my dreams. Thankfully, she fights the urge to.

When we are all finished, the waitress brings the bill and before I can grab it Liz has snatched it from the table.

"Don't even think about it," her credit card already in her hand. "This is my treat."

"But Liz…I invited *you*," I try to snag the bill, but she keeps it out of reach.

"Forget it, Autumn. I'm getting this one, you can get the next one."

"Fine. If you insist," I say.

"I do."

She pays. We walk outside and hug each other bye with the promise to get together soon with everyone.

"Remember, we are all here for you if you need to talk or vent, about anything," she says.

"I know, thank you, I will keep that in mind," I say and retreat to my car. Part of me wants to stay out and enjoy my day shopping, but I have a creative urge and need to get back in my studio to finish my painting.

Still feeling on cloud nine and full of determination, I get inside and turn the alarm off. I set my purse and everything on the table, but something in the atmosphere makes me pause. I can't put my finger on it, but something feels strange. I brush it off.

Nope, I am having a great day! I feel great, and everything is great.

I grab a bottle of water from the fridge and walk to my studio, motivation coursing through me. When I open the door, I sense something, something bad... something...wrong. *No, not now.*

I move cautiously inside the room, my eyes darting to every corner making sure that no one is in here with me. Satisfied that no one is in the room, I ignore my feelings of unease. I select the paints I will need and sit down at my easel.

That's when I see it.

I gasp, stumbling backward so fast I trip over my chair, sending my paints, and brushes flying. I rub my eyes and focus, making sure that I am seeing what I'm seeing.

Still there.

I stare unblinking at the canvas while I move my hand to pinch my arm, thinking, hoping, that I'm dreaming, willing myself to wake up.

Still there.

I inch closer to inspect it, my heart hammering in my chest. Beating a million miles a minute. Right in front of me, plain as day, lying on my easel, is a knife... covered in what I'm sure is dried blood. But that's not all. A bloody palm print is smack in the middle of my unfinished painting, right over the girls' smiling faces. Drips of blood, now dried, run all the way down the canvas to a dark crimson circle on the carpet.

I raise my shaky hand and hover it above the bloody one, not touching it, but enough to notice that the handprint is exactly the same size as my own. I don't know what to do. My chest is tightening and I am starting to hyperventilate.

What is happening?

I make a feeble attempt at taking a few deep breaths before I undergo a full-blown anxiety attack. My eyes are swimming with tears, blurring everything in front of me. I frantically wipe them away hoping that when my vision clears, what I seen won't be there anymore. No matter how many times I try, the knife and bloody handprint are still there, mocking me. I reach out with a trembling hand toward the hilt of the knife, but stop short, knowing in my heart that it is the murder weapon used in my dreams. I want to call Marc and have him rush home, but I know I can't keep making him leave work. We had such a great night; I don't want to ruin it already.

Putting my head between my knees, my only focus is breathing normally.

It's working. My breath begins to slow. I hesitantly look up, willing the knife and handprint to disappear. *If only I could be so lucky.*

A thought occurs to me. *I have proof that I'm not crazy. But what if I left this knife here after I murdered those people. My subconscious is trying to tell me I am, in fact, guilty. This is concrete evidence against me.*

I wince at my own thoughts and feel sick for thinking them. I sprint to the bathroom and throw up until there is nothing left. When I'm positive I'm done, I lower myself to the cold bathroom tile, wrap my arms around my body for comfort, and cry.

I'm not sure how long I have been in the bathroom, but all my tears have run dry. I wipe at my face, and stand staring at my blank expression in the mirror, my mascara streaked all down my cheeks. My makeup, once beautiful, is now ruined. I feel numb. I walk like a zombie back into my studio, seeing the knife and bloody canvas right where I left them.

How long have these been here? I honestly can't remember. When did I start this painting and how many days since I have last stepped foot in here? Was the knife here after the second murder… the third?

I shake my head realizing the evidence isn't the most important thing here. The most important, is why is it here at all and was it me who did it? Or maybe even worse, is it someone else and are my family and I in danger? I think about checking the security footage, but know there will be nothing but static. I walk past my easel toward the windows, locking them before drawing the curtains and shutting out every last bit of sunshine. With a final glance at my former sanctuary, I walk out, locking the door behind me. Somehow I know I will never be able to create in this room again. It's tainted with objects of sin. I need to make every effort to ensure no one can possibly get in here without my knowledge, especially the girls. I mindlessly walk to the kitchen and get started on dinner so it will be ready when Marc comes home. After we have eaten, I will bring him into my studio to show him the damning evidence it contains.

I'm setting the table when I hear Marc enter the room.

"Smells delicious, let me wash up and I'll be right back." His kiss on my forehead is so carefree and light. He doesn't take notice of my distress. I wish I could soak up his mood that is radiating off him and be equally oblivious to how much has changed in such a short amount of time.

But I can't.

When he gets back, I am already eating and staring off into the distance.

"Babe? Are you okay... hello?" he asks, waving a hand in front of my face, his good mood faltering ever so slightly.

I blink a couple of times, hesitating to look at him. My haunted look registers in his eyes. A silent knowing glance passes between us and he sits down to eat, quietly observing and waiting for any sort of communication. To his credit, he doesn't say a word. I drag out the meal for as long as I can, but a scrape of metal on porcelain indicates my plate is clear of food.

It's time.

"Come with me, I have to show you something," I reach for his hand and draw on every last bit of comfort from him.

"You're starting to scare me now, Autumn, what is it?"

Instead of answering him, I lead him down the hallway to my studio, unlock the door, and open it. I turn the lights on and wait outside the room while I urge him inside. He looks back to me, confusion all over his face, but doesn't say a word. I watch him carefully and know the exact moment his eyes land on the knife because his face changes. His eyes widen in fear, his jaw drops. He lets a gasp leave his throat, and it looks as if all the blood has drained from his face. *At least I know it's really there, and I'm not hallucinating.* He looks to me for answers, but I have none.

"Wha...wha... what is this?" His voice stammers, trying to find his words. He runs his hand through his hair while the other gestures toward the easel. "Is that *blood?*" His tone is a higher pitch than usual. "Autumn, say something!"

Finding my voice again, I meet his eyes, hoping he can see the truth.

"I swear, I found it there today when I got home from having brunch with Liz."

"Why didn't you call me?" he asks.

"I didn't want you to have to leave work again. I didn't do this... you have to believe me." My numb demeanor is wearing off and I start to feel the anxiety creep its way back into my chest again.

"I know... I do..." he stammers. "But Autumn, you have to admit this looks, this looks really bad." He throws both of his hands out, gesturing toward the blood. "Are you sure you didn't sleepwalk and put it here?" He mumbles something else under his breath, too soft for me to hear, but I'm sure it's nothing I *want* to hear.

"We have to get rid of it," he says, his voice hard and full of conviction. "Throw it away, burn it, paint over it. I don't care. Get rid of it! Immediately!" Hearing him talk like this makes me wince.

He thinks I'm guilty, and wants to cover for me. He's not even entertaining the idea that someone else could have possibly put it here.

"What about the knife?" I ask my voice small, barely above a whisper. "Should we go to the police?"

"And say what? Hi, I found this knife and I have been having these nightmares about murdering people and I think this is the murder weapon for two of those murders?" The hard sarcasm in his voice stings, but infuriates me.

"Well, I don't know Marc… what if it is me doing it and I got rid of the evidence?" I ask, confronting him. "I would be worse off than I am *with* the evidence if I were to be convicted. What if I'm a danger to all of you?" I feel like I'm spiraling. *Does he even notice? Does he want to?* "I really think we should bite the bullet and go to the police. Get this whole thing over with."

"*Ugh.* We are not going to the police! I need a minute to think!" he all but shouts before spinning around to face me and grabbing my shoulders. "You haven't told anyone else about this yet, have you?" His eyes are wide with fear.

I wince at the tightness of his grip, and he lets me go.

"No, I haven't… just you," I tell him, rubbing the spot on my arms where his hands were moments ago, already feeling a bruise coming on.

He rubs his hands through his hair a couple more times before deciding he needs to go upstairs and think…alone. I walk back into the living room and sit on the couch as I hear the shower turn on. Before, I would have gone up there and joined him, but now I sit planted on the couch, waiting for him to come back down. My mind is racing.

Does he believe me? Does he think that I murdered all those people now? What if it's not blood? What if it's actually paint and we're all over-

reacting? What about the knife though? How did it get in there in the first place, and how could it look exactly like the one in my dreams?

My thoughts are coming so fast, it's hard to keep track of them all. My darkest thought and fear, however, make their way to the forefront of my mind.

What if Marc is messing with me? I feel sick to my stomach for even thinking such a ridiculous thing. I know my husband loves me and our family. Besides, combined with my dreams, it doesn't make sense. I'm still trying to get hold of all the information and thoughts when he enters the room with his head down. My cheeks burn with embarrassment. I cast my eyes down and force myself to focus on the floor and attempt to ground myself. The closer he gets, the more potent his body wash becomes. Evergreen and citrus with a hint of cedar. When he finally speaks, I shoot a glance up to him. His voice comes out in a whisper at first, then with more confidence. Whether he is trying to convince me or himself, I'm not sure.

"We need to get rid of it."

"Okay," I say in a whisper, lowering my head. I stay glued to the couch, afraid to make any movements. "How?"

"Paint over the canvas, black. Then we should rinse off the knife, bleach it, whatever, and the next time I go into work I will dispose of it there." The confidence in his voice is comforting, but I can't help but feel in my gut that it is the wrong choice.

All I can do is nod my head in agreement. I'm afraid to ask the most important question, afraid of the answer he might give, so I say nothing. I get up very slowly and head to the studio where the canvas and the knife remain untouched. He walks in behind me, and with a gloved hand he reaches for the knife and goes into the bathroom. I turn my attention to the canvas in front of me, lay it on the table and squeeze black paint straight from the tube directly on top of it. I hate that I have to cover up what I worked so hard on. With a trembling hand, I grab my biggest brush and begin to swipe the paint back and forth. The beautiful water I painted, it took so long to get the colors exactly how I wanted them, now gone, hidden under the obsidian blackness. My beautiful daughters' smiling faces are covered next along with the dried, incriminating blood. When the whole canvas has been totally covered with a thick layer of black, I move on to the blood, staining the carpet. After lots of scrubbing and chemicals, I manage to get the majority of it out, but a faint red stain remains. To anyone else, it would look like crimson paint, but I'll always know the truth.

With nothing more to do, I go into the bathroom to wash my hands. I hadn't noticed that Marc never came out. He is sitting on the floor with the clean knife lying next to him. If I hadn't seen what was previously on the knife, I would never know it was a part of such horror and death. His only movement is to shift his eyes to mine. We remain frozen in a locked stare, until I break the spell and rinse the black off my paintbrush and hands.

When I'm finished, I sink down to the floor across from him, waiting for him to meet my eyes once more. When he doesn't, I feel a sob reach my throat and can't help but let it out. The sound jolts him to look up with a blank expression. Without words, he scoots closer and pulls me into his arms.

"*Shhhh*, babe, it's going to be okay."

"I don't know if it is Marc," I say through tears. "This isn't the first time evidence against me has shown up."

"What are you talking about?" He lifts his head in confusion that subtly turns to anger.

"After the first time… I found muddy tennis shoes in the closet with no recollection of how they got dirty." I can't look at him. "It would make sense that they were muddy if I was out there that night."

"You…why didn't you tell me?" The anger and betrayal in his voice breaks my heart more.

"I… I didn't want you to worry," I stammer with barely a whisper. I keep my head in my hands. He doesn't say anything. *He is starting to doubt me.*

I didn't know I could feel so alone with him right next to me. I hiccup my last cry and scoot away from him. Without a second glance in my direction, he gets to his feet. My heart hopes he will say something, anything, but instead, he steps around me and walks out, leaving me truly alone. Abandoned, I fear I will shatter into pieces. I wrap my arms tightly around myself trying desperately to hold myself together.

I need to get out of here!

I flee the bathroom and run upstairs to pack a bag. I blindly grab clothes and shove them inside my duffle. I shouldn't be around my family at all. What if I hurt them next?

"No! I will not allow it." I say to myself before heading downstairs in a fury.

"Where are you going?" he asks, appearing in the hallway.

"Away!" The anger I feel toward myself bubbles out in my words. "I'm a danger to everyone around me, I probably am the murderer and *you…*" I point a finger at him, "…helped cover it up for me, which makes you an accomplice."

"Stop… just stop!" he yells. "I don't think it's you, Autumn. I just… I don't know what I'm supposed to think." He hangs his head and lowers his voice back to normal. "This is all so fucked up, and I don't know what I'm supposed to do with any of the information we have." I realize how defeated he looks, "Autumn, come on. Just stay here, and we can figure it out tomorrow. I already told work that I wasn't coming in."

It hurts my heart to know I am the cause of all this. All of his pain. I don't know what else to say, so I nod and drop the duffle bag to the floor. He walks over to me to pick it up and silently takes it back upstairs. I follow him and walk in as he is taking everything out and putting it on the ottoman for me to hang back up later. I wrap my arms around him and bury my face between his shoulder blades.

"Thank you for believing in me, or at the very least, sticking by my side while we figure this out," I tell him and kiss his shoulder. "Let's talk tomorrow and try to forget any of this happened. We have to pick the girls up soon and I don't want them to sense that there is still something wrong."

"Obviously, I would love to forget this, babe… but I'm not sure I can. I need a solution of some kind… an answer."

"I know and I can try and search for one. Maybe I can be part of one of these sleep studies, or see a therapist, get hypnotized, I don't know. I can talk to my mom. She might know what we should do, or Dad. He used to be a cop after all."

"I don't know if that is such a great idea. He might not see it the way we want him to," he says, turning around to face me. "Retired or not, he would still have an obligation to uphold the law, regardless."

"I know that, but I need help here, I can't go on living without any answers. I need to know what my next steps are."

"I can see your point, but let's wait and revisit all of this in the morning shall we. We are too emotionally and mentally exhausted right now to make any concrete decisions."

"Okay, you're right, we will revisit then." I say the words he wants to hear, but in my heart, I know that I need my parents' advice right now.

15

"HEY, YOU AWAKE?" he asks in a clear voice. There is no trace of grogginess in it. I contemplate not answering, but might as well rip the Band-Aid off.

"Yeah." I tell him, rolling over to meet his eyes.

He nods and then gets out of bed, leaving me alone with my thoughts. His cold demeanor makes me feel more alone than ever. Hating this back-and-forth reaction from him, I can already feel the tears roll down the sides of my face.

He's decided I'm responsible for everything; he regrets telling me to stay.

I should have left last night and not let him convince me to stay. I wipe my frustrated tears but make no movement to get up. The shower turns off and he emerges moments later, water dripping from his hair and a towel wrapped around him.

"Are you going to shower?" He says curtly, not meeting my eyes.

His attitude makes me angry, so I don't respond.

He doesn't notice. He continues to get dressed without another word before he leaves the room without a glance in my direction.

I don't understand what happened between last night and this morning. Why is he a completely different person today?

I throw the comforter off and stand up. I grab everything he unpacked and put it back in my duffle.

If he's not going to talk to me, I will leave.

I don't bother showering. Flying down the stairs I head straight for the front door. *Guess I'll be speaking to my parents sooner than I thought.*

"Where do you think you're going?" Marc yells.

"Oh what, now you want to talk to me?" I whirl around and throw my bag to the floor.

"Don't give me that, not after what you did last night. We had a deal!" he approaches me with a finger pointed at me.

"What are you talking about?"

"What am I talking about? Seriously? Where did you put the knife, Autumn? We said we would discuss it today, and you took it anyway!" he refuses to back down. He doesn't believe that I am completely in the dark here.

"I don't know what you're talking about! I didn't take the knife anywhere! I was asleep and woke up when you did,"

He turns and stomps away, only to return a few minutes later, the tablet for the security footage in his hands.

"Look!" he says, shoving the tablet in my hands and pushes play. "Looks like you to me, don't you think?"

I sneer at him before glancing down at the screen. Suddenly the back door opens and out I come.

What? That's not possible.

I continue to watch myself. I look up at the camera before putting my hood over my head. The knife is in my black gloved hand.

I look up at him and then back at the screen.

"I didn't do this! I have no memory of it! Maybe I was sleepwalking!" I tell him looking back at the screen again.

"You look pretty awake to me," he says with anger still coloring his voice. "*Maybe* the whole sleepwalking act has been a lie from the start! How would I know?"

"Marc, I'm telling you, I don't remember doing this! You have to believe me. You know me." I'm both angry and scared all at once, talking as fast as I can to try and get him to believe me.

"Well, I don't know what to believe right now. I felt you get out of bed, but I figured you needed some time, or couldn't sleep. I don't know where you went and the cameras conveniently go dead again, so I can't tell when you came home." Grabbing the tablet away from me, he turns and runs his hand through his hair.

"Why are you not believing me now? After everything that has happened, you choose now to start doubting me?" I ask. My voice is full of hurt. He lets out a shaky sigh before turning to face me again.

"I do," he starts before starting over. "I *want* to believe you, but you have to admit, you don't look asleep, and I mean, I cleaned the knife thoroughly, but still. What if there are still fingerprints on it, or traces of blood?"

"I don't know, but I swear to you... I don't remember doing it. It's what I've been telling you the whole time, why I feel so crazy about everything," I tell him, secretly wanting him to hug me. "I think we *should* tell my parents; Dad might know what to do, or at the very least if I should turn myself in... something is happening with me and I can't explain it. I need help." My emotions overwhelm me again and tears escape from my eyes.

Seeing the tears in my eyes, his anger deflates slightly and he finally pulls me into his embrace.

"*Shhh*, it's okay, we will figure everything out, I promise," he tells me. "Until we do though, I think we should consider having your parents look after the girls another week, just in case."

"What do you mean? You don't think I can take care of them?" I ask, shocked by his insinuation. "I'm not going to harm my own daughters, Marc!"

"No, that's not what I mean. I just... I can't take any more time off of work and I never know what bad thing is going to happen next with you. I'm sorry, but I think they should stay put until we can figure everything out."

"They need to be here, with us!" I tell him. "We can figure it out with them here!"

"It's not a good idea, and you know it, Autumn. They will pick up on things, and with yesterday's findings, and last night's incident, I'm not comfortable having them here where they are possibly going to be in danger. Look, even if it's not you, at the very least, someone broke into our home to plant that knife."

Deep down I know he is right. I would never hurt my children, but I also can't take the risk. I give him a curt nod and go upstairs to unpack my things yet again.

I will figure this out if it's the last thing I do. When I get back downstairs, he is gone. A note on the kitchen table catches my eyes and for a split second my heart jumps into my throat. *He left me.* I can't grab the note fast enough.

Went for a jog to clear my head. Be back soon.

P.S. Don't go anywhere.

I read it again and again, each time filling me with more and more anger. Crumpling the note in my hands before tossing it back on the counter, I come to my own decision. *Sorry, babe, I need to clear my head too.* I grab my keys and storm out of the house. *I need advice from my parents, with or without him.*

When I get to my parents' house, my mom is outside tending to her flowers. She stops to look up when she hears my car pulling into the driveway.

"Hey, Mom," I say running into her arms. It takes all my willpower not to break down, and crumple into her arms.

"Hey, sweetie, this is a surprise, what's wrong?" she asks. She hugs me back tightly and rubs my back, trying to reassure me.

"Everything is all messed up, Mom. I don't know what's real anymore. I need to tell you and Dad something, and it's a lot, but I just... I don't know what to do anymore." I want to stay in my mom's arms forever; she makes me feel safe and brave enough to come clean about everything.

"Okay, sweetie, come inside, I'll get you some lemonade. Your father is out back. Let him know you're here and that you want to talk to us, okay?" She leans back, still keeping my arms in her hands and giving them a light squeeze before leading me inside. My phone is going off in my pocket, but I don't bother looking at it. I know it's Marc.

With both of them sitting in front of me, I decide the best thing to do is start from the beginning and leave nothing out. Every horrifying detail pours out of me, concluding with the events of last night and this morning. I take a deep breath and wait for them to process everything. Their faces are blank and hard to read. I'm worried I may have given them both a stroke of some sort. I'm seriously debating calling an ambulance when finally, Mom opens her mouth to say something.

"Oh my god! Sweetie! I had no idea this is what has really been going on with you. You should have told us sooner," she says reaching for my hand to hold it, her brows deeply furrow in concern.

"I know, it's a lot, and I feel crazy. Honestly, I don't know what to do... Dad?" I glance a look at him, but his face is unreadable.

Mom looks over at him, and nudges his knee with hers. He looks at her before finally meeting my gaze. Under the scrutiny of his gaze, I feel like a child again, about to be reprimanded.

"Well, I agree with your mother, you should have told us sooner, especially when you first found the knife," he says disappointedly. "That is a huge deal, Autumn. It could possibly be key evidence or at the very least, evidence that would have exonerated you. Are you sure you don't remember leaving the house with it?"

"I'm positive, Dad! Marc has video of me from the cameras we installed, but I don't remember doing it. He's mad right now, thinking that I actually got rid of it without consulting him, but I don't remember."

"And you say he went for a run?" my dad asks skeptically.

"Yes, but Dad, he said it was to clear his head. He has been calling me nonstop since I got here. He wasn't sure talking to you would be a good idea, you having a duty to uphold the law and all," I say almost embarrassed.

"I see. Well… dreams about murdering people and actually doing it are very different, but knowing your history with sleep-walking definitely doesn't bode well for you. Now this knife is showing up in your house, which you should not have cleaned by the way… any way that all would make me skeptical."

"Oh Howard, be serious, you *know* our little girl is not capable of the heinous things that she has dreamt about," I'm relieved that my mom is defending me. "There is no possible way she could be involved with any of this. I don't know what to make of it, but I know she couldn't have done these things."

"I know Mary, hang on, let me think," he says. He places a hand on his chin and paces in front of us. "You say this is the first time the security footage shows you leaving the house, correct?"

"Well, yes, every other time the system was offline or turned off.

There was nothing but static," I tell him, confused about where he is going with his question.

I'm about to ask him when I get another call, followed up by a text. I open it.

Why won't you answer me? I know you're probably at your parents. I'm coming over. I hope you haven't told them anything yet.

I close it and feel sick to my stomach. I hate when we fight.

"Listen, I have a few buddies left on the force who owe me a favor. I'll do some digging around, see if I can't get some information on the three victims. I'll find out if they have the murder weapon in evidence, which would solve the whole *is that the real murder weapon business* right away," he says using air quotes. "Hell, they might even have someone in custody already and haven't released the information to the public yet."

"Thank you, Dad, I really appreciate it," I say.

"Don't thank me yet, sweetheart, if this does somehow end up being you... I will have to turn you in... you know that, don't you," he says looking at me with sympathy. I lower my head to respond, not wanting to look in his eyes.

"Yes, Daddy, I know." Against my efforts, a rogue tear falls down my face. I wipe it away before they can see.

"Oh, Howard, stop, it won't come to that... our baby is innocent!" my mom says, swatting him lightly on the back.

"Thanks, Mom."

We all hear the car pull up at the same time and look at each other, *Marc*. I know he won't be happy that I told my parents, but so what? I stand my ground and hold my head high when I answer the door.

"How was your run?" I let the sarcasm drip off every word.

"I figure you already told them," he says, ignoring me. He looks more defeated than anything but, the lingering anger is still present in his words.

I move aside so he can walk in the door and be confronted by my parents. I stand next to my mom and wait for him to explain himself.

"Look, I'm sorry I didn't believe you and that I didn't want you to tell your folks," he says, gesturing to my mom and dad.

"You're damn right she told us... something you should have wanted to do as well, mister," Dad says. His eyes flash with anger and Marc winces.

"I know, I just... it's a lot," he hangs his head, taking the full weight of everyone's disappointment. "Well, you know, at least I assume she has told you everything by now."

"Yes, I did. I didn't leave anything out," I tell him, crossing my arms. *How dare he insinuate that I would leave stuff out.*

"Come on, Howard, let's leave these two to talk for a moment," Mom says. My Dad doesn't follow her right away, so he grabs his hand and leads him outside.

Feeling parched from all the talking, I go to the kitchen and pour myself a glass of lemonade. I am fully aware that Marc is watching me, waiting for me to speak.

"Dad is going to ask his buddies on the force for information on all three victims and if they have recovered a murder weapon."

To me, this is good news, even though it might paint me as guilty. At least I will have some answers, but a strangled look flashes across Marc's face. He recovers quickly and smooths his facial expression back to blank.

I know I saw it.

Before I can confront him, Mom walks cautiously back into the room.

"Sorry to interrupt, but it's almost time to pick the girls up. Why don't you two stay here and talk while we go get them. We can pick up some dinner and eat together. How does that sound?" Mom asks as she moves to grab her keys off the counter.

"That would be great, Mom. Thank you."

As soon as the door shuts behind them, I face Marc.

"I can't believe you left to go for a run and didn't even tell me, or that you didn't believe me when I told you I don't remember getting rid of the knife... because I don't," I say glaring at him.

"I know... that was shitty, but Autumn, I needed to get out of there. It was too much and I needed to think. This is all a lot," he says.

"Yes, I know. It's all a lot for me too! I'm the one living it. There is a possibility that I am actually a murderer."

"It's not only you living it, Autumn! We all are! I know it is *happening* to you, but don't think for one second that it doesn't affect all of us!" Every muscle in his body is tense.

"I know, I'm sorry... this whole situation is extremely messed up," I tell him, holding my head in my hands. "Dad is going to look into it and see if it could be me. I will stop taking my medication so I can take the girls to school, and we can go from there. One step at a time."

"I think we should ask your parents how they feel about that, because I for one am still against possibly putting the girls in danger."

"Fine, but I would never hurt my own children, and it hurts, you could ever think otherwise."

"Given the circumstances, Autumn, I think my concerns are warranted."

I purse my lips together to keep me from saying anything I might regret.

The silence lingers and from the tightness in his mouth I know he is as uncomfortable as I am. We are already on thin ice, and need to control our anger before the girls arrive. He slowly lets some of his tension go and sits down next to me. I want to be happy with his olive branch, but I still feel betrayed. For the sake of the girls though, I put those feelings aside and try to be civil.

"Okay… we wait to hear what your dad has to say. Until then, let's make everything seem as normal as possible for the girls' sake. We will take them home after dinner and have a normal weekend and try to find the piano we promised." He pauses. I give him a small nod to communicate that I'm with him so far. His face becomes softer and his eyes kinder before he continues. "Okay, as for the medication, I think you should stop taking them… you're drowsy and you still had a nightmare. We can see how the weekend goes without them and call the doctor on Monday to reevaluate everything. However, if anything else comes up over the weekend, the girls will be staying with your parents, deal?"

"Yeah… okay, deal," I tell him.

For now, things have calmed down between us. He pulls me into a cautious embrace.

"I'm sorry for how I reacted, that wasn't fair to you. I know you're going through a lot right now. None of this is easy," he whispers in my ear.

"Thank you, I'm sorry too." I breathe him in, loving the feeling of being in his arms and for now, not feeling alone in this crazy situation. Things still feel tense between us, obviously, but I know when all of this gets figured out, we will be fine; we have to be.

I count down the minutes until my parents arrive. *I am beyond excited to see my Gemini Stars.* Luckily, I don't have to wait long. The door opens and they rush through the door into my arms.

"Mommy!" they both yell.

"Are you taking us home?" Ada asks. Hope is written all over her face.

"Yes, sweetie! After we eat we can go home." I am grateful I can make them so happy.

Mom and Dad bring in the two large pizzas they ordered.

"Who's hungry?" my dad asks.

"We are!" we all say in unison.

It looks delicious and I am ravenous. We eat as a family and act as normal as possible for the girls, who don't seem to think anything is wrong as they talk excitedly about their day and how they can't wait to go look for pianos tomorrow. When we are finished eating, Marc loads their bags in the car and gets them in their car seats while I linger inside with my parents. They try to reassure me that everything will be okay. Dad will let me know as soon as he finds anything out about the victims or if the police have the murder weapon.

"Thanks, guys, I really appreciate it. Everything is so messed up right now. I want all this to be over," I tell them.

"Don't worry, sweetheart, it will be over soon. I'm sure it's all a big coincidence and doesn't mean anything. You'll see. They probably already have the murder weapon and a suspect lined up. However, if I were you, I would look into getting a handle on the sleepwalking," Mom says as she looks to Dad for support.

"Yeah, your mother's right, everything will be fine. I will let you know as soon as I find out anything. Don't worry," Dad says with his reassuring grin.

I thank them and walk out the door to get in the car to head home.

16

I AM DREADING shopping for pianos. Too much is going on right now and I want to be home in case Dad has any leads for me. However, seeing how my Gemini stars light up in anticipation, well, nothing beats that and I can't take the adventure away from them. Things between Marc and I are still tense and I have no idea what he is thinking. His face is a blank mask that I can't read. I should have told him about the shoes from the beginning instead of trying to keep it a secret. *I'm honestly lucky he hasn't taken the girls away from me and had me put into a psych ward. I need to try and keep it together until I can find out more answers.*

Unable to contain their excitement, the girls run inside, eager to play notes on every piano they see. They love how they all sound. We tell them they have to stick with the upright ones, so they move to look at those. A salesman comes up and offers us help with finding a perfect piano for beginners. We tell him what we are looking for and how much we are willing to spend, so he leads us to the discounted pianos in the back.

"These are used, but since your girls are beginners, it shouldn't be a problem," the man says with a hint of annoyance.

"Okay, thank you," I tell him.

Getting the girls' attention away from the new pianos to these is a little challenging, but they reluctantly listen and begin trying these out instead. To my immense relief, they immediately fall in love with the second one they lay their hands on.

"This one! We want this one!" They both squeal with delight. "Can we get it, Mommy, please," they plead before turning to their father. "Please, Dad!"

It's a beautiful, black Yamaha upright. The salesman tells us it is a great brand and choice for aspiring musicians. I look at Marc, give him a slight nod that he returns.

"Okay, you sure this is the one?" I ask them seriously.

"Yes, Mommy! We love it!" They both say, unable to contain their excitement.

"Well, if this is the one, I guess we will have to buy it, won't we?" Marc chimes in, smiling at them.

They are over the moon, and all but tackle us with hugs. They continue to play at the piano they chose while we do all the paperwork and figure out a time and day for delivery. Since they have lessons on Wednesday, we try to get it delivered for Tuesday. Thankfully, they have an opening at noon. We pay and leave with two very excited girls.

"Well, that was quick. I didn't think we would find one so fast, or that cheap either," I tell Marc as we get in the car and head for home.

"Yeah well, I thought we would browse around different shops and compare prices before we decided to buy." His hands grip the steering wheel tightly and I know he is annoyed.

"I thought we were in agreement," I whisper, so the girls can't hear. "Do you not think we got a good deal?"

"We did, but I would have liked to shop around, is all." He sighs before looking at me. He loosens his grip and reaches for my hand. "I'm sorry, I'm still on edge, but everything will be okay, we will get through this." He winks and gives my hand a final light squeeze before placing it back on the wheel.

"Well, hopefully my dad will find something out soon," I tell him. I keep my tone light and hopeful, not only to convince him, but myself as well.

His only acknowledgment is a curt nod. I tune out his negativity and focus on the girls chatting about their new piano. Their only complaint is they have to play the keyboard until it arrives.

We try as hard as we can to keep everything normal and upbeat for their sake, but I am finding it challenging. I'm mentally and emotionally exhausted, as well as filled to the brim with anxiety wondering when my dad will call with news. I want to put all of this behind me and get on with my life. The only thing keeping me sane right now is the fact that I haven't had any more dreams of murdering people or forgetful episodes.

We have been checking the security footage feed every day to make sure that no more time has been missed. Thankfully, the system is working as it should be now. However, I still can't figure out why it was acting up and only at times when we would have been shown the truth. I don't acknowledge the obvious reason...

Me.

When Monday comes around, Marc and I are back to semi-normalcy, seeming to have put all of our issues behind us, at least for the time being. He heads off to work while I get the girls ready and drop them off at school. When I get back home, I can't bring myself to go into my studio to start a new painting. As much as I long to create something from start to finish, it's too soon. Instead, I busy myself with chores around the house, keeping myself preoccupied so I don't spiral into my thoughts.

It's a beautiful day, so I take a break and sit outside in my favorite rocking chair with a nice cold glass of sweet tea. I try to finish a book I am reading while the warm sun beats down on me. I face the sky and soak in every ounce of sunlight I can. Releasing a deep breath, a tranquil calm falls over me. I am brought out of my serene state when the harsh trill of my phone goes off in my pocket, bringing me back to my daunting reality.

It's my dad.

Anxiety comes to the surface. *Breathe, everything will be fine.* Working up the final bit of courage I have, I answer the phone and slowly lift it to my ear.

"Hello," I whisper.

"Hey, sweetie, I have some news for you." His tone takes on a serious note and my heart begins to hammer in my chest.

"Oh yeah?" I ask nervously.

"Yeah, it's nothing too damning, but I thought you would like to know that they have not recovered the murder weapon from either crime scene," he tells me calmly. "However, they did recover fingerprints at both scenes and are running them to see if they can get a hit on a suspect."

"Oh… okay… so when will they know what the results are?" I ask. I don't realize I'm biting my nails until it rips a little too far down, sending a surge of pain through me.

"Well, I'm not sure, I told them to let me know when they had a hit. Anyway, that's all I have for you for right now. I'll let you know if I hear anything else."

"Okay thanks, Dad. This means a lot," I tell him.

"No problem," he says before ending the call.

I sink down into my rocking chair and mechanically reach for my iced tea, suddenly feeling too hot underneath the scorching sun. The waiting is brutal and taking a toll on my mental health. I down the rest of my sweet tea, not even enjoying it, and debate calling

Marc. Not wanting to get in the habit of keeping things from each other again I decide to bite the bullet.

Cooling off in the air conditioning, I prepare myself to make the call. Marc must have known I was about to call because my phone starts to ring in my hand. His name pops up on the screen, and heat rises up in my cheeks and my heart rate quickens.

"Hey, I was actually about to call you, what's up?" I say trying to sound as casual as possible.

"Not much, I was just on my lunch break and wanted to call and see how you were doing," his words are fine, but his tone is off.

"Well, that was nice, it's always good to hear from you."

"So, what were you going to call me about?" he asks.

I get the sense he already knows, but he waits for me to bring it up before saying anything.

"Well," I say nervously, "my dad called today. The police don't have a murder weapon, but they found fingerprints at both crime scenes and they are running them now for a match."

"Well, that's good right? Now we will know who is really behind all of this." He tries to sound confident, but I can hear doubt in his voice, making me more nervous and uneasy than I was before.

"Thanks, I'm glad to hear you are so confident in me," I tell him, ignoring the doubt I heard.

"Of course, babe." I wish he would elaborate more to calm my doubts.

"So… will you be home when the piano gets delivered?"

"Unfortunately I can't, I have taken off too many days already."

"Okay, that's fine." The small talk is painstakingly awkward. "Well, I'll let you get back to work then."

We end the call and I am relieved, and excited I will be the only one here when the piano arrives. I remember having lessons years ago. It might be fun to mess around on it before the girls take over.

After we end the call, all I want to do is unwind a little before getting the girls.

I attempt to go back out and enjoy the nice weather. Another glass of tea in one hand and my book in the other, I relax, escaping into my story once more, wanting to live anyone's life besides my own. The time creeps closer, so I close my eyes and savor the final minutes before I'm forced back into reality.

A feeling of unease creeps up the back of my neck. I try to ignore the feeling by keeping my eyes closed.

But I can't.

It feels like someone is standing right in front of me.

I snap my eyes open to confront whoever might be there, but to my confusion and relief, no one is there. I sit up and shield my eyes from the sun so I can get a better look around, but still nothing. No one. *How strange.* Brushing off the feeling, I head inside to grab my purse and keys, but they are nowhere to be found. *Seriously?*

I try to think back and retrace my steps to see where else they could be, but come up with nothing. I search more frantically knowing that I'm running out of time. I open every drawer, move every pillow, look outside, upstairs, still nothing. *Ugh, I don't have time for this.* I take my phone out and type in my mom's number. Luckily, she picks up on the first ring.

"Mom! Hey!" I say frantically. "I can't seem to find my keys to get the girls. Can you swing by and pick them up? If I find them, I will come get them or I can send Marc to get them when he's on his way home."

"Okay, sweetie, that's fine, if you want though, your father and I can drop them off at your house so they get home faster," she tells me.

"Thanks, Mom! You guys are a lifesaver!"

"No problem, Hon."

I am still searching for my keys when my parents pull into the driveway. I run out to greet the girls and apologize for not being there. To my surprise, they don't seem to mind, they just run inside laughing. I thank my parents again, and ask if my dad has heard anything else.

"Um, no I haven't." He casts his eyes down and fidgets with his keys. "We should be getting back. Bye now."

"Okay… bye," I say.

His strange behavior sets me on edge, but I shake it off and get back inside. The girls have started their tea party upstairs already, so I have to call out to them to start any homework while I prepare dinner. Their little feet patter downstairs. They grab their books from their bags and head toward the table.

"What do you girls feel like having for dinner tonight? Any requests?" I ask them

"I want pizza!" Anna yells.

"I want spaghetti and meatballs!" Ada yells.

"Okay," I laugh, "how about we pick one of those."

They look at each other, deep in thought, their little eyebrows furrowed with such a big decision. It's so cute, the hardest decision for them is to choose what they want for dinner. Suddenly their faces smooth, and they look back up at me.

"Okay, we pick spaghetti," Anna says.

"Okay, spaghetti and meatballs coming up," I tell them, "Start on your homework and it will be done before you know it."

While they work on their homework, I try to settle my thoughts. I keep coming back to my missing keys in the process, *Ugh, I hope I find those soon,* and Dad's weird behavior. Those two thoughts swim in my head until I give myself a migraine.

"Hey girls, do you happen to know where Mommy left her car keys?" I ask.

"No, Mommy, haven't seen them," they both say, not even looking up from whatever it is they are working on.

"Okay, thank you, my sweets."

As the food is done, Marc walks in the door to greet us. Perfect timing as always.

"*Mmm*, something smells delicious," he says sniffing the air. "How are my girls doing today?" He puts his briefcase down and loosens his tie.

"We're doing good," the girls say.

"I'm good. Hey, you don't happen to know where I might have left my keys do you?" I ask him.

"What do you mean?" He looks at me confused.

"I mean I had to have my parents pick them up because I can't find my keys," I tell him as we start eating.

"Oh... well no, I haven't seen them, but I can help you look for them when we're done eating."

After an hour of looking with no luck, I'm starting to get nervous. They have to be around here somewhere. It's not like I can leave the house without them.

"Have you checked your studio?" he asks after we have scoured the whole house.

"Hmmm... you know, I haven't, I haven't even gone in there since everything," I tell him. "I'll go check now."

I walk down the hall, hesitating when I get to the door. I unlock it and slowly bring my hand to the knob and take a big breath before opening the door. I walk inside, my eyes scanning the room and immediately spot my keys on the table. Unfortunately, that's not all I see. Sitting next to my keys is a plate of chocolate chip cookies. The blood drains from me as the memory of the last murder comes to mind when I witnessed myself eating the freshly baked cookies from the woman's kitchen.

No! Don't go there, this is not that. They can be from anywhere. Maybe the girls left them in here or something. I walk out feeling numb, holding the plate of cookies in my left hand and my keys in my right.

"Oh, good you found them," Marc says, getting up from looking under the couch again.

"Yeah... you didn't happen to leave these in my studio, did you?" I ask him, showing him the cookies.

"No... why?" Comical confusion is written all over his face.

He doesn't bake.

"No reason, I just... I didn't do it, and my keys were sitting right next to them, and I know I haven't been in there since... well you know." I ended on a whisper so as not to alarm the girls.

"Well don't worry about it... you probably just forgot, or decided to bake in your sleep," he chuckles, trying to make a joke of something I really don't find funny. "No big deal. Come on, we're all going to watch a movie."

I wander into the kitchen, and put my keys on the counter. I debate whether I'm overreacting. It is just a plate of innocent cookies, but what they represent leaves a bad taste in my mouth and I throw them in the trash without a second glance. Marc only raises his eyebrow at me in silent question, but continues to make the popcorn. The buttery smell fills the room and makes my mouth water.

"Can you make me a bag, just for me?" I ask.

"Oh, yeah I can. I figured we would all share, but I can make you your own."

I nod thanks, shuffle to the couch, and cozy up with my girls.

Everyone is focused on the movie and long finished with their popcorn, but I continue to pick at mine. My thoughts begin to drift to more unpleasant things no matter how hard I try to focus on the movie. I find myself trying to think of every possibility and explanation of how and why my keys were found in a locked room. I haven't stepped foot in there since the incident. Or why, a plate of the exact cookie I ate after murdering a woman ended up in the same room. Before I know it, the movie is over and we are tucking the girls in for the night.

Ugh, I need to stop thinking about this. Maybe I baked them in my sleep. That's hardly the worst thing I might have done while sleeping, so I should be relieved.

I go to bed convincing myself it was nothing more than that, but deep down there's a nagging feeling I can't shake.

With the arrival of the piano today, it takes a lot of convincing to make the girls go to school since they wanted to be home when it arrives. Reluctantly, they gather their things and let me take them to school. I'm not home long, when I get the call that the truck is five minutes away, sending a surge of excitement through me. I move stuff around in the family room so they have plenty of space to maneuver the piano against the wall I chose. I was finishing when the doorbell rings and I all but run to answer it, feeling like a kid again. I open the door and see two men standing there, the truck in the driveway with another man opening up the back. There it is, the piano, shiny and new… to us.

"Come in come in, I'll show you where we want to put it," I tell them, ushering them into the family room to present the wall. They take a few measurements before walking back out to the truck to unload it. It takes all three of them to get it inside and place it where I want it, but it's done, and it looks as if it belongs here.

Heck, I might start taking lessons again myself.

I thank them as I walk them out, and then run back to where the piano sits. I run my hand along the stark white keys, which make a beautiful contrast against the obsidian blackness of the rest of the piano. I can't help myself. I sit down at the bench and raise both my hands to hover above the keys. I play a few notes that turn into a song I thought had long been forgotten, my muscle memory still intact. The beginning of *Fur Elise* is the only song I remember from when I used to play, but it's something. *I can't wait to see the girls' faces when they walk in and see it here and ready for them to play.*

———

As I suspected, they come running out as I pull up. They are already opening the door to get in the car before I can even get out of the driver's seat. They demand that I hurry so they can get home to play with the piano, which makes me laugh and hustle to buckle them in. When we arrive home, they sprint out of the car and head for the front door.

"Mommy, hurry!" Ada demands.

"Yeah, Mom come on," chimes in Anna.

"I'm coming, I'm coming, hold your horses, girls," I tell them. Their pure joy brings a genuine smile to my face and I pick up the pace to unlock the door for them.

They immediately beeline to check out the piano. I have one foot in the door when music fills the house. I find them sitting on the bench side by side, each playing different notes simultaneously. It doesn't sound good, but I don't care.

They don't leave the piano until I practically have to pry them away to eat dinner. *So glad we got them into lessons.*

Marc walks through the door minutes after I finally get the girls to tear themselves away and come sit at the table. He too makes a trip by the piano to look at it.

"Wow, it looks really great right there," he says, setting his briefcase down. "Did you have any problems with the guys bringing it in here?"

"No, no problems at all. It was fairly quick and painless," I tell him

"That's good." He snags a plate of food and sits down with us. "I'm starving."

The girls scarf their food, despite my telling them three times to slow down so they don't choke. That doesn't stop them; they eat everything on their plate and run to the piano again to play some more. Marc's eyes meet mine and they mirror my joy. We finish up our food and make the girls do their homework, much to their disappointment. *Luckily, they will get a book tomorrow so they can play some real songs.*

17

THE GIRLS CAN'T WAIT for their lesson tonight; that's all they talk about while they get ready for school. I can't wait for some alone time today; it's possible Dad will call with updates on the fingerprints. *The wait is killing me.* Part of me still can't get what Ren told me out of my head. I don't know how one forgets about sleepwalking with a knife in high school at a sleepover. Every time it pops in my head I start to feel guiltier. I decide it's time for me to rip the band aid off, so to speak, and work in the studio. I hope it will be able to occupy my mind so I don't watch the clock all day.

Walking down the hallway gives me pause and sends shivers down my spine. Every time I go in here, something has been wrong. I hesitate before opening the door, but I refuse to be afraid of the one room that is supposed to be my sanctuary. I push through and open the door with confidence, ready for anything, but find nothing.

Nothing amiss, nothing strange. *Good, maybe I can do some painting today.*

I play some upbeat music to keep me motivated while I start on yet another totally new painting. I get everything set up and begin.

Before I know it, I'm mixing paints, switching brushes, frantically moving my hand all over the canvas while holding another paint brush between my teeth until I'm ready to switch to it. I am in the zone, more than I have been in a long, long while. I wipe at the loose strands of hair that dare to cover my eyes and feel the wet swipe of paint I left behind on my forehead. I know with certainty it is not the only place that paint covers me.

My eyebrows are furrowed in concentration. All my emotions pour out of me into my work. I feel absolutely invigorated — until my phone rings, breaking the spell and making my hand pause mid-brush stroke. I take a deep breath and glance over to the screen, getting slightly anxious that it could be my father, but see it's only Marc. I'm a little annoyed that he has interrupted me when I am on such a roll. I let out a frustrated groan before putting my brushes down, and wipe my hands of as much paint as I can before answering.

"Hey, what's up?" I say making my tone light and happy.

"Not much, just wanted to check in on you, see how you are doing," he says cautiously.

"Well, no worries here. I'm doing really well today, been painting all morning."

He seems surprised by my carefree attitude, pleased I'm doing much better today.

"Well, don't let me keep you, happy painting," he says and ends the call.

I take a step back and admire my work. *Not bad; I really love it.*

The piece is full of different colors and abstract emotions that leap off the canvas. The painting tells my whole turmoil story with the use of colors paired with my deliberate brush strokes. Anyone would be able to feel the raw emotions of fear, guilt, anxiety, yet also happiness and joy mixed in throughout. It's a huge weight lifted from me to have it all out on my canvas, like the painting is helping carry the load of those feelings. Upon further inspection of the piece, I only have a few more brush strokes to add before I deem it the perfection I am looking for. I center myself, focusing to bring myself back to my previous emotional state. Opening my eyes, I instantly know what else it needs.

Reaching for my pallet knife, I mix more colors and apply the thick paint, layering over what is already there, adding even more texture. I am beyond proud of myself for completing what I perceive as my own masterpiece. I clean up my paints, wash my brushes, and move my painting to the drying rack. With a final glance, I decide to take a picture of it in case anything were to happen to it. The alarm goes off on my watch alerting me that it is time to get the girls. There is no time for lunch, so I grab a granola bar from the cabinet and head out.

———

Arriving at Mrs. Lang's sweet little cottage, the girls run to knock on the door while I follow behind them. She opens the door to let them inside, and I stand on the steps to give her the money for the month's lessons, apologizing again for missing last week's lesson. I'm grateful that she accepts the apology, allowing the girls to be back on track. Having a couple of hours to kill now, *no pun intended*, before I have to pick them back up, I might as well treat myself to a little shopping spree around town. I could use some retail therapy, and it can double as a celebration for finally finishing what feels like my most accomplishing work of art to date.

I park in one of the only empty spots downtown. I plan to work my way from one side of the street and then the other. The first boutique I go into has amazing clothes, all hung in a way that draws you right in, giving the illusion that every article of clothing would look fabulous on you. The workers are very friendly and offer to open a fitting room for me if I should need it. I happily take them up on the offer.

Before I know it, I have tried on at least half the items in the store and surprisingly, everything fits and looks amazing on me. It's not my usual style, but with how I am feeling now, it needs to be. I recklessly grab everything, and walk to the counter to pay. I know I went overboard, but I don't know how much until they tell me the total. My jaw drops when I see the total. Recovering quickly, I put everything on a credit card I never use. *I deserve to treat myself.*

Weighed down with all the bags of new clothes, I have never felt more alive. A quick glance at the time and I realize I was in there for over an hour. It's already time for me to head back to pick them up from their lessons. *So much for hitting up every store downtown.*

I drive slightly over the speed limit to make it back to Mrs. Lang's cottage with five minutes to spare. I wait for them until they come running out grinning from ear to ear. I get them in the car and we head home.

"Mommy, you have to see the new book Mrs. Lang gave us!" Anna says excitedly. She holds it up, waving it, expecting me to grab it.

"I will check it out when we get home okay? Mommy has to keep her eyes on the road right now."

"Okay, but we have to play you the new song we got to learn right when we get home!" Anna says.

"Yeah, like, right when we get home, Mommy," Ada adds.

"Well, let's hope Dad has dinner ready for us. After we eat you can play the song as many times as you want for us, okay?" I tell them glancing back in the rearview mirror to look at them.

"Okay," they grumble, upset they have to wait so long.

When we walk in the door, I'm extremely grateful to smell food already cooking.

"Hey! We're back! It smells amazing in here!" I yell from the doorway. I haul all my new clothes inside and set them at the foot of the stairs. *I'll take them up later.* "Why don't you girls start setting the table while I help Daddy with dinner?"

"Okay, then we can play after we eat, right?" they ask.

"Yes, as soon as you're done eating, but that doesn't mean speed eating, got it?" I warn as I turn my attention to Marc.

"Hey, thanks for getting everything started," I say while giving him a hug. I breathe him in and relax in his arms.

"No problem, I see you had an eventful day," he says nodding to the bags of clothes.

"Yeah, well I decided to treat myself for a job well done for finishing my painting and to keep my mind off not hearing any updates from Dad yet," I say shrugging.

"That's good, you deserve to treat yourself babe," he says, as he moves to kiss my temple.

Despite my warning, the girls gobble their food so they can show us the new songs. To keep it interesting, they are each learning a different song so they don't get bored and they can motivate each other.

Once everyone is finished, they take turns playing their songs, and they sound pretty good. They are both beginner short songs, but they play them fluently without much hesitation. After what feels like an eternity of hearing the same songs over and over, we have to tell them it's time to go to bed. After a bunch of "one more times," we finally get them tucked in for the night.

"Come with me, I want to show you my painting," I tell him, grabbing his hand.

"Okay, lead the way," he says, trailing behind me. We head down the dark hallway and I go inside, this time with no hesitation at all. Before I flip the light on, I second guess whether the canvas will still be how I left it. *Only one way to find out.*

I pull the canvas out from the drying rack, relieved when I see that it is exactly how I left it, and now fully dry. I'm hit again with how much I love it.

"Wow babe… that's really good! I love all of the colors," he says. His eyes wander over the canvas in amazement. To see his reaction is the greatest feeling for an artist.

"Thanks, I put all of my emotions from everything that has been going on into this piece. It's my abstract emotion," I tell him feeling extra proud of myself.

"Well, it's amazing, I love it," He says as I put it back on the drying rack so he can pull me into his arms.

"Thanks, I'm really proud of it," I tell him as we head back upstairs. "I think this could be the first of many in a series of some sort and they would do really well hanging up in a gallery. Don't you think?" I'm so giddy of the mere thought of my work hanging in a gallery again, I'm basically on cloud nine.

"I think they would definitely look amazing in a gallery, babe…" He hesitates before asking the next question that I didn't want to think about tonight. "Do you think we will have an update soon about everything?"

"I don't know, I hope so. Can we talk about it later? I want to stay in my happy bubble for a little while longer."

"Sure thing. Let's talk more tomorrow."

We tell each other goodnight, but try as I might, my happy bubble, has popped, and I can't seem to get to sleep. All I do is toss and turn. I can't seem to get comfortable. I don't want to disturb Marc, and I'm not going to sleep any time soon, so I decide to go downstairs, get some water, and watch some tv for a while until I get tired.

I lie down and put a blanket on, mindlessly watching the news, periodically closing my eyes in hopes I will drift off to sleep and not caring if it's on the couch. I can barely hear the news anchors talking. Something they say brings me back to my conscious self.

"A match from the fingerprints collected on two recent murders—"

Hearing this, I jolt upright, no longer on the verge of sleep. I rewind the tv and turn the volume up just in case they are talking about the murders I might have committed.

"A match from the fingerprints collected on two recent murders has identified thirty-year-old Ashley Wood as the prime suspect for the murders of Gwen Frost and Carol Sanchez. A BOLO has been put out in hopes of locating the suspect. She is considered armed and dangerous. If anyone has any information about this woman, please contact your local police department."

I'm so elated. They *finally* have a suspect and it isn't me. *I wonder why Dad didn't call me today with the news. Maybe he doesn't know yet, oh well.* I glance at the time because I want to tell Marc the good news! I'm so distracted that I almost miss the picture they post on the screen. My whole body becomes rigid; my vision blurs and black spots swarm my vision. My breathing is shallow and I feel like I might pass out. I reach back for the couch and collapse onto it. Looking back up the picture is gone. I quickly rewind and pause on it again, hoping I am just seeing things.

I know this woman.

The name is different, but I know the woman on the screen.

It's me.

She looks *exactly* like me, every detail of her face from her almond brown eyes to the porcelain color of her skin. She even has the same shaped nose and mouth. If her name wasn't different, I would swear the picture I'm seeing on the screen is one taken of me. *We could be twins!*

I'm still in shock and disbelief, but every time I look, my face is still on the screen. I get up and approach the tv, studying the woman's face to make one hundred percent sure I'm not losing my mind.

Everything is the same.

My brain frantically goes through a hundred different explanations as to why this woman looks like me.

Doppelganger, perhaps. Everyone supposedly has one. Perhaps I'm more tired than I realize; maybe I'm dreaming or just seeing my own face in place of this woman's because I feel guilty. I have to get Marc; I don't care what time it is; I'm waking him up.

I still have the woman's photo paused, however, it does not show her name. I'll let him look for himself, and see if he sees what I am seeing. I run upstairs, taking the steps two at a time, trying to get there as fast as I can. When I reach him, he is still sound asleep, and I am fully out of breath, but manage to call his name and shake him a little too violently until he wakes up, startled by my harshness.

"Marc! Get up! Come on, it's important!" I say in a loud whisper so I don't wake the girls.

"Wha— babe? What is it? What's wrong?" he asks confused and groggy, but the alarm on my face triggers an instant turnaround from asleep to wide awake. "The girls? Are they okay?" He's already getting out of bed and heading for the door.

"The girls are fine; they are still asleep. Come downstairs I need to show you something." Relief washes over his face, but is quickly followed by annoyance that something else could be important enough for me to react this way.

"Okay, okay, I'm coming."

We get into the living room and I run ahead to stand in front of the still paused tv, and face him.

"Okay, tell me who you see, okay?" I move aside so he can get a full view of the screen, but he rubs sleep out of his eyes looking annoyed and confused.

"Pay attention and look!"

"Okay, I am," he tells me, slumping on the couch.

I know the moment he registers the photo on the screen, his eyes go wide, he rubs his eyes and blinks again at the screen.

"What is this? Why is your face on the tv? What's going on?" he asks as he gets up from the couch, his voice becoming increasingly louder.

"Okay, you see my face? You see me on the tv?" I ask urgently.

"Yes, it's you! Why are you on the... *oh my god!*" he says with realization coming across his face.

Before he can freak out too much, I hold up my hands for him to wait as I resume the tv, so the woman's name come across the bottom

"I just wanted to make sure I wasn't crazy in thinking that we looked exactly alike," I tell him. "This woman's name is Ashley Wood. They found her fingerprints at both of the crime scenes."

"Wait... so that woman, isn't you?" he asks, sitting back down again, rubbing his hand through his hair. "She looks exactly like you."

"I know, it's crazy... I don't know what's going on."

The silence overwhelms us as we process what is on the tv, trying to make sense of it in our own way until he ultimately breaks the silence.

"Do you have a twin you didn't tell me about?" he asks. His eyes are wild with confusion. "Or a secret identity?"

"What? No! I think I would know if I were a twin. You know I'm an only child," I tell him. "And no, of course I don't have a secret identity."

"Well, I don't know. You really do look exactly the same for it not to be you or your twin, " he says incredulously.

"Well, they say that everyone has a doppelganger." A humorless chuckle escapes me in a poor attempt to lighten the mood, but he is still unconvinced.

"Yeah... but don't you think looking alike and dreaming of

committing these murders yourself is a little too bizarre of a coincidence?" He pushes, forcing me to entertain this ridiculous idea.

I stay silent so I can process what he said. He does have a point; this is really bizarre.

"Well, I know I'm an only child, but I can go and talk to my parents tomorrow. I think they will be as thrown off as we are," I tell him confidently. *My parents would never keep something like this from me.*

"Okay, yeah, that sounds like a good idea," he says. "Well, I am not going to be able to go back to sleep after this, so how about I make us some early breakfast?"

"Sounds good," I tell him and hurry to turn off the tv so we don't have to look at my face anymore. We make breakfast together in complete silence, the tension between us evident in the way we move around each other. Neither of us wants to speak, or knows what to say. We're too engrossed in our own thoughts. When we are finished, the silence continues as we go through the motions of eating. I can't taste the food in front of me, but continue to eat until every last bite is gone. Before we know it, it's time to get the girls up and moving and he needs to get ready to leave for work, much to his disappointment.

"Let's try not to worry until we have to," I tell him. "I will let you know immediately what my parents say."

I'm not only convincing him, but myself as well.

"I hope you're right." He attempts to give me a hopeful glance but shadows of doubt lay beneath.

I get the girls ready and off to school in a blur. My mind is still racing as I drive to my parents' house. The adrenaline is wearing off and I'm starting to notice how truly tired I am, but I need to focus, and I need answers. I drive in complete silence, trying to think how I'm going to approach the question of possibly having an unknown twin in the world. My anxiety habit kicks in and I start to bite my nails,

Should I just show them Ashley's photo? Rip off the Band-Aid and confront them directly. Do I have a twin?

This all seems so surreal; I realize I haven't factored in the worst part of the whole thing: having a twin who is a murderer and trying to cope with that. *Is that why I sleepwalked with a knife all those years ago? Was it Ashley, which is why I have no memory of it? Or do we have more in common than I want to admit?* My thoughts are endless and I am spiraling as I get closer and closer to having to confront my parents.

Maybe Dad already knows and he is simply afraid to tell me? Dread sets in as I round the corner and pull into their driveway. I sit in my car still chewing at my nails and try to muster enough courage to get out of the car, walk the few steps to the front door, and knock.

Don't be a coward.

18

WALKING up the driveway to get to their front door is the longest walk I have ever had to make. My heartbeat quickens and my palms start to sweat. Confronted by their door, it looks daunting, which is ridiculous. *I'm simply asking my parents a question, nothing more.* I knock on the door, but there is no answer. *Hmm, they should be home.* I reach into my purse, pull out my spare key, and slowly open the door, peeking my head in to look around before stepping all the way inside.

"Hey. Mom? Dad? It's me, are you home?" Silence. I wander the house looking for her. "Mom, are you here?" Finally, I see a glimpse of her and dad out in the backyard, so I step outside.

"Hey, Mom, what's up?" I'm trying to keep my voice as even as possible, but my anxiety is slipping out.

"Oh, hey sweetie, not much. We thought we would step out and get some sun for a bit. What's wrong? You sound a little frazzled," she says with a hint of tension in her voice.

I pick up on it and wonder if they have already seen the picture of the woman who looks like me and decided not to tell me?

"Oh, it's nothing. I only wanted to show you this picture I saw last night on the news. See if you see what I see." The change was subtle, but it was there on her face. Her smile faltered ever so slightly and she darted her eyes away from me for a split second toward my dad. I reach in my purse to pull my phone out to pull up the picture, but she reaches out and grabs my hand. She looks back toward my dad who slowly walks over to us.

"Let's go inside and I'll make us some tea." The tightness in her voice is unmistakable, and my dad refuses to look at me at all.

We walk inside and I pull up the picture on my phone while she puts the teapot on the stove. Dad is sitting at the table, staring at a fixed spot on the table, arms crossed. His mouth has formed a hard line. I wait until she comes back from starting the tea so I can show them both at the same time. I see her eyes get slightly wider. She glances at my father, almost as if they expected what I would show them, and know what I'm about to ask.

"Does she look like anyone to you?" My eyes are trained on both of them to see if I can read what they are thinking.

My mom takes the phone with trembling hands and looks at me a beat longer before she glances back to my dad. The change in her is subtle, but it's there. She's too stiff, rigid even and her face looks like she has seen a ghost. Her eyes, however, harbor a sadness as she stares at the photo on my phone. My voice comes out in a rush.

"So, what do you think?" My question breaks her eye contact with the phone, allowing her to smooth her features before looking back to me. I take a look at my dad, and he is still hard to read, his face completely blank. "She looks like me, right?"

She takes another look toward the phone before looking back up at me and I notice a small, single tear sliding down her cheek, giving away how immensely sad and heartbroken she is. I suddenly feel stupid. She must think it's me in the photo. That's why she is acting like this; she can't bear the thought of her daughter being a murderer.

"Oh, *God. No, Mom*. It's not me; it's a girl named Ashley Woods, see. Doesn't she *look* like me though."

I say my words in a rush hoping she will look up with relief, but she is still frozen while Dad slowly gets up from his rigid position and moves to stand behind her. He puts his hands on her shoulders, still not meeting my eyes.

"Mom? Dad? What is it? What's wrong?" My mind is reeling. *Maybe I really am a twin*. No that would absolutely be wrong; my mom would have told me. Still, I hear myself asking.

"Mom. I'm not a twin, am I?"

As soon as I say the words out loud my mom looks at me, guilt all over her face and I know. Her eyes are still damp with tears, but they are wide open, fixed on me. Dad finally dares a glance in my direction, but quickly looks away. Anger and betrayal bubble up inside me. My whole life has been a lie.

"Oh my God! Mom! Dad! I'm a twin?" I can't help but shout, looking at both of them with not only outrage, but also with sadness in my eyes as well.

My mom looks away nervously confirming my thought. My voice is more frantic as I grab her hands and look her in the eyes so she will hear me.

"Mom! Dad! Answer me," I say. I stare at both of them and will them to speak — to give me some sort of answers. I deserve something.

She slowly lowers her eyes to the floor and her voice is barely audible when she says, "No. Autumn, you're not a twin."

I'm almost relieved when she says that, but her reaction is so strange. I start to ask,

"Mom, then wha—"

Before I get the words out, she cuts me off and looks back to my dad, who gives a slight nod of his head, which gives her the courage to look back at me, resolve on her face mixed with slight hesitation.

"Autumn, you're not a twin. The day I gave birth to you, I also gave birth to *two* other daughters... You're a triplet."

I stare at her thinking I must have heard her wrong, but one look to Dad, and know I didn't.

"Wha...what?" I manage to stammer out before she reaches toward me to pull me into her embrace. I'm too shocked to pull away from her.

"Oh honey, I'm *so* sorry we never told you. We didn't think it would matter; they went to separate states and we didn't see any harm in your not knowing."

"You were never supposed to find out like this... if at all," My dad chimes in suddenly finding his voice.

Anger gets the better of me and I tear away from her. I whip around, unable to face them, still in shock. She moves to grab my shoulder, pleading with me, but I barely hear her. My thoughts are reeling.

I feel sick.

"What do you mean I wasn't supposed to find out? How could you keep this from me?" I yell at them. My face is hot and burning with anger and hurt. *My whole life has been a lie.* Black spots swarm my vision. "I need to sit down." The room spins before me and I'm afraid I might pass out.

My mom runs to get the tea made that has been whistling in the background for some time, only I'm just now hearing it. She comes back with two mugs and sets one in front of me while she holds the other one in her hand. She tells me to drink the tea, but I'm frozen in place, mesmerized by the steam rising up from the cup.

"I'm a... triplet?" I say almost to myself. "I have two sisters..." This all feels so surreal.

"Yes," my mom tells me in a soft, comforting voice as she reaches her hand toward mine

I let her hold my hand, taking comfort in the warmth against my icy cold hand.

"Autumn, I'm sorry… when I found out that the fingerprints matched Ashley, and I became aware of who she really was, I was afraid to tell you… for obvious reasons," my dad tells me. He fidgets with his hands and is obviously uncomfortable with the whole situation. *I wonder if he ever wanted to tell me before this whole incident.*

The comment sends a jolt of fresh anger through me. *So, he did know who the fingerprints belonged to and simply didn't want me to find out.* I glare at my parents.

"How could you not tell me? You both lied to me my entire life! You cheated me out of having sisters!" Angry tears threaten to spring from my eyes against my will.

I let my mom wrap her arms around me, while dad stands a few feet away from us. She rubs my back trying to console me, but all I feel is numbness.

"Sweetie, you have to understand, it was a difficult time for your father and me when I was pregnant. We didn't have the means to take care of one baby, let alone three." She pauses nervously before she continues. "We did what we thought was best for all of you girls, hard as it may have been." I manage to clear my mind enough to realize what she was saying.

"Wait…is it purely a coincidence that I stayed with you while my sisters were shipped off to live with new families?" I say pulling away from her embrace. I look from my mom to my dad, a fresh flash of hurt crosses my face. *They probably just flipped a coin.*

"Sweetie… I…" My mom has tears forming in her eyes now, and my dad reaches to comfort her.

"What your mom is trying to say is, yes, it is technically a coincidence. We instructed the nurse that helped deliver you to take all three of you away and come back with one. The other two were immediately given to the head of the foster care system and they were adopted within a few days. We didn't even see them, or know what family they went to. Our only request was they be in separate states and their name to begin with the letter A, if possible," my father explains in a voice like he says this type of thing every day.

"See, Autumn, you have to understand, to us, you *were* the only child we have ever known or seen," Mom chokes out between her tears.

Stunned into silence, I attempt to process the information. I feel my phone buzzing. I blink a couple of times before grabbing it.

Marc has texted, *Hey, how's it going at your parents' house? Any news?*

I read his message over and over; he has no idea exactly how much information I have received.

"I need a minute; this is all just too much," I tell them while I rub my temples feeling a migraine coming on.

Mentally drained, I don't know what to believe anymore. I not only found out that I am a triplet, but also, one of my sisters has been committing horrendous murders while I dreamt about them. This is completely messed up. The walls in my childhood home are starting to close in on me, and I bolt out of the house before my parents can say anything else.

Once in the car, I peel out of their driveway. I call Marc. *I cannot be alone with this.* It rings and rings, no answer. *Come on! Pick up.* I try again, but still, nothing. I'm shaking and feel like I'm going to lose it when he finally calls back. *Thank god.*

"Hey babe, what's up, sorry I was in a mee—" he begins to say before I can cut him off.

"You need to come home right now!" I tell him, my voice

shaking with a mix of anger, anxiety, and fear. I try to keep my tears at bay while I drive home, but I'm seriously considering pulling the car over. I'm probably not in the best state to be driving, but I really need to get home.

"Why? What's wrong?" he asks, concerned.

"Just get home… I need you." This is all I can manage to get out before I hang up. If I say anymore, I will lose it and I need to at least be out of the car and not driving when that happens. I shake my head trying to focus and swipe at my eyes to catch any tears falling down my face.

Marc is calling me back, but I can't answer.

My sole focus is to get home, and it's taking all of my effort. My hands are gripping the steering wheel so tight, they start to cramp. I take multiple deep breaths, but nothing is making this ultimate feeling of betrayal and disgust go away.

How could my parents lie to me my whole entire life!? If none of this had happened, they would have let me live my entire life without knowing that I have two sisters. The only consolation I have about the news is knowing it wasn't me who committed the awful murders. *But what on earth would make my sister do it in the first place?* I feel a small sense of relief as my turn comes into view. I am less than five minutes from my house. I can only hope Marc took me seriously enough to come straight home after I hung up.

Getting out of the car so fast I almost leave the engine running, I run for the front door. I get inside and close the door. Luckily, I remember to turn off the alarm before I slide my back against the door and sink to the floor. The mad rush of tears I have been holding the entire time suddenly bursts out of me. The dam containing them has finally been shattered. The intensity of emotions is almost unbearable, bringing on an anxiety attack for me to try and navigate through as well. In the process of attempting to ground myself and focus on my breathing, I begin to get flashes in my head, images that don't make any sense.

Am I finally having the psychotic break I have been dreading?

The weight of the truth starts to crush me, which makes it challenging to see the images clearly in my mind's eye. None of the pictures makes sense. What I am able to make out leaves me more distraught than before. *This can't be real.*

I'm still trying to understand the flood of images and feelings flashing through my brain, when all of the sudden, as quickly as they appeared, they vanish. It's hard to catch my breath. I feel a warm sticky substance falling from my nose. I reach my hand gingerly up to inspect it, and realize my nose is bleeding. I manage to pull myself from the floor and make my way to the bathroom to try and stop it, wondering what caused it in the first place.

Once I have it under control, I splash cool water on my face to help focus and try to remember the images that were once playing in my mind like a movie. They come back in bits and pieces. I'm confused and hurt by what I see. I don't understand what it means or how I am even seeing what I'm seeing. *Am I dreaming again?*

I can't be sure anymore.

Not wanting to take any chances, I frantically reach for my phone and begin to type out a letter. I know I don't have much time to spare to put my plan in motion.

Just in case.

Checking the time, I know Marc should have arrived by now, and I'm starting to get worried.

Maybe he didn't take me seriously.

I walk through the house in a daze and find myself heading toward my studio wanting to gaze at my work of art, somehow hoping it can take the burden of my emotions away. I wish I had the time to start a new one to carry these new, possibly worse, fears and emotions, but I know I don't. Pulling me out of my thoughts, I hear a door open, but it sounds like the back door instead of the front.

How strange, he never comes in through the back door.

19

I HEAD to the kitchen to investigate, hoping it was nothing, or Marc, but when I walk in the room, I see movement out of the corner of my eye. I whip my head around startled and see myself staring back at me pointing a gun. My eyes are wide; with disbelief and fright. The reality is so surreal it takes me a minute to raise my hands in self-defense, blinking a couple times to make sure the person I'm seeing is real.

She has the same oval face, same brown eyes, but her hair is cut shorter with pink streaks in it. She has heavy eyeliner on, making her brown eyes appear darker than mine, almost black. She also has a nose ring, something I always wanted, but never had the guts to do. Though there are a few differences, I know for sure that this is one of my sisters. The fact that she is pointing a gun at me tells me, it's Ashley.

"Wow, you really are a jumpy mess, aren't you? Guess all my effort in messing with you these past few weeks really took a toll," the woman who looks like me says as she snickers. "Take your phone and set it on the counter,"

I do as she says, careful to not make any sudden movements in case she is trigger happy.

"So, you're the one that's been in the house moving things around? Placing murder weapons and baked goods for me to find," I say. "It wasn't me sleepwalking this whole time then?"

"The one and only." She smirks. "Aren't you relieved to find out you're not crazy?" She moves closer to me with the gun in her hands pointing right at my chest. "I had you going in that direction, didn't I? I bet you were *this* close to committing yourself into the nearest psych ward, huh?" Her eyes dance with amusement. I ignore her questions; I won't give her the satisfaction of an answer.

"How did you manage to get around the alarm system?" I ask, trying to stall in hopes that Marc will arrive soon.

"We will get to all that in due time... *sis.*" She spits out the word like it is toxic on her tongue.

"Ashley, please, you don't have to do this. Just put the gun down and we can talk about this," I plead with her, my eyes still fixed on the gun in her hands. "Please, my husband will be home any second now and I don't want any trouble. I didn't even know you existed until today."

All she does is glare at me with only hate in her eyes.

"Trust me, your *husband* will not be coming anytime soon." She giggles and lowers the gun slightly only to raise it back up and train it at my chest.

"What do you mean he's not coming? What have you done to him?" I cry out taking a step toward her, but retreat back when she raises the gun higher and moves a step toward me.

"Stay where you are, bitch," she spits out.

I raise my hands in defense again and step back.

"Okay, okay, but please, where is my husband?"

"Relax, he's fine... for now," she says comically, making me uneasy about what she means or what she has done to him.

"Okay, so what do you want with me, how do you even know about me," I ask, careful not to make any sudden movements. "What has the purpose of all this killing been for?"

"Oh, honey, I've always known about you. The *chosen* child our parents deemed worthy enough to keep." She looks at her nails, uninterested, but I can tell it bothers her. "I on the other hand was unlucky enough to grow up in a poor home in Florida with an angry drunk dad, and even drunker mom. She let it slip one time that she wished she had never taken me in, or that one of my other two sisters would have been better than me. *Ha,*" she says full of disgust and hate.

"You've known this long and you never wanted to search for us sooner? Instead of doing all of this? Have you found our other sister?" I hope I can keep her talking since she tends to lower the gun every time she does. Part of me wants to know what happened, but all I can think of is how to stall her so I can figure out a plan to get out of here, or look for a weapon of my own to defend myself.

"Oh yeah, I found our sister alright, I spent my whole life tracking down the people responsible for how I ended up. Then what do I find... I find out that our parents, *my* real parents, decided to keep *you!* What made you more special than us? Than *me?* Sure, at first I was hurt, but that didn't last long before the rage set in. I was initially going to team up with our sister and together we were going to take you down, but then I find out that dear Ashley grew up with the higher rich class, silver spoon and all that. I got the short end of the stick! Tossed aside! Like a piece of trash!"

"Wait, Ashley? I thought you were Ashley?" I ask her hesitantly hoping I don't reveal how confused I am, but failing. Hearing Ashley's name gets her to stop dead in her tracks.

"Oh honey, I'm not Ashley, my name is Ainsley, but everyone calls me Z," she says slyly and winks at me. My thoughts are racing.

Not Ashely. Not Ashley. Not Ashley. Ainsley?

"But… the news said the fingerprints found were for Ashley's," I say almost to myself, trying to understand the situation. She looks at me, mischief and deviance dance in her eyes before a slow, wicked smile spreads across her face.

"I know, I planted them there," She tilts her head to the side, she's enjoying this. "Pretty clever of me, right?"

"You… she… you're both a part of this?" I think I'm going to be sick. How could two women, my sisters, who I didn't even realize I had, hate me so much. How could someone want to cause me so much pain?

This gets her to reel back in anger and raise the gun as she walks all the way up to me and presses the cold barrel against my head. Every muscle in my body freezes, fear most certainly apparent in my eyes. I squeeze them shut and pray this isn't the end.

"She is not a part of anything!" she spits out. "Haven't you been paying attention at all? I killed that rich bitch first! Wrapped my hands around her pretty neck and strangled her in her sleep. You should have seen the look on her face as she looked at me before the life left her eyes." She pushes the gun hard into my head and then retreats leaving me stunned.

"You… killed her?" I whisper. Grief washes over me for a sister I never knew and never will. Then it dawns on me — the first dream I had: a stranger's vice grip around my neck wasn't a stranger at all.

It was Z.

Her grip was actually around Ashley's neck. Mixed emotions dawn on me as I realize that I *felt* how Ashley felt as she died.

"Oh please, don't cry for that bitch; she had it better than both of us. She had anything she could ever ask for. She deserved to die and be blamed for the other murders," Z says.

"Are you going to kill me too?" I ask in a whisper and look to the floor, unable to meet her eyes.

"Not yet… besides, I need someone to frame for poor Ashley's murder, and who better than her long lost twin that's been dreaming of killing people and acting like a complete mental case for weeks now. It's perfect, besides, we have to take a drive to go say hi to dear old Mom and Dad. Really sell how crazy you are. Killing your own parents, now that is mental, huh?"

"What? No! Leave them out of this! Come on, it was thirty years ago, they were young and didn't do it to hurt us," I say in a rush. "They didn't even know which one they were keeping; they took us all away and let the nurse choose." As I say the words, her eyes shift from dark humor to pure hate.

"Why do you think I killed the nurse after I killed the doctor that delivered us? They all deserve to pay for ruining my life!"

It all starts to make sense now; the three people I dreamt of being killed, was me somehow seeing Z's actions. It wasn't my reflection I had seen in the window; it was hers. The people weren't random either. I know the third victim must have been some part of her adoption as well. I'm hoping if I can make Z see that we are connected in some way, she will be inclined to spare me and my family.

"We're connected, Ainsley… Z." I start to move toward her with my hands outstretched. "I dreamed it was me committing those murders, like some sort of twin vibe. My daughters do the same thing; they have their own secret way of communicating. Please, it doesn't have to end this way. I'm so sorry our parents made the decision to separate us and you went to an awful home, but please, let it end with Ashley. No one knows we are all sisters; it's not in the records." I stop mere inches away from her, closer than I ever dared, nervously waiting for her reaction. I feel a huge triumph when she starts to lower the gun a little.

"Yeah, I knew you were able to sense when Ashley died. I could sense you being there; it kind of felt like I killed both of you, but as she drew her last breath, I couldn't sense you anymore. That's why I decided to mess with you so much." She lowers the gun all the way. "It was intriguing to me you could do that, and the fact you have twins of your own... well. How could I resist?"

She looks down before looking back up at me; her eyes have softened a little. "I can't have kids. Yet another thing I didn't have in my life that you got instead." She's trying to hide the sadness, but I can see it in her eyes.

"I thought for sure your kids caught me one night when I snuck in, but I was wearing a wig and some clothes you would wear, very mom of you by the way. Anyway, I told one of them to go back to bed and it worked." She chuckles. Anger courses through me. The thought of her interacting with one of my daughters disgusts me and threatens to send me over the edge. It takes every ounce of self-restraint not to show my anger. I have no doubt she will kill me on the spot.

"It's been you in my house all this time?" I ask, shocked and confused. "But how did you get in? We installed a security system." I'm desperate to know the answer.

"Like I said, in due time, but I also sense things about you too," she says proudly.

"So, I take it you're an artist too, because you finished the painting I was working on with no problem," I tell her, changing the subject.

"Well, not actually, but when I picked up the brushes you used, it was like you were painting it instead of me. Pretty cool huh?" She laughs to herself, more relaxed now, and less menacing, but quickly recovers.

"I didn't call my mom and cancel my girls piano lesson, did I?"

Her only response is a wink.

"Enough stalling. Let's go and see our parents; I have a few things I would like to tell them." Her eyes grow black with anger again.

"Wait, please, my daughters. They need to be picked up from school soon, and you said you have Marc somewhere. If we go to *our* parents, no one will be there to pick them up," I plead with her. She waves me off with a click of her tongue.

"Oh, please, I called their friends' mom pretending to be you and asked them to have a playdate," she says as she ushering me out of the house. "Now hurry up, we don't have all day. Leave the phone; I don't need you doing anything stupid on the way." She shoves the barrel of the gun hard against my back.

"Okay, okay I'm going," I tell her and grab my keys, leaving my phone on the counter like she instructed. I internally kick myself for not letting Marc set the watch up on its own so it could make calls without being in close proximity to the phone. It's basically useless now. "I appreciate you arranging for the girls to be somewhere else for all of this truly." I'm trying to appeal to what little humanity she may have. Unfortunately, I can tell the second the words leave my mouth, they were a mistake. She reaches out with her chipped nails, grabs a handful of my hair, and yanks my head back.

"I did *not* do that for you! Or out of the kindness of my heart! You intrigue me, that's all but don't think for one second that I don't plan to kill you," she snarls. "Besides, maybe I'll even pretend to be you and play house with your family for a while. Who knows." She lets my hair go and pushes me out of the door.

I nod my head and don't say anything more as I walk to my car and get in the driver's side, while Z gets in the back seat, the gun undoubtedly still aimed at me through the seat. Her words bring back the memory of what I saw in my… vision if that's what it was. I push it aside and focus on figuring out a way to save my parents. My heart is pounding against my chest as I put the car in reverse and slowly back out of the driveway and head toward my parents' house. My hands are so sweaty I have to keep wiping them on my jeans so I can have a good grip on the steering wheel. I'm half-tempted to speed in hopes a cop will pull me over, but that probably won't work. I wrack my brain thinking of how I can alert someone to the danger I'm in, or if I can somehow run us off the road.

Would we both survive? Would I? What if she is the only one left?

The outcome is too uncertain and I can't afford her surviving and not me. I have to protect my family from her.

"You know, your thoughts are very loud," Z says calmly. I freeze at her words, clenching the steering wheel tighter, and glance in the rearview mirror to look at her. "I think we would both probably survive, but do you really want to put yourself through that?" She looks bored.

"How did you do that?" I ask her, keeping my eyes on her through the rearview mirror.

"I don't know," she says. "I've had lots of practice, being around you, getting to know you. I guess it helped make the connection stronger." She shrugs.

I look back to the road and try to keep my thoughts as blank as possible, but my curiosity gets the better of me.

"So, can you hear everything, I think? Or is it just bits and pieces?" I ask her, but keep my eyes on the road this time.

"Just bits and pieces, but I have to concentrate; it's definitely not as strong as the connection your daughters have. However, it's possible ours is too. You were able to feel every time I killed someone and when our other sister died. You didn't even have to try." There is a hint of jealousy or envy in her voice, but I can't tell which.

"That may be, but I was asleep when that happened, every time," I tell her.

I see her shrug in the mirror and look out the window; she's not interested in the conversation anymore. I start to wonder: if she can read what I'm thinking, maybe, just maybe, I can get bits and pieces of what she is thinking too.

20

I EVENTUALLY ARRIVE AT MY PARENTS' house, pulling into their driveway like so many times before. Only this time, it's life or death. My movements are slow and I exhaust every last minute until I have to get out of the car. I still haven't come up with a plan yet. I hear her yell at me to hurry up. She appears next to me and holds the gun inconspicuously against my ribs as we both walk up to the door. Her eyes are darting around the neighborhood, making sure no one is around to witness us out in the open. It would ruin her plan. I take a deep breath before I knock on the door. *Please don't be home. Please.*

Unfortunately, I hear rustling and footsteps approaching the door. I assume it will be my mom who answers, but when the door swings open, there stands my dad. His face changes to something like shock and confusion and his eyes go wide when he sees us both standing there. Z pushes me inside and walks in behind me raising the gun in front of her.

"Hello, *Dad*," she sneers, closing the door behind her. "Where's dear old Mom?"

My dad stumbles against the couch, still in shock from seeing his long-lost daughter. He recovers quickly and his protective instincts kick in. He steps slightly in front of me, keeping me out of range of any stray bullet.

"Hey, Mom! Where are you!" Z calls into the house still keeping the gun trained in our direction.

"Hang on, sweetie, I'm coming, trying to finish up some gardening," Mom calls back. She doesn't even know who she is really talking to.

When she appears in the doorway wiping her hands on her apron, she's still smiling until she looks up and sees the scene before her. Her smile fades and she lowers her hands to her sides. Dad pushes me across the room behind him, reaching out with his other arm to put Mom behind him as well.

"What do you want?" he asks Z in a serious voice.

"What do I want? *Hmmmm* let's see. I want you all to pay for giving me up when I was a baby! That's what I want," Z says angrily, raising the gun higher and taking a deliberate step closer to us.

"That's what this whole thing is about?" Dad demands. My mom and I both put a hand on his arm to calm him down, keep him from provoking her further.

"We had no choice; we couldn't raise three girls. We didn't even know who we kept; we didn't even meet you; the nurse simply brought us *one*," Mom pleads as she comes out behind my father, pushing him aside when he tries to pull her back.

"Yes, that's why I took care of all the hospital staff that was involved in your little secret. At least it was only the three of them. Could you imagine the blood on your hands had more of them been involved in separating us?" Z's voice is flat.

Mom puts her hand in front of her mouth and lets out a small gasp. I step beside her and put my arms around her, trying to comfort her.

"Please, Z, like I said, it can all end with Ashley. You don't have to do this *please!* Do you want money? Is that it? We can give you whatever you want to start over with a new life. All you have to do is put the gun down." My voice trembles. I squeeze Mom's hand and draw strength from her to suppress my fear.

"I don't want your stupid money," she snaps back. "I *solely* want you all to suffer like I did my whole entire life! The least you all could have done is make sure I went to a good home like Ashley, but no, I got sent to hell on earth." Her face contorts as she says this and her hands begin to shake. I know she is becoming more and more unstable.

"I'm *so* sorry," my mom whispers. The guilt is apparent on her face.

"It's too late to be *sorry,*" Z spits out.

My eyes go from her to the gun. Dad tenses up beside me and I know he is planning on making a move. I try to signal him not to do it, but it's too late. He lunges for the gun when her focus is locked on our Mom. It all happens so fast. I grab for my Mom and scream, pulling us both to the ground. She lets out a strangled, "*No!*" and I grab her arms to hold her back.

Bang!

I jump and freeze in place, scared to look at who the bullet hit. I don't feel any pain, and my mom is struggling beside me to get up, but my arms are wrapped tightly around her still. I look up at my dad, hoping that he succeeded.

No!

Blood spreads through my dad's light gray shirt as he crumbles to the floor. My mom lets out a scream and rushes to his side. My arms release her and I sit frozen in shock, disbelief washing over me. I glance up and see Z's face. She's enjoying this and moves to pull the trigger again, this time with our mom as the target. I have just enough time to act while her focus is on my mom and lunge forward as fast and as hard as I can.

I don't know how, but I manage to knock Z off balance enough to make her lose her grip on the gun and send it skittering under the sofa. We fight each other for control while I scream for my mom to call 9-1-1 and grab something to restrain Z until the police arrive.

Trying to keep her underneath me, I see her face as my own. *Some weird sort of poetic justice is here somewhere.*

Her face, however, has much more malice and anger. It distorts and becomes very different from mine. I think I have her, but right when I get confident, she head butts me leaving us both dazed. I try to recover, but she is a half a second faster. She jumps on me and lands blow after blow to my face. I have never been punched before, so my skills are purely instinctual at this point. Anything to stay alive. Mom approaches, vase in her hands and smashes it over Z's head knocking her to the floor. She is still conscious, but dazed.

Mom and I tie her hands and feet together and wait for the police to arrive. Once we are sure Z isn't going anywhere, Mom goes back over to Dad and puts pressure on his wound while I stand guard over Z.

A vision pops into my head. My husband isn't fine. He is locked up somewhere dark. He's bound to a chair, his face bloody and swollen. I lean down inches from Z's face,

"Where is he!" My desperation is evident in every word. She simply peers up at me, smiles, and spits blood from her mouth. She knows she has won.

"If I'm still here by the time the cops are, you will never find him, or know what my associate has done with him," she sneers. I want so badly to be wrong about what I have seen, but now I am convinced I am not. Marc is in danger.

I am unable to hold in a gasp. I look at Mom.

"Autumn, she could be lying as a way to get you to set her free," Mom says. I look back at Z and somehow know, she is not lying. I sigh and look back to my mom, my eyes pleading with her to understand.

"I'm sorry, but I can't take the risk. Tell the police everything when they get here, but I have to go and save my husband," I say. I look at Z, ready to untie her. "Take me to him."

"Now wait a minute, Mommy Dearest," Z sneers, "if you tell the cops anything about me, I will kill her, her husband, and your granddaughters. *Mark my words.*" Mom winces at the truth in her words.

We only have seconds to decide because I can hear the sirens coming down the street and getting closer. We are out of time and I have to play by her rules.

"Do as she says, Mom, I will be okay." I try to sound confident. I am anything but. "Get Dad to the hospital. Tell them it was an unknown burglar or something." I am positive my mom will do exactly as Z says. She would never do anything to put me or my girls in danger.

I untie Z and give my parents a sad smile before we race out the back door. I am determined to save my husband, even if it's the last thing I do.

"My car is in the front, so there is no way we can drive," I tell her, hoping to throw a wrench in her plan. To my surprise, she grabs my arm so tightly I cry out in pain. She leads me to the back of the neighbor's house and orders me to get in the old, semi restored Camaro. Realizing she is going to hotwire the car, I open the door to the passenger seat.

Where could she be keeping Marc?

I focus on the old smell of the car and try to calm my thoughts, which is a lot easier since she no longer has the gun in her possession. I try to get in her head for more information. Coming up blank, I decide to ask.

"It's only us now. I'm here, like you wanted. You can tell me where we are going."

I am met with silence. I steal a glance at her face; it is hard as stone. I know she won't tell me until we are there. Accepting this, I use the time to prepare for any possible scenario. I have no weapon, no phone, and no defenses. I know she has another person working with her and assume the accomplice is armed. There are a lot of unknown possibilities. I hope the paramedics get to my dad in time. I couldn't live with myself if anything happened to him.

Wherever Z is taking us is farther than I anticipated. We make a turn down a dirt road I don't recognize and dozens of trees fly past us. Before I know it, we hit an end to the road. I expect her to stop or slow down, but she does neither. She continues to drive through a small open field. We go through some woods before we come up on an old, worn down barn. Calling out for help will be useless; we are in the middle of nowhere.

"Once we get my husband, you will let him go, right? You already have me, which is what you really want." I follow her lead and get out of the car, closing the squeaky door behind me.

"Sure, he can go and you can stay," she says without looking at me. I know she is lying or hiding something, but when she smiles at her own thoughts, I begin to fear what or who is actually inside these old, abandoned doors.

I can't see anything once we are inside. She grabs tightly onto my arm and half-drags me through the barn. It smells like moldy hay and decomposing flesh from some unfortunate animal. *At least I hope the smell is coming from animals. How big is this barn anyway?*

Continuing in the dark, we come up against a door. She gives me a sidelong glance before opening it. The door creaks and opens into a dimly lit room. It takes a minute for my eyes to adjust, but when they do, I see him. My Marc, slumped over, tied to an old chair. His face is covered in blood.

"Marc!" I yell, running to him. I kneel in front of him and gingerly take his bruised, bloody face in my hands. "Marc! Wake up! Please baby, wake up!" I sob and stroke his face.

"Autumn?" he manages to whisper.

"Yes! It's me! I'm right here!" I tell him before surging to my feet and whipping around to glare at Z. "How *dare* you hurt him! Untie him! It's me you want. Not him. He has *nothing* to do with this."

"Now why would I do that?" she asks. She is enjoying the pain and angst she is putting us through.

"You know what would be fun?" she asks with a devilish grin on her lips. Walking a circle around us. "If we add Marc here to the people that you killed as well."

"No!" I roar. Suddenly she has a gun in her hands. *Where did that come from?*

"Autumn, it's okay. Run!" Marc coughs out. He glances up at me through swollen bruised lids, his eyes pleading. I look back to Z, hoping to bargain with her. Buy us time. But it's too late. She squeezes the trigger.

Bang!

I whirl back to Marc. He is no longer looking at me. Instead, he is crumpled over, not breathing.

"No!" I scream. Wrapping my arms around him and choking back my sobs, "Marc! Baby please, open your eyes, look at me!" I search for his wound in hopes of stopping the bleeding.

Where is it? Where's the wound?

"What's the matter, *sis*?" Z asks innocently. "Can't seem to find a bullet hole?"

"What did you say?" I rise to my feet to face her.

"Damnit Z! You were *this* close to shooting me!" Marc shouts from behind me. I forget all about Z and turn with relief.

"Marc! You're alive!" I say ecstatically before realization stuns me into silence. *How does he know Z's name?* He gives me an evil grin and my blood runs cold. He is out of the chair and walking toward Z. *How did he get untied from the chair? How is he not dead? What is going on?*

My thoughts fly through my mind at a million miles per second. Nothing is making any sense. I feel hands on me, shoving me into a chair. I can't bring myself to stop them; I'm too stunned to move. I don't see the blow coming, but I feel its impact and I am dazed enough to give her time to tie me to the chair.

"What is going on?" I ask, still woozy. I try to focus, but the room is spinning. Marc looks at me and then turns to Z and smiles before reaching for her and kissing *her* right in front of me. I am so shocked and confused, a strangled noise comes out of my throat.

What is happening?

That's when it hits me like a blow to the chest: my husband's been in on it from the start. The awful realization of the truth stops my breath. They break apart and all I can do is look back between them before Marc smiles and reaches out to run a thumb over my cheek. I pull away, not able to stand his touch.

"Oh, Autumn." He chuckles. "You should see your face right now. I'm sure you have lots of questions." He sounds like the Marc I know, but there is something different, more of an edge.

"Marc? What is this?" I ask my voice barely a whisper while tears start to form in my eyes. "What are you doing?" I swallow a sob. Nothing makes sense. *Is everything in my entire life a complete lie? How could I not have seen this coming? How could I not have known he was involved?* The questions come faster and faster and I have no answers for any of them.

"Well, first of all, my name isn't Marc, it's Axel," he says with a daring grin. "Marc was my brother who unfortunately died in a tragic accident when we were kids." His tone takes on a somberness at the mention of the brother I never even knew he had. "I must say, this has *definitely* been a long time coming. I was beginning to think we were going to have to continue this charade forever." He looks at Z, who rolls her eyes.

"Oh please, you knew how long it was going to take and I'm sure it was a complete hardship playing house with a woman who looks exactly like me," she scoffs.

"Oh, love, don't be jealous. You may have similar features, but she is *nothing* like you, nor does she have your *look*," he tells her as he runs a hand down her face, gripping her chin, and bringing it to his mouth for a kiss.

"But... your face..." is all I'm able to stammer out. Z looks at me with amusement in her eyes.

"Oh babe, keep up." Marc says, annoyed that I interrupted them.

"Good, right? Had to make it look real so you would think he was in danger," she says.

"Yeah, you really didn't have to make it look *this* real though," Marc counters as he gingerly touches his face, wincing when he touches the ugly bruise on his cheek.

"You'll be fine," Z snaps back.

Try as I might, I can't stop the tears from running down my face. *This must be another dream. I will wake up any minute now with Marc lovingly lying beside me.* I close my eyes as tight as I can and will for this sick dream to be over, but when I open them, all I see are Z and "Axel" staring at me in amusement. Taking a deep shaky breath, I try to settle myself and focus on my next move: getting out of here alive.

"This... this was all a lie?" I ask them, my voice barely a whisper. The feeling of betrayal shakes me to my very core.

"Who do you think told Axe about you, and everything needed to win you over?" Z says using his nickname. "I *might* have understated my connection to you. See, I have been planning, watching, and building this twin connection, or whatever you want to call it, for a long, long time now. However, I couldn't have pulled it all off without my Axe, of course." She smirks and kisses him again. She wraps her arms around him while he presses her tightly against him.

"That's how you were able to get into the house," I say, the final piece coming together. "And it was you that made it seem like I had blood and paint on my arms... You did all of this."

"Very good. See, I told you it would make sense in due time. Oh! And don't forget the added steps to your watch." She leans into Axel for another hungry kiss. "That was all Axel's idea," she says, looking proudly at him. "I wasn't able to do *everything* myself; Axe helped quite a bit. I did all the *heavy lifting* if you will, but it was most definitely a team effort." Her triumphant grin not only makes me want to throw up, but also to punch her in the face until my knuckles bleed. I have never felt such sadness and rage simultaneously.

"You should have seen her face when she brought me the plate of cookies you baked; it was priceless. It took everything I had not to lose my cool," Marc adds.

"And to hear you threw them away. That was rude, I spent hours making those you know," Z says. Sarcasm dripping from every word.

I try to ignore her and look into Marc's eyes, the man I have loved and been married to for eight years.

"Oh, honey, you think eight years is long? I met Axe back when we were in junior high. I was already a mess and had a shitty childhood, but Axe here was my savior," she says looking up to him lovingly. "He was my shelter from my hellish life at home. He protected me and showed me what love was when no one else did. I love him. We are destined to be together." She turns to him as she talks, and leans in for another kiss; he eagerly obliges. Once they come up for air she continues with her story. "He also came from a shitty home, so we connected right away. We were always looking for a way out. We wanted to start over with our lives and be happy together, just the two of us. When I told him what had been done to me at birth and the revenge plan I wanted to unleash on all of you, he was my number one supporter."

Axel grins and holds her tighter.

"Of course I was, love. You are the only one for me," he tells her through a genuine smile. It makes me sick to my stomach. He's never looked at me the same way.

"When it was time for him to meet you at college and get you to fall in love with him, I didn't care how long it took. He would forever love me and be mine. Never *yours*." She curls her lip at me. "Besides, he has had plenty of long hours at the office or on 'business trips' where we could *reconnect*."

I listen to her while I fight with the ropes, hoping to loosen them enough and somehow break free. No matter how hard I try, the rope digs further into my skin. I can feel blood drip down my fingers.

"But we have children together, Marc... or Axel or whatever your name really is. If this is all a sick, drawn-out game to frame me for murder, why are we married? Why do we have two beautiful daughters?" I ask. Rage is coursing through my body. He only looks at me with a blank expression.

"My dear," he kneels in front of me, "having children with *you* doesn't mean anything to me. My love can't have children and you, her twin could. Think of yourself as our surrogate." He shrugs as if he didn't say the most disgusting thing I have ever heard. I hate how his words cut deeper than I let on. I won't give him the satisfaction of my pain. *My beautiful Gemini stars.* It takes every ounce of will I have not to break down.

"Don't you see?" Z says. "I have made your whole life a lie and taken everything from you, exactly how my life was a lie and everything was taken from me. You had to suffer as I did. Axe was not fond of the idea of being away from me for so long at a time, but it must have helped that we look the same."

"Trust me, Z, none of it was *easy*. She might look like you, but she will never be you." He kisses her with a passion I've never experienced. All I can do is watch, my mind reeling. He comes closer and gets inches from my face. "You have to admit though, *babe*," his face reflects unvarnished contempt, "I deserve a *fucking* Oscar for my amazing acting skills, and the ability to be the *perfect* husband for *soooo* long. You have to admit, I was great." I can't repress my rage back any longer.

I spit in his face.

"Where are my daughters?" I demand. He comically wipes my spit from his cheek, amused. His hand holds Z back from dishing out another blow to my face for my actions.

"Calm down," he chides, "They are safe at their friends house, as Z told you before. They won't know the difference or be affected by anything. You and I were undoubtedly a lie, but I love *my* daughters very much."

"This is never going to work; I will tell the police everything! So will my parents! You are not going to get away with this," I scream.

"Oh, sweet sister," Z says, "I know everything there is to know about you. I know how you walk, dress, talk, and think. Becoming you is why this process has taken so long. I can take your life, and no one, not even *our* parents will know the difference between us. Even if they do suspect, you have already paved the way. After all, you are unstable, forgetful, and you have crazy dreams. It's no wonder some things might be a little off." She lets out a triumphant shout before looking back to Axel. "Besides, my loving husband here will always stand up and advocate for me. He will convince everyone of my identity." She changes her facial expression. Now she looks exactly like me. She winks.

"Who says that the police will even find your body to even hear your side of the story anyway, " Axel says. The two of them look confident. I get a glimpse of Z's thoughts. She wants Axel to be the one to pull the trigger.

"You were never going to frame me, were you? It was always your plan to steal my life and get rid of me." The daunting realization suffocates me. *How could I have been so stupid?*

"And here I thought you were never going to catch on," Z mocks.

I look to the man I have known as Marc, the man I have built a life with, had children with, and I hope some of what we had has been true enough that he can't do it.

"Please, Marc," My eyes search his for any trace of the man I love, "you can't do this. We made a beautiful life. I love you. Think of our girls. They need me. I am their *mother*. Everything we have or ever said and went through couldn't have all been a lie."

A flicker of his hardness melts, showing a small glimpse of the man I love still in there. My heart leaps at the hope that I can talk him down. The more I look, the more his face falters ever so slightly. Unfortunately, Z notices the change as well. Annoyed, she steps in front of him and takes his face in her hands.

"Axe, baby, come on, we have worked too hard, waited so long for this very moment. Everything has been in preparation for right now." He waits a beat too long to answer. Her posture turns rigid before she turns to me, her face contorted in anger and hatred. *He's never killed anyone before, he won't be able to pull the trigger on me.* I'm filled with false hope until she yanks my hair back and gets inches from my face.

"Fine, I will have the pleasure of killing you myself then. I already killed one look alike; what's one more?" She sneers and walks to the corner of the small dark room and picks up a different gun from the table.

"No! Please, Marc, don't let her do this! Please!" My voice is frantic, my eyes wide, and I struggle harder against the rope. I have to get through to him or break free to defend myself.

Marc's eyes flick to me, then to Z, who is walking toward me with the gun raised right at me, smiling as she gets closer. It's no use, the ropes are too tight. The Marc I knew won't even look at me. All that is left is Axel, who stares at me with a sickening grin on his face as he watches the woman, who is supposed to be my sister, about to murder me. I feel defeated and stupid for believing this was going to end any other way. It was deluded to believe that simply because he couldn't pull the trigger himself, he would have any problem letting someone else do it.

All I can do is hang my head, say a silent goodbye to my children, and hope my Plan B works. I open my eyes and look at the end of a barrel aimed right at me. I won't give them the satisfaction of showing them my fear anymore. *Let her look into my eyes as she pulls the trigger.*

"Any last words?" Z asks. "It's more than I gave our other sister." She cocks the hammer back and puts her finger on the trigger. A rogue tear runs down my cheek as I try to accept what is about to happen.

"Tell the girls I love them, and, Marc, I loved you too. It might not have been real to you, but it was real to me." I look one last time into his eyes, wanting to believe he is still in there.

Everything happens so fast. The last thing I hear is the sound of a gun going off before my whole world turns to black...and nothingness.

L. A. Brink

They say that before everything ends, your whole life will flash before your eyes and you get to see all the major highlights life had to offer. However, that is not what happened to me. All I saw was what was in front of me: a sister I never met, full of hatred, and the man that was supposed to love and protect me, but did neither because it was all a set-up from the beginning. The only good thing was the image of my beautiful daughters I conjured in my head. There was no pain, only darkness. I hope my daughters will be able to see the monster that is impersonating me.

One day, maybe justice will be served.

21

Three Months Later

THE MEDIA FRENZY surrounding the horrendous events has finally started to die down, allowing everything to get back to semi-normalcy. Dad is making a full recovery with his shoulder, while Mom continues to fuss over his every movement. Luckily, the girls don't fully understand what has happened and seem to be taking everything in stride. They were acting a little weird around me right after everything, but luckily, they seem to be back to normal. We have tried to shelter them as much as we can from recent events.

Even their teacher, Mr. Young, has been diligent in keeping the rumor mill quiet, which can be hard when the murder suspect looks exactly like their mom. After the blur of our escape, Z disappeared and hasn't been seen or heard from since. The search for her still continues. Fortunately for the family of Ashley, the truth of Z's plan has been brought to light and Ashley's memory and reputation have been restored. It's a small comfort since she was taken away from her family in such a violent way.

It took a week to find her body where Z buried it in a field near the property where she'd been staying. As for me, escaping from her clutches with Marc was a harrowing tale and has been the talk of the town. We had news vans parked outside our house for weeks trying to get an interview. Neighbors we have only ever talked to a handful of times suddenly became experts on us as well as our best friends. When I think about it, we were very lucky to escape with our lives, even though we both suffered some wounds. I had severe rope burns and a gunshot wound to my shoulder, instead of the death blow I would have gotten had Marc not grabbed for the gun at the last minute and saved me. Marc got the worse end of it. He sustained multiple bruises to his face as well as an orbital rim fracture and bruised ribs. He saved me that day and I will never know how to thank or repay him.

I feel blessed to have our family on the mend. The house we lived in felt tainted and robbed of its safe feeling, so we have decided to move. Mom hates the idea of being farther away from the girls and me, but she understands what's best for our family.

When we first approached the girls with the idea of moving, they wanted nothing to do with it. It took a lot of convincing; they didn't want to leave their friends or stop with the piano lessons, but they eventually came around to the idea when they found out their new house came with a pool in the backyard. It's only an hour away and we told them we could come back and still make play dates with Sarah on the weekends if they wanted.

By the end of the week, we will fully be moved into our new place equipped with a full security system as well as a security guard for the whole subdivision who drives around making sure everything and everyone are safe. We even found another piano teacher for the girls so they can continue their lessons. They were sad about Mrs. Lang not being their teacher anymore, they really liked her, but are excited they don't have to give up the lessons all together.

"How's everything coming in here?" Marc asks me.

"Good, I am almost done, and I can't wait to be rid of this place," I say, wiping a bead of sweat from my brow. "All the girls' things are ready to go as well, and then I just have the rest of my paints to pack."

"That's good. Well, I'm about to start on supper, any requests?" he asks. He strides in the room and greedily pulls me into his embrace.

"Surprise me." I savor his strong arms around me and allow him to give me a swift passionate kiss before I wave him out of the room.

He leaves and gets started on dinner, leaving me alone up here with my thoughts. The reason I'm not done packing is because I can't stand anything I own anymore. They say after you have gone through a traumatic experience, you might want to change everything about yourself. I'm finding that to be true. I hate the way my hair looks, and every article of clothing I own. My friends have been nothing but supportive. They try to get me to go with them on shopping sprees, or help me pick out a new hairstyle they swear I could "rock," but, is it what I really want? I'm not sure.

I finish packing and head to my studio. Walking in, the air feels different; the room is mostly bare. I pick up the abstract piece I painted — it seems so long ago now. I am glad that one good thing came out of the whole ordeal. Being slightly famous for surviving a murderous attack has put my art back on the map and galleries are dying to put my abstract piece on their walls; they want a whole series. I don't mind this piece going in a gallery, but I'm not sure I'm ready to make it into a series since all I want to do is forget every feeling, lock them in a box, and bury them so I never have to feel them again.

Until I officially decide, the galleries are more than happy to have the single piece. I take one last look at it before gingerly placing it in bubble wrap, then inside a box so it doesn't get damaged. I must have been in here longer than I thought because Marc is already done with dinner.

"Mommy, look what Daddy made," the girls say excitedly.

"*Oooo,* this looks delicious," I say to them, but look at him out of the corner of my eye, thankful he went to the trouble of making such an extravagant meal.

The steak is cooked to perfection, as are the homemade garlic mashed potatoes, and the Brussel sprouts. The girls don't care for those, so they get homemade mac and cheese instead. Everything looks delicious. I scoop healthy portions on my plate and dig in.

"Now don't eat too much, I have special desserts waiting for you guys afterwards as well," he says. He's proud of himself.

"Babe, you really didn't have to go through all this trouble really, you're still recovering," I tell him, but I'm so glad he did. Everything is so amazing. "Besides, now I know what you're capable of, I'm going to want this kind of treatment all the time."

"Anything for you, love," he says winking at me.

"So, what's this special dessert?" I ask. I take another bite of the delicious steak.

"Well, for you my love, I have tiramisu, your favorite," he says before turning to the girls. "And for my monkeys here, I have a delicious chocolate cake."

The girls go crazy for chocolate cake, and they instantly demand a piece.

We are finally in our new home with almost everything unpacked. The girls love their new room, which is down the hall from ours — upstairs exactly like before. They are excited about decorating it themselves, and can't wait to go paint shopping over the weekend. I hope they can come to a decision on the color. Ada wants purple, but Anna wants the brightest yellow there is, so it should be interesting to see them compromise.

I am excited to make our master suite homier and have decided to paint the walls a calming blue. I have selected a more oceanic blue for the master bath, which I absolutely *love*. The master bath is much larger than the one before and includes a shower with dual heads, and a huge tub big enough for both of us. Don't even get me started on the walk-in closet, because it is enormous and everything I have ever wanted.

I can't wait to go shopping for my new wardrobe.

After a couple of days in the new house, getting everything settled and forming new routines, I finally decide to get my new studio put together. I will need the space to produce the series the gallery owner has been requesting. I decided if I'm really going to start over and fully enjoy this fresh start, I have to get out all past emotions and let the canvas carry them. After I get all my supplies, Marc takes the girls to see a movie so I can shop for a whole new wardrobe and get a brand-new hairstyle. Feeling bold, I tell the hairstylist to cut it short, and dye it a completely new color, her choice. It is now a radiant honey blonde, and I am completely obsessed with how it looks. I look and feel like the brand new me I always wanted and needed. When Marc comes to pick me up after their movie, he almost falls over.

"You look absolutely *stunning*, love!" He pulls me into his arms and kisses me right there for all to see.

"Really? I'm so happy you love it because I adore how it turned out," I tell him. I feel absolutely radiant. "Do you think the girls will like it?" I am suddenly self-conscious.

"They will love it, come on, let's show them."

Their eyes go wide when they see the new me, but don't look like they hate it, so that's a plus.

"What do you think of Mommy's new hair girls, do you like it?" I ask.

"It's very pretty, Mommy," Anna says.

"Yeah, Mommy, it's pretty," Ada says, but she seems less convinced.

"Thank you, girls, I'm so glad you like it," I tell them as I get in the car so we can head back home. "Hey, while Mommy was shopping, I picked out a few new outfits for you girls as well. Do you want to try them on when we get home?" They gasp and clap.

"What did you get us?" they ask at the same time.

"Well, you will just have to wait and see when we get home," I tell them, pleased they are so excited.

"I can't wait to try everything on," Anna says with excitement written all over her face. She *loves it when* she gets new clothes.

"Did you get us matching ones, Mommy?" Ada asks.

"Oh, um, no honey, I thought you might like different outfits so you didn't have to match all the time," I tell her trying to spin it into a positive, but I can see both their expressions fall. *They are disappointed.*

"Oh."

"But, Mommy, you always buy us matching outfits," Anna says, pushing the subject.

"Well, how about you look at them, try them on, and keep what you like. Tomorrow we can buy the matching set," I tell them eager to earn their happiness back.

Thankfully, it works and their smiles return.

Arriving home, the girls run out of the car and upstairs to their room so they can try on their new outfits. They end up loving every single one. *Now I just have to buy a second of every outfit. No problem!*

This day has been so wonderful, one minor hiccup, but overall amazing. I can't wait to spend the rest of our lives exactly like this. Happy and together. Everything before is becoming a distant memory.

Once we settle down for the night, alone with Marc at last, I roll over to him. He is already reaching out to pull me closer to him.

"I could get used to this," I whisper to his shadowed figure, not being able to make out his features in the dark. "I have waited a long time to have this life."

"Is it everything you ever wanted, my love?" he asks. He cups my face in his hands and kisses me.

"It really is," I tell him.

I kiss him again, so grateful for him, and everything he has done for me.

EPILOGUE

20 years later

MY SISTER ANNA and I have always had a strong twin connection and a strong connection with our mother, though when we were very young, the connection abruptly felt severed and we could never place why. She came home with our father one day after a terrifying incident. We didn't get all the details until we were much older. Once we finally did, we brushed off the feelings we had and chalked everything up to trauma. Life seemed to go on as usual, but we never forgot that moment.

Today, on our twenty-sixth birthday, everything makes sense…

…and our world implodes.

Our grandma calls us to tell us we have received a birthday letter. Not knowing who it is from, my sister and I decide to take a detour from our birthday plans and head over to her house to retrieve it. Afterall, it's only an hour away and our party doesn't start until later. We haven't seen our grandparents in a while, so it will be nice to catch up with them. Anna, of course, drives. She claims her skills are superior to mine, which is a lie, but I'm happy sitting in the passenger seat getting to glance out the window. I belt out singing without a care about the other cars around me. Anna rolls her eyes in annoyance, but she ultimately joins me.

We finally arrive and pull into the driveway. Their house hasn't changed one bit. Walking up the sidewalk, it's like Grandma already knows we are here. She greets us at the door with our favorite cookies, a constant every time we visit.

"Happy birthday, girls!"

"Thank you, Grandma! These are delicious as always," I tell her through a mouthful of snickerdoodle. I haven't even swallowed the one I'm eating and I reach for a second one as we sit down on the sofa. "So, who is this letter from?"

"Well, I'm not sure, but if I didn't know any better, I would say it was from your mother," she says with some hesitation. "Why she had it mailed here, I'm not sure. I'll go get it for you, hang on."

"Happy birthday, girls!" Grandpa says as he comes in from the backyard looking like he was working hard in the heat.

"Thank you!" we both say as we continue munching on the cookies while he gets himself a glass of lemonade and then retreats back out into the heat.

Grandma returns, holding the letter out to us. Anna takes it first, looking it over, while I peer over her shoulder.

"Thanks, Grandma, I think we're going to sit on the porch and open it. Can we have some iced tea while we're out there please?" we ask standing up from the couch.

"Of course, here you go," she says, pouring us both a large glass. "Tell your grandpa to come inside while you're out there though; he's been outside too long in the heat."

"Will do."

After Grandpa heads inside, we make ourselves comfortable on the back porch. We turn the letter over in our hands, not knowing why, but it feels like something will change as soon as we open it.

"Why would she send the letter here? She could have simply handed it to us herself," I say.

"I'm not sure, but let's find out," Anna says. She starts ripping the envelope to reveal the typed letter inside. I hold it out in front of us so we can read it together.

My dear, wonderful daughters,

I hope this letter finds you well. This website says it can send letters in future time. I have to believe that is true, because it is the only way I can get this letter to you safely. Please forgive me for choosing such a lengthy time for you to find out the truth, but I had to make sure you were old enough to understand the gravity of what I'm about to tell you. It will be very hard to read and understand, but here it goes.

The person you now call your mother is not me… my hope is I am wrong and that you will never have to read this, but if you are reading it, then I, your true mother, was murdered long ago by the woman who is now pretending to be me. Your father was involved as well. My dreams have been coming true a lot lately and I have recently had another, though this one was different. I wasn't sleeping when I had it. It was more like flashes of a movie. It felt like something that was destined to come to pass. I can't be sure if it is real because it seems so preposterous, but I guess I will learn the truth soon and I hope I am wrong.

You may or may not know that I am a triplet. One of my sisters, Ashley as she is called, is the person behind all the murders you heard about — and mine as well. Since we have the psychic connections that you two experience, I was able to dream about the murders she committed.

If I am not wrong, she plans to murder me and take my place. The sad truth is that the person who has been helping her this whole time is, in fact, your father. I don't know how or why he would do such a thing, or how he even knows of her, but he does. I know this is a lot, but please, when you finish reading this letter, go to the person you now call Mom and ask her what my secret nickname has been for you since you were little.

Only you two know what it is; not even your father has heard it. If the woman cannot remember or does not know, then she is actually Ashley. No matter how much time has passed, I, your true mother, could not and would never forget. I hope you take your knowledge to the authorities so I can have justice, but if you choose not to, I don't blame you at all. A lot of time has passed, and Ashley has fooled a lot of people. The decision and choice are completely impossible and I am truly sorry to put this burden on you. Whatever you decide, know that I could never be mad at you and I will understand. I will always love you my "Gemini stars."

Love,
    Your Real Mother

We finish reading the letter at the exact same time, frozen with the gravity of the situation. Nothing could have prepared us for such unbelievable information. We know that Ashley was actually murdered by Ainsley or Z as everyone called her. Mom must not have known yet, that this was actually Z behind the murders. We re-read the letter at least two more times, wanting to make one hundred percent sure we understand it. My hands shake as I lower the letter to my lap and look at my sister, seeing my exact reaction reflected in her face.

How is this even possible?

A memory dawns on us — the "severed connection" we felt when "Mom" came home.

She didn't "feel" right. She didn't know we wore matching outfits. She has never called us her Gemini stars since.

She is not our mother.

Lost in our individual, yet shared thoughts, we clutch each other's hand. A silent nod passes between us and we know instantly: the letter is real. Hand in hand we walk back through the house, careful to check our emotions. The goodbye to our grandparents sounds mechanical even to me.

Did they know? I wonder *How could they not?* My sister answers through her thoughts, *We can only hope they didn't.*

The car ride to where our "mother" awaits is a silent one. Both of us work to check our emotions. We have to be careful not to give anything away. Anna grips the steering wheel turning her knuckles white. Her grip only loosens when I place my hand on her shoulder hoping to calm her.

Just breathe.

Stepping into the house we walk over and reluctantly hug the imposter we have lived with for so many years. Trying to act as normal as possible, we are hoping against hope that we are wrong. I look over at Anna. I cannot be the one to ask. Thankfully, she senses my hesitation and does it for me.

"Hey, Mom, Ada and I were just talking and we remembered something from when we were little. You had a nickname for us, but for the life of us, we can't seem to remember what it was. Do you?" Anna asks. Her tone is flawless. Not even a tiny hint of ulterior motives.

She stops what she is doing and gives a curious look before continuing.

"What do you mean?" she answers brightly. "Oh, you must be thinking of your father. He used to call you 'monkeys.' That's what you must be thinking of. What a random question."

"Yeah I don't know; it just popped in our heads," Anna says.

"Okay, well anyway, come on, your cake is all ready for you to blow out the candles."

She leads us into the dining room where our dad puts the cake on the table with twenty-six candles lit on top.

I look at my sister, and she echoes my thoughts.

This woman is Z, and we are going to do everything in our power to bring our true mother the justice she deserves after all of these years.

We give Z an innocent smile, hold each other's hand, and blow out our candles.

ACKNOWLEDGMENTS

I would like to thank everyone at Paper House Publishing for making my lifelong dream of publishing my first novel come to life. A special thanks to my editor Art, who helped me become a stronger writer throughout the editing process. I really appreciated all of your notes. To my husband Colin, who consistently encouraged me to keep writing, even though some days I wanted to quit. My sister Lindsey, who was always eager to read every draft, and to my parents, who's belief in my abilities from the very start gave me the courage to write in the first place. I love you both! I would also like to thank my beta readers, who gave me their opinions as well, Kayla J, Kayla H, Mel, Jacob and Stacy. Shout out to Jacob for helping me stage and take the photo for the cover. And finally, thank you to all my readers for picking my book off the shelf and giving it a chance. It truly means the world.

ABOUT THE AUTHOR

L.A. Brink lives in Illinois with her husband and son. She has a Bachelor's in Photography, but writing has always been her passion. This is her first novel.

Printed in the USA
CPSIA information can be obtained
at www.ICGtesting.com
BVHW052055220823
668748BV00008B/22

ABOUT THE AUTHOR

L.A. Brink lives in Illinois with her husband and son. She has a Bachelor's in Photography, but writing has always been her passion. This is her first novel.

Printed in the USA
CPSIA information can be obtained
at www.ICGtesting.com
BVHW052055220823
668748BV00008B/22

9 781088 212172